THE PURPLE PLAIN

THE PURPLE PLAIN

H.E.BATES

CASSELL&CO

Cassell & Co
Wellington House, 125 Strand
London WC2R 0BB

Printed and bound in Great Britain by
Cox & Wyman Ltd., Reading, Berks.

1

Shy flocks of small banana-green parrots had begun to come back to the pipul trees about the bombed pagoda. But across the rice-fields, scorched and barren now from the long dry season, only a few white egrets stepped daintily like ghostly cranes about the yellow dust in the heat-haze. Nothing else moved across the great plain where for three years no rice had grown.

Somewhere down the line of tents beyond the pagoda a sergeant kept a tame monkey, and Forrester, sweating and naked on the bed in his own tent, could hear it crying in the heat of the afternoon. It cried piteously as he lay watching the low mountains that rimmed the plain in the haze of heat and dust like long crests of thunder-cloud. Now and then these mountains seemed to dissolve in gigantic explosions of sulphur dust against the heat-discoloured sky and the whole plain melted away under the glitter of dust and sun. And then when it cleared and came to life and the white light burned glassily down again it was always to create for Forrester the same illusion. It gave him the impression that besides the white egrets there moved across it, in the pitiless heat-haze, a spark of purple flame. This flame seemed to burn itself forward on the burning dust, quivering and dying and brightening in the dazzling air until it became at last a group of people: a solitary line of Burmese peasants, tiny and brilliant in waist-cloths of vermilion and violet, travelling south to the villages of the river.

When Forrester turned over and lay on his back and stretched his long legs and felt the sun strike down through the brown canvas tent-flap like an acetylene lamp through a piece of gauze, the splintered glare clashed into white stars on his eyeballs and jerked out of his body a new rush of sweat. And when he moved as if to wipe it off with his hand it was only to find

5

that his hands, too, were streaming with that small exertion. He lay for another moment or two gasping for breath. Then he turned and lay right over on his side, his face to the tent wall, away from the downward glare of light, feeling immediately the slight relief brought about by shadow. And as he did so he caught sight of Blore.

Blore was sitting with cool immobility in the far corner of the tent at a small table of teakwood, writing with spectacled eyes held at a careful distance from the page. He was still wearing his bush-hat, the strap buckled under the chin, and his face had something of the look of a pudding tied with string. The table had been crudely made by Burmese carpenters at the bazaar and it was now neatly filled with the steady precautions of the older campaigner: the bottle of yellow mepacrine tablets, the glass of salt water, the Thermos flask wrapped round with a wet towel. There was a singular absence of heroism in Blore. To Forrester he looked less like an officer than a sort of ecclesiastical horse. But it was too hot to say so. He only turned over again and shut his eyes slowly against the sweat that was now pouring down into them like bitter water.

'Don't tell me you find it hot,' Blore said.

Sweat was running down over the closed lids of Forrester's eyes and joining in a single stream the sweat of his face.

'This is really the spring-time,' Blore said. 'March – this is the pleasant weather. The real heat begins in June. With the rain.'

'I bet you love it,' Forrester said.

'I do not love it.'

'I bet you get really warmed up then and get your letters written home.'

It seemed sometimes to Forrester that Blore wrote a hundred letters a day.

'The trouble with you is that you don't understand anything outside your own business,' Blore said. 'You flying people. You're young. You don't care. That's the trouble with you.'

'That's the trouble with us.'

'Well, have you?' Blore said. 'I mean – '

'I don't know what you mean.'

'Well, for instance, what I told you,' Blore said.

'I don't know what you told me.'

'A wife in England,' Blore said. 'That's what I mean. Wait till you've been out here three years and then you'll know what I mean.'

Forrester turned away and stared at the blank brown wall of the tent. Momentarily the intensity of his anger blinded him so that the canvas seemed to rock backwards and forwards. He shut his eyes. His feeling against Blore, in which was wrapped up his feeling against the heat, the dust, the crying of the monkey, and the glare of the plain outside, had gone beyond the edges of irritation; it had become boundlessly and personally hostile. He frantically desired to hit Blore with the Thermos flask.

'Oh for Christ's sake!' he said.

He clenched his hands and thrust his face down into the pillow that was already like a lump of warm moist sponge. The short movement of his head brought out a fresh break of sweat over his entire body. Even as his face touched the pillow it streamed down and wetted still further the linen where he lay. He tried not to think of Blore, thinking instead of the simple fact that he had been waiting for three weeks for a navigator to come over from Calcutta. It was a three hours' flight over the delta, the sea and the mountains to the central Burmese plain. It was a very simple thing; it was all arranged; and yet no one came. It was so far arranged that he had even known for some time the name of the man who was coming, so that each morning now he drove across the ruined town to the bombed bungalow where a clerk dealt with the outer mysteries of posting to inquire if there were news of Carrington. There was never any news. There was something queer about it. Carrington, who had become for him a living fact, seemed also to have become somewhere swallowed by a vast and fatalistic disregard of time, part of the mysterious and senseless way of the East, where one day of molten and dazzling daylight flowed into another exactly like it and then into another and another. Time seemed to go quickly and to have no importance and the missing navigator had become part of the timelessness and the confusion and the stupidity of war. He had grown to be an expression of the officialdom that posted men about the mountains and jungles and swamps and plains of the earth as if they were nothing but bags of nameless offal: so that although he had never seen him Forrester had now come very near to hating him. His constant absence had become, like the system that created him, a presence to be loathed, one with the dust, the heat, and the glittering deadly light of day.

In the stupor and sweat of thinking this it occurred to him suddenly that Blore had spoken something and that he had never answered. He opened his eyes. It seemed to him suddenly that the older man, in his loose green bush jacket with the single blue flying officer tapes ill-fixed on the shoulders, had something of the chalky obese aloofness of one of the many Buddhas squatting about the half-jungle that in the years of occupation had swamped the town.

'I thought you said something,' he said.

'Ten minutes ago.'

'It couldn't have been important or you'd have said it again.'

'It is important and just for you I'll say it again,' Blore said. 'I'm posted.'

'Good Christ.' Forrester sprang suddenly into a sitting position on the bed, so that the violence of the exertion brought a fountain of sweat from his face down on to the bed and his hands. 'That's wonderful.'

'Thank you very much,' Blore said. 'I'm glad too.' He seemed to speak with involuntary sadness.

'Where?' Forrester said.

'Well, oddly,' Blore said, 'a little nearer home.' Forrester felt suddenly almost touched by an air of helplessness in Blore, who had stopped writing and was gazing at the tent wall. He seemed all at once like someone old and tired, a man of another generation, a lost body who had wandered by mistake into a tropical campaign that was not of his making. Forrester's irritation became dissolved for a moment into pity that he did not want to show.

'Yes: a little nearer home,' Blore said. 'Not much. But something. Back to Akyab.'

'They say it's nice there. By the sea.'

'I'm to be there by the twenty-first,' Blore said. 'That's four days from now.'

Forrester did not speak again. Lying down again on the bed

flat on his back, shading his eyes from the white acetylene glare beating vertically down on him and feeling the bite of it transferred to the back of his hands, he felt intensely glad that Blore was going. Already he could look forward to the security and comfort of the tent, alone. It occurred to him already that he would move it; forty or fifty feet perhaps, to somewhere between the row of blistered palms and the small white and gold pagoda, partly shattered now, where children came sometimes to play among the broken images of Buddha that war had smashed into a wreckage of cheap white plaster. If he moved it there he could be sure of a little shade from the pipul trees in the late afternoon; he would be sure, hidden away from the tents of the rest of the section, of a little privacy and quiet in the night and the heat of the day, and he would be a little farther from the monkey that woke him every morning with its shrieking childlike voice before the sun rose. There would be nothing to disturb him there but the parrots. He would settle himself before Carrington came. By the time Carrington did come the apparatus of his isolation would be complete: no more Blore, writing eternal letters home, taking eternal mepacrine tablets, no more talk, no more arguing, no more company. Perhaps he would be able to bear a little better then the long ferocious days of fatalistic glare, heat and sweat and dust, but above all the dust: dust explosive against the sun, dust blown everywhere by vehicles and the furious winds of aircraft coming in and taking off, dust in your hair and your throat, in your eyes and mixed like grey mud with the sweat of your body, in your food and your water, in your bed and your belongings and, finally, and worst of all, creating moments of the most frenzied irritation, in your mind.

His gladness that Blore was leaving and the idea of being alone at last made him suddenly get up off the bed. He picked up his cap, blue once but now dusted over with a dry creamy bloom like powdered cement, and put it on. He slipped his feet into a pair of laceless canvas shoes and tied his green bush towel round his loins and then, without saying anything to Blore, went out of the tent into the sun.

In the immediate moment of coming out of the thin shade the heat came straight down and hit him flatly, with a vicious horizontal blow, as if it had actually solidified and had been waiting to fall on him like a hot iron. It was as if he had no covering on his head at all. He shook his head like a man staggered by something and then walked away to the pagoda, impressive once with its two obese smooth Buddhas but ruined and deserted now, its graceful broken tiers of dead white plaster rising to about half the height of the palms that were motionless as if slit out of black steel against the dust-discoloured sky. Over in the pipul trees the small green parrots hid themselves in the shade. Under the trees and about the pagoda lay the wreckage of low jungle shattered to tinder by vehicles and men, dark with the kind of desolation that comes after burning. Shrubs and vines had been hacked away for tent room and what remained had been cut by Indian boys for fires. The palms alone remained, too high to touch, and a few lower trees whose name he did not know, green with soft new leaf and tender crowds of sweet white flowers, heavy and scented, that clotted the night air with a honeyness sweeter than lime.

He walked round the pagoda, blasted so that the cheap brick core of the Buddhas lay revealed under the smooth outer gilding and emerald and ruby glass of the surface jewellery, to where there would be a little shade in the later afternoon. He knew already where he would pitch the tent. He would get Ali, the boy, to fix it up as soon as Blore had gone. He could take his bath under the shadow of the Buddha. It was even possible that he could get Ali to arrange something in the way of a shower-bath by the wall.

In the narrow slice of shade that lay at the foot of the wall like a strip of smoky glass in the dust he stopped for a moment and leaned against the pagoda. Burma still remained for him a strange, empty, broken country. All over it, but especially in the central plain, the heat was rising steadily and now, in the middle of March, it was reaching a hundred or more by the middle of the day. He felt himself to be lost in the centre of a vast and dusty arena blistered by relentless sun. The newspapers that reached him were a month, sometimes two months old, so that the talk in them of victories was stale and meaningless and he felt cut off from the central channel of the war: an isolated and fragmentary part of a conflict already fought. The continent of mountain and jungle and paddy-field that lay all about him seemed anonymous and no one seemed to doubt that the war stretching over it far eastward and southward would last for another two or five or even ten years.

As he leaned against the wall he heard sounds coming from the farther side of the pagoda and as he moved along the wall, out of the narrow shadow into the full glassy stab of sunlight again, to see who was there, he came suddenly on a small Burmese girl of six or seven playing idly with a green-brown lizard on the broken steps of the pagoda. She was letting the lizard run for a few inches along the stone and then frustrating it with her hands. It ran with quivering electricity on the white stone so long as it was free and then as it reached her hand it seemed to die where it stopped, liquid body solidified, tiny quivering hands suddenly rigid and transfixed. The child as she half-lay on the steps brought her bright almond-flat eyes to the level of the lizard's own eyes, as if she were trying to mesmerize it. And then for a moment she would sit up, looking away for an instant so that the lizard could run. Then when it ran, darting like a flicker of green lightning on the dazzling white hot stone, she brought down her brown hand and stopped it again. Each time it died with the perfection of instinct and fear and lay there like a piece of imagery painted in the sun.

He squatted down beside her, bringing his cap down over his eyes. He thought she was one of the children from the temporary settlement by the river; she had no business to be there. As he sat down she turned up to him her flat smiling face, almond-brown and genial and squinting because of the slight Mongolian slant of the eyes, and gave him a grin as if he had been sitting there for all time. He grinned back. In an instant her hand was out towards the lizard, light brown fingers outstretched, to capture it before it could run the distance of her thin dust-creamed rosy arm.

He spoke to her in English. He had succeeded in mastering fifteen or sixteen words of Burmese, but none of them seemed adequate for the game he was watching now.

'Are you going to kill it?' he said.

She looked up and grinned, very pretty and blandly devilish and squinting. He thought she was going to kill it.

'Where are you from?' he said.

As she held her face up to him and then averted it sharply to watch the lizard again, the grin became wider, a little flatter, a little more genially devilish. The lizard did not move. For some seconds both she and Forrester watched it with great intensity. During this watching, as he forgot the heat of the stones and became almost part of the game, it occurred to him suddenly that the child might always have played there. It struck him that he was about to pitch his tent on her playground and it was, after all, he thought, her country. No one else had any right here. The town had been blown to pieces. There wasn't a single bungalow with a roof on except the one with the white veranda, by the rice-mill, where the nurses lived. The rest was desolation.

He knew that he ought to send her off; the thing to do, of course, was to be hard with these people. You could not, by all the rules, be too hard. They were exceedingly friendly and smiling; they had all the charm of liberated friendship; but behind your back they probably spat on you and covered you with curses appropriate to an invader in a different kind of uniform.

The child let the lizard run again, this time a little farther than ever before, cruelly, so that it almost escaped. Forrester was intensely fascinated and sat down completely, his legs under him, watching her bring down her hand in a calm swift stroke of frustration.

If she doesn't kill the thing it will die of fright, he thought, and he sat there for some time mesmerized by the immobility of the lizard and the life of the rose-brown hands, so that he forgot to talk to her again.

Watching her in this dazed way, he began to think of England and of something Blore had said. It had been very like Blore, wrapped up like a fat cocoon in the problem of personal exile, to hit on the truth of things and not to know it. 'Of course you haven't a wife in England,' Blore would say as he sat at the teak-wood table writing countless letters home. 'It makes all the difference in the world.'

It occurred all at once to Forrester that Blore would now never know exactly how much difference, how deeply, how sharply and how continuously, it did make. He felt very relieved. He did not want Blore to know; he did not want anyone to know. Sometimes the whole affair had a finer sharpness than the plain, with its delicate white egrets feeding about the paddy-fields, as he saw it from the tent. Much more often it had the brooding vagueness of the far mountains. Very occasionally it came down and hit him with the blinding shock of the sun as it hit him when he came out of the shade. Mostly he tried not to think of it, and mostly without success.

He had once had a wife and now he began all at once to think of her quite sanely and without pain as he watched the rose-brown hands of the child. They seemed to soothe his powers of memory. He even found himself watching her with a partial smile.

They had been married very young: she only nineteen and he a little over twenty. There had been one or two small parental objections, nothing very much, mostly from his side because he was a pilot and so young, and in the end they had been married on the twentieth of January, 1941, at nine o'clock in the morning, and in the afternoon they took the train to London for the honeymoon. She was a girl with very dark wavy hair, pale skin that had a touch of sallowness in it and a way of smiling magnificently with her eyes, without moving the rest of her face. They went straight to the hotel and afterwards they had dinner. It was a very good dinner, except that the mushrooms on toast were burnt; and after dinner she went upstairs to change her dress. She put on a black silk gown with huge scarlet artificial blossoms of some sort across the breast, and they went out in the blackness of London to dance. They had five days in which to dance and make love and be happy before he went back on fighter operations. All the time he could taste the burnt mushrooms.

The child let the lizard run farther than usual, so that she had to grab wildly across the pagoda steps to catch it. He saw then what was the matter with it. It had lost some of the toes from one foot, so that it was a little lame and ran very slightly crab-like, sideways. As her hand came out he saw it become still as death in the sun.

London in those days was very noisy but unless the noise

became intensely local you went on dancing or eating or loving or walking, wherever you were. The noise on that night seemed to come mostly in thumps and barks of gunfire from the suburbs and down the river. Forrester remembered it as nothing much more than an extra drum in the orchestra. He and his wife had nothing to do with the blackness outside; it seemed to them momentarily that the war had stopped for them. If he now remembered anything more vivid than this feeling of the personal suspense of war it was the feeling of his wife's tender body through the thin silk dress, and the flavour of burnt mushrooms.

They were dancing quietly, not talking, when the bomb fell. He did not hear it falling above the noise of the orchestra. He remembered only that one moment his wife was there, face to face with him, dancing, and that the next moment she was not there. In the moment of an enormous darkening blast that sucked the breath out of his body and then drove it back again like the heat of a furnace she was gone for ever. He never saw her again.

As he sat thinking he saw the child smiling up at him. He saw it as a smile in return for something. He became aware that all the time his own smile had become fixed on his face, and suddenly he felt something extraordinarily compassionate about the way she sat there, sparing a little time for him from the absorbing game of torment with the lizard in the sun.

The consequence of the bomb was that he had tried to get himself killed. He began to bring to the business of ending life a frenzied deliberation. He wanted to do it in the ordinary course of combat, so as not to give to his parents a more complicated pain. Because he was flying fighters it seemed that it might well have been a simple thing. But it was not simple. And nothing, as time went on, could make it simple. He took his aircraft about the sky in a cold frenzy of purpose, determined to wreck it. He seemed suddenly to have a kind of sinister charm about him. He became involved in a series of fantastic escapes until in the end it became inevitably construed in the proper quarters as bravery of a deliberate sort and they gave him a decoration with a magnificent citation declaiming his splendid valour and leadership over Havre. The consequence was that he went out and

14

got very drunk over the medal and had hardly ever felt less like leadership and still less like valour.

Now, at last, the purely personal attempt at death was over. He was waiting for a man named Carrington, and life, in Mosquitoes, was to be very different now. He did not know how different; except that from now onwards death, if it came, would have to come accidentally.

'Hullo; so this is where you hide yourself.'

Looking up, shading his eyes with his hands, he saw Harris, the Squadron doctor and senior M.O., a short cherubically bald man with a face burnt to a violent brown.

'Hullo,' he said. He looked at once away to the child. She was looking at the lizard in a cruelly fixed way, rose-brown hands ready to strike again.

'Blore said I'd find you here,' Harris said.

'Something you want?'

'I wondered if you'd care for a trip.' Harris said. 'Village across the plain. Christian community.'

'And what made you think I had anything to do with Christian communities?'

'It's just a trip,' Harris said. 'Half an hour.'

'You go.'

'Really nice people,' Harris said. 'Really very interesting. Pure Burmese. They speak English. I buy fruit from them.'

'Buy me a nice cold melon.' Forrester was still watching the child, who in turn had spread both hands in the form of a brown cage.

'I wish you'd come,' Harris said. 'Seriously, I wish you'd come.' He made suddenly a very astonishing statement. 'I'm going to help choose their hymns for Easter Sunday.'

'Good God,' Forrester said. 'And what have I to do with that?'

'You could help.'

'Ah, I see,' he said. 'A new form of doctrine. Mepacrine and seraphim.'

He suddenly got up, holding the towel about his loins, dancing up and down a little as his thin soles touched the scalding dust, and as he did so the child for a moment forgot the lizard and looked up, laughing, as if in turn she were mocking him.

'What is she doing?' Harris said.

'To kill or not to kill,' he said. 'That's all. That's the question.'

He moved a pace or two away from the pagoda steps, lifting his hand slightly in farewell to the child.

'No business here,' Harris said. 'Probably a damned carrier of something.'

'None of us have. Lousy country,' Forrester said.

'Think so?'

Forrester did not answer and began to walk away. Each step across the dust burned up through the thin rubber soles of his shoes. He resented Harris, though more in amusement and less harshly, as he had long resented Blore and already resented Carrington. He had been happy alone, watching the child. 'You should really come,' Harris said, and in that moment Forrester was startled by the brutal slap of the child's hand on the stone behind him and he turned to see what she had done.

This time she had come down too sharply on the lizard as it had run to escape, and now it lay immobile on the stone for the last time. And seeing him look down she smiled her flat genial undisturbed smile up at him as if nothing had happened.

'It'll be good fun,' Harris said.

Will it indeed? Forrester thought, but did not answer. He stood instead looking back at the child. Now because the lizard was dead she was trying to make it run again. When she saw that it could not run she pulled it by one of its hands across the stone, animating it crookedly, sideways and then backwards, quickly and then slowly, until in sudden spasms it looked more living in death than it had done in its life of fear. At last she let it lie still again. And then for the last time she grinned up at him, quite serene, almond eyes soft and bland, rose-brown hands rubbing themselves together as if rubbing the feel of death from them.

By this time, too, Harris had turned back to look, the sweat standing in fierce brassy drops on his amiable face as he looked down at the lizard lying dead on the stone. Already in that terrific heat it seemed to have shrivelled where it lay.

'Funny the fascination death has,' he said. 'Very funny.'

'Very,' Forrester said. 'Perhaps that's why you became a doctor?'

'Well!' Harris said. He turned away towards the tent, waving his arms in mock anger, making noises of punctured pride.

'Well! Now for that last bloody insult you shall come.'

'Good old doc.' Suddenly Forrester did not mind. 'The good old mepacrine and seraphim.'

'You can come and see what civilization did for this country before war busted it up,' the doctor said. 'You can come and see the real country. The real people too.'

'The good old yellow peril,' Forrester said.

They had reached the tent and now as he held back the flap so that the doctor could go in he stood for a moment longer, looking back in the fierce dazzle of light to the broken pagoda and the child. And he saw her still smiling, still trying to bring the dead lizard back to life in the sun.

But what he did not see was the way Harris and Blore were looking at each other. They were looking at each other very seriously, and Harris was shaking his head.

2

The doctor drove out of the town by the perimeter road on the south side, past the great monastery, towards the plain, driving fast between deep double rows of trees that shaded the lower bullocks tracks running parallel on either side. Two gigantic elephants that stood in front of the greater temple, white and scarlet and gold, blazed with cheap and dazzling fire against the dark shadow of the immense banyan tree that seemed quite black, in turn, against the white pagodas behind. Along the road small gangs of Burmese labourers with a few Indian boys were shovelling truck-loads of stone into craters left by bombing, and at these points the doctor dived the jeep into the bullock track and down on through the bottomless dust of it until the road was clear again. A continuous fine fall of dust lay on all the brown naked backs of the boys so that the skin was bloomed to rosy cream and as they looked up their eyes were bitter and dilated with the sting of dusted sweat. Forrester clung to the side of the jeep as the doctor dived in or out of the bullock tracks, keeping his head down against the dense cream fog of dust that obliterated every few moments the groups of slow and wondrous Burmese villagers, brilliant with waist-cloths of purple and vermilion, trekking heavily with a broken bullock or a water-buffalo and a cart, towards the plain.

'I've made a sort of dispensary for these people,' Harris said. 'Very jolly.' He wore dark sun-glasses which did not conceal the restless boyishness of his face. He seemed to regard the entire reoccupation of Burma as a huge fraternal joke.

Forrester did not speak and the doctor drove at this moment out of the bullock track, so that the jeep lay back at a steep angle, wheels churning violently in hollows of dust a foot deep. It hung for a few seconds poised like a cat at the crest of a high wall. Then the doctor threw it into emergency gear and it leapt over the edge of the track to the metal road with an explosive bound. The doctor, impassive behind dark glasses, seemed to take no notice of it at all.

'You're quiet,' he said. 'You seem off colour.'

'Perfectly all right,' Forrester said.

'Look tired. Take your salt water?'

'No.'

'Take your mepacrine tablets?'

'No.'

The doctor did not say anything. He drove on for some moments as if considering a new way of approach, but finally, after lifting the dark glasses off his eyes and taking a quick look at Forrester from beneath them, he simply went on with the old:

'You really ought to take those tablets. Important.'

'And turn yellow,' Forrester said.

The doctor adjusted his glasses and seemed to think of something else. 'You ought to wear glasses too,' he said.

'I'm sure.'

'It's possible to get sun-stroke through the eyes,' Harris said. 'I suppose you know that?'

'No.'

'Then you should know. It can be a most terrible thing.'

'Well, well, well,' Forrester said.

The doctor gave up. Driving on in silence, he took the jeep off the road again and down into the bullock track and then up with a roar to the road again until at last he had thought of something quite fresh and distant from the subject of Forrester's health to say.

'I hear Blore is leaving you,' he said.

'Yes: I'm bloody glad,' Forrester said.

'You really are off colour, aren't you?'

'No.'

'Remind me to give you a box of a new thing that's come out,' Harris said. 'Secret as yet. Over from Calcutta yesterday. A temperament killer.'

'You think of everything,' Forrester said. 'I suppose you couldn't prescribe two cases of beer? Iced, for preference.'

The bitterness in Forrester's voice, more acid in its fineness than Harris had yet heard, drove the doctor into silence again. He put the jeep into the bullock track and after a quarter of a mile or so drove it out for the last time. The road and the bullock track had become one. The narrowing half-metal track began to stretch out without shade, glittering and nakedly intolerable in the full glare of the plain.

Instinctively as they came out from the shade of the last trees Forrester put up his hands. It was to shield himself from the vicious downward blow he knew the sun would give. Before he knew what he was doing and before the doctor could look at him he lowered very slightly the peak of his cap. It brought the smallest relief to his eyes. And in a moment the entire sun-beaten mass of the plain, fantastically hazy in a glare of light that seemed to rock back from the crystalline dust as if from minutely broken glass, came brutally into focus. He suddenly saw the plain as he had not seen it before. He became aware for the first time of its vastness. The road had become like a mark of darker burning traced across it. And when after a mile or two a single narrow gauge track of railway appeared suddenly out of the dust its two glittering slashes of silver line seemed to disappear each way into distances that had no horizon. There did not seem to be a living leaf or branch in the cloud-like level crystalline distances of haze between the moving jeep and the cloud-like mountains.

But after a few moments, in which the doctor did not speak again, he saw that he was mistaken. The near distances had become broken by trees. Colourless at first in the glittering haze and shapeless against the purple mass of horizon, they became clearer, greyer and finally greener as the jeep went on. When the road at last reached them, nothing but a track in the dust now, they stood like an oasis of skeletons, flowering green at the high tips. Soon the dust beneath them gave way to earth, and high wild banana trees shone tenderly and softly, with silkiest green, above the shade. Finally he began to see the village: brown palisades of dry palm fronds, fences and hovels of cleft bamboo, bashas and huts of bamboo thatched like the fences with wide brown fans of palm.

The doctor drove to the first of the palm fences and stopped. Immediately there came out from behind the fence, as if they had been waiting there all afternoon, about a score of small cream-brown boys, laughing and shouting. The doctor became very excited and stood up in the jeep, talking rapidly, partly in English and partly Burmese.

'My patients!' he said. Forrester grinned in reply.

'Several Christian boys!' the doctor said. The boys began climbing on to the jeep. They sat on the hood and the mud-guards and wherever they could find a hold. The doctor was jubilant with excitement. Forrester turned round and grinned at the packed creamy-brown faces laughing with flat almond eyes. 'Pilot!' the doctor shouted, and made wild gestures, as of flying, with both arms. All the boys laughed at once in a great shout and Forrester laughed too.

'Fine boys!' the doctor said. 'Magnificent subjects for research! I should like to stay here. Honestly, Forrester, I love this country. I love the people.'

He suddenly sat down, put the jeep violently into gear and drove on. The sudden shock of movement threw all the boys sitting on the mudguards and the hood into the thick dust of the road. All the boys began shouting for the doctor to stop but Harris drove on, pretending not to hear. The boys continued shouting in a frenzy of delight. Suddenly the doctor slapped his hand to his head as if remembering something awful and stopped the jeep so sharply that all of the boys who had not fallen off the first time now fell off into the dust with the rest.

'Do it on purpose!' the doctor said. 'Every time!' The sweat was pouring down from the rim of his bush hat as if the hat were full of water. His eyes were shining with tears. Behind him the boys were climbing back on the jeep, brown bodies powdered now with yellow dust, laughing and shouting.

'Wouldn't believe how they love it!' Harris said. 'Wouldn't believe!'

The road narrowed under the deeper shade of banana and palm and tamarind trees between brittle palisades of palm fronds. Little shadowy wooden houses raised up on low stilts began to appear in small compounds of bamboo. In the shade Forrester felt his first relief from the staggering violence of the plain and the sun. The doctor drove the jeep on through the narrow dusty track until the houses on either side were a little larger, with wider verandas and larger compounds and roof thatch of newer, cleaner palm.

He stopped in front of one of these houses with violent use of the brakes, so that all the small boys, laughing hysterically, fell off into the dust again. The trousers of the very smallest boy, hitting the dust with a flat explosion, fell off completely. And for one moment he stood there laughing up at Forrester with friendly almond eyes, trousers over his ankles, buttery brown belly quivering with laughter.

There was a great shade tree over the house and Forrester, looking up, saw it covered with the same small creamy white blossoms, already sweetly fragrant, but not with the full sickly honey-sweetness of evening, that he had known on the trees in the town. He got out of the jeep and stood by himself against the palisade of the compound. The tree had the coolness of a great green rock: the shade of it was solid and yet in some way liquid too. He felt it pouring down on him greenly and moistly in heavy waves, giving him comfort. The voices of the boys seemed suddenly cool too and for the first time that day he did not care about the heat, the sweat and the glare of sun.

As he stood there waiting for Harris to unload his two black leather cases of medical supplies he turned and saw a woman walking across the compound from the house. She was a very pale Burmese woman of forty. She was dressed simply in a skirt of dark purple and a blouse, almost European in style, of banana-yellow silk, high in the neck, where her dignified black hair lay at the back in flat rich coils. The skirt was tight on her narrow hips, folded so that the slit in it was hardly visible at the side. She walked with only a slight swing of the hips, with suppressed and shy grace, her bare legs moving smoothly in flat brown shoes. As she came across the compound she began to smile and the pale handsome quiet face grew more living at every step, and at last she was holding out her hand.

'Ah! yes, yes,' the doctor said. 'This is Dorothy.'

The woman held out her hand and Forrester took it and smiled.

'Mr Forrester. Squadron Leader. A pilot,' the doctor said.

He was pushing through the small swing gate of the compound with the bags of medical supplies.

'Dorothy is from Rangoon.'

'I'm glad to know you,' Forrester said.

'And I am happy to know you,' she said.

'You see!' the doctor said. 'Perfect English! The most wonderful English! You would never know.' He turned on his heel in the dust of the compound, trying to wave the bags about in triumph.

Forrester held open the gate so that the woman could walk into the compound. She went through it silently in the soft dust and then waited for him to shut it. He shut it behind her, keeping the brown laughing boys outside, and then walked with her across the clean swept compound to the house.

'I was at the University of Rangoon,' she said.

'Yes,' he said.

'My sister too. My sister has a degree.'

The doctor set down the medical bags on the steps of the veranda. He wiped his face and the inside of his hat with his handkerchief. Forrester came with the woman and waited.

'Please sit on the veranda,' she said.

'Thank you,' Forrester said.

'There are chairs there at the back and I will get you something cool to drink.'

'Some lime?' the doctor said.

'Some lime – whatever you wish.'

'Please, the lime. Forrester, the lime is wonderful.'

For a moment longer the woman stood in an attitude of service, hands together below her small waist, and then turned and went across the dark veranda towards the door of the house.

'And where is Anna?' the doctor called.

She turned at the door to answer him.

'Oh! She is here. In the village. She will be back.'

'And you think there will be fruit for me?'

'Oh! There will be fruit for you, yes,' she said. 'Plenty.'

She went into the house before the doctor could speak again. He sat down on one of the light bamboo chairs at the back of the veranda, where the shade was doubly black and deep from the palm roof and the great tree. 'Glad even to sell fruit,' he said. 'Sell you the most wonderful melons and bananas and limes. Glad to do it. Everything gone. Came up here stripped of everything. Bloody Japs. All the way from Rangoon.'

Forrester leaned back in the bamboo chair. He felt tired and took off his hat. Its wet brim had scarred his forehead and he rubbed the skin slowly backwards and forwards with one hand. Beyond the edges of the great tree he could see segments of sky, pale hazy blue and glittering with heat and far away. They reminded him of the plain that lay below it, with its miles of bitter, shadeless dust and its illusion of having no end. All the harsher effect of it seemed suddenly to have slipped away. He shut his eyes for a moment or two and rested, once more feeling the liquid fragrant shade pour down on his face, and in a few seconds he could not believe in the bright brutality he hated so much. He let his hands fall to his sides. And slowly he went off into a doze that was tranquil and dark in its restfulness.

He roused suddenly to hear the doctor say 'Lime!' and to see the woman standing by him, smiling, with a tray of glasses.

'I'm sorry,' he said. The shade of the tree seemed to have grown darker, as if the sun had begun to go down.

'Nice nap,' Harris said. 'Do you the world of good.'

'Sometimes you talk the most drivelling nonsense, Harris,' he said.

'You've been to sleep,' the doctor said.

'Complete drivel,' he said. He leaned forward, putting his head, clean of sweat now, into his hands, gently rubbing himself into wakefulness, still not quite sure whether he had slept or not.

And then, a moment later, he knew that he was not sure. He looked up from his hands and saw that the colour of the woman's skirt had changed. It was no longer dark purple. It was a soft melon shade of green, and the slit of it was folded still further across her body, still more in the European way.

It was the change of colour made him drop his hands to his knees and look slowly upwards. He could not believe that she was not the woman he had seen go back through the door into the darkness of the house. He seemed to be looking at a paler, slighter reflection of her. The bright banana-yellow blouse had turned to white. It was made of some fine material like organdie and the cream of her arms and narrow shoulders shone through it softly. And seeing it he got up so sharply that he knocked over the bamboo chair.

The doctor lay back in his chair, legs spread out, his belly just across the line of his jungle trousers quivering with laughter. 'She won't eat you, Forrester. Honestly, Forrester, she won't eat you!'

'I thought – ' Forrester said.

The girl was laughing too. There was none of the Mongolian flatness in her face except the very slightest pressing out of the pale cream cheek bones, and her paleness was so pure and soft that she seemed to have kept all her life out of the sun. She stood quite upright in the deep shade with the tray in her hands. She laughed at him quietly from behind the glasses and the green jug of lime, without mocking. Her head was held very straight and in the right side of the smooth black hair, just above the ear, was a cluster of pinkish-scarlet buds of flower.

'My God, the funniest thing I ever saw!' Harris said. He rolled off his chair and tried to quieten himself by walking up and down.

'I really have been to sleep,' Forrester said. He looked straight at the black, slightly elongated eyes of the girl and smiled. It was like coming to life in a strange world.

'You really have,' she said.

'I'm sorry.'

'You were very tired and no one wanted to wake you.'

'It was very rude of me.'

'It was very very rude and no one minded at all.'

She held the tray with one hand and began to try to pour the lime-juice from the jug into one of the glasses with the other.

'No: let me,' he said.

'Thank you so much,' she said.

She held the tray with both hands and he picked up the jug. 'You see, this is Anna,' the doctor said, 'the younger sister.' Forrester was not really listening. He was pouring the lime-juice from the glass jug and through the glass was looking at the pale cream shoulders of the girl. He felt suddenly quite nervous and could not look directly at her face. He filled the glass to the brim and set the jug slowly down. Then he took the glass and said 'thank you'. She stood there without any attempt at going away. And suddenly before he lifted the glass he made himself look at her face. The black eyes were watching him very softly. 'You must have been very tired. You look very tired,' she said. He did not speak but he knew without resentment that what she said was true. He was tired with a long deep tiredness that went exactly like the long dusty arid road of the plain far back inside himself.

Then he realized suddenly that she stood holding the tray so that he could drink again. He drank the long fresh glass of lime eagerly, feeling the coolness of it wash away the dust of his throat. 'That's the most wonderful lime on either side of the equator,' the doctor said, and Forrester filled the glass for the second time.

'Not so tired now?' she said.

'No,' he said. 'Not so tired.'

She took the tray and set it on a small bamboo table at the side of the veranda, by the door of the house.

'Please sit down,' she said.

'If you sit down,' he said.

'You can both sit down,' Harris said. 'I'm off to my brand new basha dispensary to mix a prescription or two.'

'You were to mix hymns too, don't forget,' Forrester said.

'I'll be back for that.'

'Always at work,' Forrester taunted him. 'Body and soul.'

Harris, carrying the two bags, walked down the steps of the veranda and across the compound. The girl watched him go and then sat down. Forrester sat down too. As he did so he looked up at the space of sky visible beyond the great tree overhanging the house. He was surprised to see its change of colour: already the pale haze of day was drawing out from it and the deep tawny purple of late afternoon spreading up in its place.

'You thought I was Dorothy,' the girl said.

'Yes,' he said.

'She will be glad of that,' she said. 'There is twenty years between us.'

He sat entranced by the little touch of imperfection in her English. The glass of lime was very cool in his hand. The girl had nothing to drink and sat empty-handed and the coolness of her slim cream arms lying along the sides of the chair was something that fascinated him. And as he sat wondering what to say to her he heard a stirring of air in the dry palms of the palisade across the compound: the first breaking of the oppressive sun-killed day by the wind of evening blowing in from the river. He lifted his face and caught the breath of it, sweetened as it came by the scent of the tree.

'What tree is this?' he said.

'This is a margosa tree.'

'It is very beautiful.'

He leaned back and looked up at the darkening branches. He breathed the heavy fragrance of the little creamy flowers and caught with it the finer fragrance of the half-open cluster of buds in her hair.

He wanted also to ask her the name of the flower she wore. But suddenly he felt nervous again and could not speak. As if she were shy too she spoke formally. She had a way of putting her head slightly to one side, the flower upwards, as if she feared the flower would fall. And he began to think it would fall too and watched it, fascinated, half hoping it would fall, so that he could reach forward and catch it in his hands. But it did not fall all that evening as he watched it. The rosy-scarlet buds remained tightly suspended in the black hair and all the time he felt a deep suspense in watching them and a wonder in the thing that never happened.

'Have you been here for long?'

'For nearly three months now,' he said.

'Do you like it?'

He hesitated for a moment. He did not want to offend her, and said, 'I'm not sure if I know it yet.'

'No one knows it,' she said. 'All of Burma. No one knows it all.'

'No,' he said.

'It is very beautiful here in the dry belt in the cool weather,' she said. She still spoke with delicate polite correctness, as if she were talking from a text-book. 'But no one knows it all.'

'Rice and rubics,' he said, 'that was all the Burma I knew. Before I came.'

'There are stones here if you wish to buy them,' she said.

He did not know what to say. He did not want to buy stones;

he was not interested. Sometimes he thought he was the only serving man in the entire East who did not possess a small horde of gems in cotton wool.

'We could go to see them if you wish,' she said.

'You are very kind,' he said.

'It is not far.'

He did not know what to do. He was bored by the thought of looking at useless collections of coloured stone, and thought of the doctor, busy with prescriptions and hymns, and said:

'The doctor will want to get back.'

'Oh no,' she said. 'He goes late. Always. He never bothers. It's all the same to him.'

'All right,' he said. 'I would be glad.'

She got up at once and walked to the door of the house, opening it and calling a few words inside without waiting for an answer. Forrester finished his lime and got up, leaving his cap on the table. He had not recovered from the surprise of seeing her there on the veranda after his sleep, and now as they walked together across the compound and through the gate and up into the dusty track that was the street of the village he sometimes let her walk a pace or two in front of him, so that he could look at her fully again. She was very small beside him, her hips in the light green skirt almost straight, her breasts hardly lifting the transparent stuff of the blouse. She walked with slow grace in the dust of the track, not speaking much, turning only sometimes to smile at him with eyes that the smile itself seemed to press a little flatter.

As they walked up through the village, between rows of low cane houses and fences of palm, he could see the dull bronzy-purple rim of evening horizon growing like solid smoke between the gaps of the trees. He saw villagers lying or sitting in the deep shade of the houses, like flashes of white and magenta shadow against the dull orange of evening, and he heard the wind slowly flapping again in the long shining banana leaves.

'We go in here,' she said, and he followed her across one of the near compounds towards a hut of cane and palm, and went into it after her.

Shade from tamarind trees and palms made it almost dark inside the hut, where a Burmese woman of old grey face sat on

28

the floor. The girl spoke to her and she hurriedly got up in a wonder of shy excitement at the presence of Forrester. Her flat lips trembled so that she could not speak but after a moment or two a man of forty-five or fifty, wearing a green felt hat and black trousers and a bright red shirt, came in from the compound.

'They are mother and son,' the girl said. 'They had a house in the town once but it is gone now.'

'Pleased,' the man said. 'Good.' He shook hands energetically with Forrester and smiled with shy flat cordial face. 'Pleased. Good.'

'They will get the stones,' the girl said.

From a wooden cabinet on the wall the old woman began to bring out very small folded packages of brown paper and lay them on a teak table in the centre of the room, opening them there with trembling hands. The son talked to her swiftly as if wanting to hurry her but she would not be hurried and laid out each package with slow care, unfolding its under-covering of cotton wool until the small seeds of red and emerald and white and blue lay clear. The old woman spoke eagerly to the girl, and the girl spoke to Forrester. 'She would like you to sit down,' she said. The jewels were spread out on the teak table on white nests of cotton wool and Forrester sat down to look at them. It was growing twilight in the little room and he could not see very well and as if sensing it the son brought a small tin oil lamp and set it on the table.

'These are rubies,' the girl said. 'But you know them.'

'Yes,' he said.

'These are white sapphires, and these are golden amethysts.'

He picked up some of the stones and held them in his hands under the light. All of them were small and the cutting was bad.

'Perhaps they have something better,' he said. He was embarrassed by the eager, trembling face of the old woman and the smiling eagerness of the son, and he wanted to be polite.

'They say tomorrow,' the girl said.

He did not know what to say. The old woman began talking to the girl very quickly again.

'They say if you will come tomorrow they will have better stones. Zircons and emeralds perhaps.'

He looked down at her face, very pale in the lamplight of the darkening room. Her black eyes were intensely penetrating and he knew suddenly that she knew what he was thinking: that he was embarrassed and did not want the stones and did not know how to refuse.

'Tell them I will come again,' he said.

'Tomorrow?'

'If it is possible,' he said.

'Try to make it possible.'

Before he could speak again she began talking to the old woman and the son. 'Pleased!' the son said. 'Good!' He suddenly took off his hat to Forrester and bowed.

'They say they will have beautiful stones for you,' the girl said.

'Thank them very much,' he said.

He got up from the table and shook hands first with the old woman and then the son. With his hat held above his head like an umbrella the son came to the door with Forrester and the girl, saying over and over again, 'Pleased! Good-bye!' bowing to them very slowly, like a man before a shrine.

Outside the sun had already set and under the trees the short twilight, broken now by a breath of wind, was almost gone. Whenever the breeze died for a moment under the thick sweet trees the air was profoundly still and he could feel the silence begin to spread vastly over all the plain. It seemed to wash away at last, as it always did, the brutal clamour of the day.

'You did not want the stones,' the girl said.

'No.'

'I am sorry.'

'I have no one to give stones to,' he said.

'No one?'

'No one,' he said.

'Then there is no need for you to come again,' she said.

'All the same I would like to come,' he said. He walked entranced by the silence of the rapidly falling darkness and by the little lights coming everywhere now among the trees. She did not speak again for a short time and he knew by her silence that she was thinking of what he had said. He felt he had spoken hypocritically but there was a gentleness in the silence that did not press on him. And sometimes as they walked past the light of a house or a fire burning in a compound he looked at her calm unaverted face, with its slightly flattened eyes that seemed always to be on the verge of smiling, and felt the last irritation of the afternoon slipping away.

'Do you mean you have really no one to give the stones to?' she said. 'Or only that you have no one who would like them?'

'I have no one to give them to,' he said.

With the repetition of her question he felt the beginnings of his irritation come back. She was going to start to be stupid, he thought, like the rest. She was going to catechise him and push him and fret him with curiosity. She was going to behave with the same infuriating inquisitiveness as Blore and Harris.

'You are the first officer who has come here and not bought jewels,' she said.

'Am I?' he said. He spoke almost sharply and then in the light of a house as they passed it he saw her smiling and in a moment his irritation was gone.

'All of them come for that. I thought you had come for that too. That is why I took you.'

'No,' he said. 'I don't care for them.'

'I'm sorry. It was my fault,' she said.

'There is nothing for you to be sorry about.'

'It was very stupid of me.'

He was suddenly touched by the humility of the way she spoke and he did not know what to say. He felt for the first time slightly ashamed of himself. The feeling jolted him physically. And without having the slightest idea why he did it he swung out both hands and said:

'It's really very wonderful here.'

'Most of them hate it. They long for England,' she said. 'Don't you?'

'No,' he said. 'I don't long for England.'

'Never?'

'No,' he said. 'Sometimes I think I'll never go back.'

She turned her head as if startled. Before he was aware of it and could do anything to stop it the word England brought back the idea that he was going to kill himself. Its violent suddenness almost frightened him. He looked at her quickly as if thinking she must have heard what was going on in his mind, but she was not looking now. She was walking in the same smooth calm way as before, and he knew that all that was wrong was his own stupidity.

'We are at the house,' she said.

He saw a light in the small windows behind the veranda, and smelt the deep heavy fragrance of the tree. He held open the gate of the palisade and she said:

'There is a light in the dispensary still. That must be the doctor.'

He followed her across the compound to where in the far corner was the hut that Harris had made into a dispensary. The girl opened the door. Inside the hut Harris, sleeves rolled high up his sun-red arms, was bending over a white enamel bowl of hot water in the centre of a long teak table. Behind him stood a few rows of shelves neatly filled with bottles.

Forrester was surprised to see that the hut was big enough to hold two beds, in one of which a small Burmese girl lay looking upward with staring scared eyes in the lamplight. Harris said, 'Hullo. She was brought in by Dorothy,' and wiped his hands on a towel. The girl went over to the bed and knelt down by it, talking to the child in whispers, holding her hands.

'She didn't take her mepacrine,' Harris said. 'But that was scarcely odd, because the poor little devil had no mepacrine to take.'

'Poor kid.'

'Let it be a lesson to you,' Harris said.

'Why don't you prescribe *Onward Christian Soldiers* three times a day in water?' Forrester said. 'For the good of my soul?'

'Stop talking cock,' Harris said. 'I want you to go back to H.Q.'

'Medical orderly,' Forrester said. 'Promotion.'

'Take the jeep and go back to my tent and see Johnson, the corporal. Give him this list and let him have the things ready and drive the jeep back to fetch me at daylight.'

Harris gave him a folded paper. Forrester took it and toyed with it in his hands.

32

'Some day you must tell me what H.Q. thinks of M.O.s who start private hospitals for the natives.'

'H.Q. can go to bloody hell,' the doctor said.

'That,' Forrester said, 'is practically the most sensible remark I've heard in Burma.'

'It'll cost you a drink,' the doctor said.

The girl, smiling, came over from the sick-bed, and suddenly Forrester remembered the plain. He was not sure of the road going across the vast expanse of dust in darkness.

'I'm not sure of this road,' he said.

'There ought to be a moon,' Harris said. 'Otherwise of course there's a thing called navigation.'

'I never learnt it.'

'What is wrong?' the girl said.

'He is not sure of the road,' Harris said. 'He is very young to be out at night.'

'I could show him.'

'Oh no,' Forrester said. 'Thank you all the same.'

'It is a little difficult to the end of the village but after that you make for the railway and it's all right.'

'Please,' he said. 'I can find it.'

'You'd better go with her,' Harris said. 'At least there'll be one good head.'

'You wouldn't like the corporal to bring the harmonium?' Forrester said. 'No trouble.'

'Just keep your mind on your work,' the doctor said.

'No trouble,' he said.

He followed the girl out of the little dispensary into the darkness of the compound. The night was very warm and the scent of the tree had closed down like a too-sweet sickly cloud. There was no air moving in the dry leaves of the fences, or in the leaves, or in the thatch of the house, and the dust was silent as solid velvet everywhere.

He switched on the lights of the jeep and waited for the girl to climb into the seat in front. He got in too and started the engine.

'I'll turn round,' he said.

'There's no need,' she said. 'I will take you out another way.'

'It's very kind of you,' he said.

As he drove the jeep through the narrow fenced track between the lighted houses and the trees, she said nothing except an occasional word to guide him. He drove in low gear, quite slowly, but enough breeze came in the open sides of the vehicle to blow her blouse flatly against her body, that looked all mellow cream now in the reflected light.

Gradually the track widened and there were no more houses and in a few moments he saw the last of the banana trees, like a huge column of green glass in the headlights, go past him into the darkness. He saw before him the beginnings of the plain, the yellow dust distinct in its vast flatness under the softest sky of black-purple, already wonderfully thick with stars. The moon was not up yet but he could see the faint glow of it beginning to whiten hazily the sky above the rim of mountains and he knew that it would be easy now to find the way.

He stopped the jeep and got out and went to the other side, to help her down. 'I shall find it now,' he said. 'Will you be all right?'

'I shall be all right,' she said.

He did not know what else to say to her and stood for a moment awkwardly beside her, looking at her face in the lamplight, its flatness without shadow, the hair intensely black about it, so that the skin was whiter and purer than any English girl he had ever seen.

'I must go back,' she said.

'Yes.' He held both her hands as she climbed down, and then let them go. Almost at once she gave him her right hand back, shaking his own.

'Good night,' she said.

'Good night,' he said. 'It has been a wonderful pleasure.'

'You are coming again,' she said.

'Yes,' he said.

Before he could say anything more she turned away and began to walk back again along the track. She turned and smiled for a moment and he lifted his hand, standing for a moment or two longer to watch her go.

When he could no longer see her in the darkness he got up into the jeep and drove out across the plain. He did not drive very fast. It seemed to him that he had suddenly all the time in the world to drive across the great stretch of dust that was becoming lighter and lighter now, with a flush of rosy orange, from the rising moon. The night was very beautiful and there was nothing to fret the edges of his mind as he thought back to the girl, the way he had slept on the veranda of the house and had woken in dumb surprise to see her there. He could even bear the sound of the jackals, the only sound across the plain, howling and crying like stricken voices in the hot darkness, almost without rest.

3

He got to the camp about eight o'clock, and, not realizing he had not eaten, went straight to his tent. The glow of the moon coming up behind the palms had a fantastic and sombre splendour that dwarfed the brown tent, the palms and the broken chalky pagodas into the shadowy paltriness of ruins left by an advancing army. He saw the end flap of his tent open and hooked back and inside it the golden glow, very like the colour of the moonlight flooding the dust outside, of the two hurricane lamps hanging from the poles above each bed. Close by stood his green canvas bath, filled with water put there by the boy Ali, ready for the bath he had not taken.

He knew that Blore would be reading in the tent, and he determined not to stay inside more than a moment or two. Late as it was, he would come outside again and take his bath, washing away the day's dust in the light of the moon.

He went into the tent and came at once to a dead stop just inside it. Blore was reading on his bed, under a mosquito net still thrown back at the edges, propped up on one elbow as Forrester had expected him to be. His own bed, with its mosquito net that always reminded him of an enlarged meat-cover and infuriated him constantly because it let in a single disastrous mosquito every night, was neat and ready too. But at the end of the tent, placed cross-wise, with its mosquito net already fixed, was a third bed. In it lay a very young officer. And he knew at once, even before his anger came rushing up at him to overcome him with impotence, that it was Carrington.

Startled and troubled, Blore leapt off the bed. He began to speak at once, nervously changing his book from hand to hand. 'I thought you were over at Ops. I couldn't find you anywhere.' He seemed to Forrester quite frightened.

The young officer in a very leisurely way got off his bed. He was slight and small.

'This is Carrington,' Blore said. 'He got in by Dak from Comilla about seven.'

Forrester did not move or speak. The young officer had an extraordinarily high aristocratic head, with long blond hair sliced back like glass. It gave him in Forrester's eyes an expression of maddening aloofness.

'This is Squadron-Leader Forrester,' Blore said.

'Good evening,' Carrington said. He had the single thick blue stripes of a flying officer on his shoulder and his navigator's badge on his chest.

'Who gave you authority to sleep here?' Forrester said.

'The camp commandant,' Blore said.

'Then the camp commandant should mind his own bloody business!'

'I'm sorry,' the boy said.

'It's rather late to be sorry.' He looked savagely round at the confined space of the tent, that seemed now to be nothing but an oppressive tangle of men and mosquito netting. He felt that it stifled him even more than it had done in the awful heat of the afternoon.

'You know how it is,' Blore said. 'Everywhere is as full as it can stick.'

'So I see! So I see!' He began savagely to unbutton his bush jacket. Without speaking again, he took it off and threw it through the loose mosquito netting on to the bed. Underneath it his thin singlet was grey and wet with sweat-soaked dust. He took that off also and stood with it screwed up in his hands, as if ready to throw it with the jacket.

'And another thing.' It seemed better in the height of his anger to reveal the entire mass of his grievances. 'Where have you been? We've been waiting three weeks for you – the whole bloody show held up for a navigator.'

'I thought you knew,' Carrington said. 'I was taken ill at Comilla. Dysentery. They yanked me into hospital before I knew.'

'And before we knew. Didn't they ever tell you about a thing called a signal?'

'We did signal.'

'Then where in Hell and God's name did it get to?'

'You know how it is,' the boy said. 'India.'

'I don't know how it is! Tell me!' Forrester said.

'It was probably some clot of an Indian kid who was supposed to have sent it and didn't. You can never depend on anybody.'

'No?' Forrester said. 'So it seems.'

He threw the wet mess of his under-vest that was like wrung-out dish-cloth down on the bed, and turned abruptly away. Before either of the men could speak again he picked up his soap and bush towel from his table by the bed-head and went outside. The heat of the plain was not yet humid enough, even down on the river, for mosquitoes to be anything like a scourge and he was far too stinking and clogged with dust and sweat not to think of bathing, even though it was long past the hour. He slipped off his socks and trousers and stood naked in the canvas bath. The water came just above his ankles. It would have been poured in by Ali, quite hot, about six o'clock, and now even after nearly three hours it was still unpleasantly tepid and dead. He picked up his soap and began to lather it in his hands, turning nervously round and round in the yellow glare of the moon, not knowing quite what he was doing, aware of being furiously angry and of behaving badly and yet of being able to do nothing about it. All the tension and irritation of the earlier day, so explicable to him but of utter unreasonableness to others and only calmed and dissipated by the few hours with the girl in the village across the plain, now came back, black and heavy, on the full tide of the bitterest memories, complete with the haunting longing for death that had always seemed to be its only end.

He flung the soap down into the water at his feet and then sat down. The actual physical feeling of water against his sweat-tired body had for a moment a curiously calming effect. He sat relaxed, with his head in his wet hands, staring at the fragmentary gold reflection of the moon in the water between his legs. And then his first moment of calm was broken as he looked up.

'I came to say I was sorry I put up a black.' He looked up to see Carrington standing there. The young aristocratic fair face, with its too-oiled, too-precise hair, still angered him. He knew with perfect rationality that this was the moment in which to end all the differences, the frictions and the misunderstandings between them: that it would be a simple thing, a right thing, and a final thing for him to get up out of the bath and say, 'For God's sake, don't let's go on talking cock' and end for ever the childishness of something that was of his own making. He had, after all, to fly with this boy: to know him, to give and to gain confidence, to share the physical and mental experience of operating over a vast country of river and mountain and jungle, practically roadless in the parts outside the plain, in which if anything were to happen to them there would be practically no hope for them at all. He was rationally aware of the necessity for that. And yet as he sat there in the small ridiculous bath, tired of his own anger and even of himself and knowing that a single moment of polite decency would wash away the stupid mess of it all, he could do nothing that would even take him as far as the accent of reconciliation.

It was Carrington who tried again. 'I'm sorry we got off on the wrong foot,' he said. 'I had a message for you from Comilla.'

'Oh?' Forrester tried vainly to recall anyone he might possibly know in that squalid and dislikable air-junction beyond the Delta.

'A nurse in the hospital there,' he said. 'Miss Burke.'

'Good Christ,' Forrester said.

'We talked a lot of you,' the boy said.

'Oh, you did?' He resented suddenly the idea that the boy, fed on hospital gossip, might have arrived with some idiotic damnable preconceived notion about him. He resented Burke too. She was an angular, short-haired Irishwoman of forty, quick-tempered and tireless and fond of whisky, who wore trousers and had built up about herself an iron barrier of man-hatred. She was known always as Burke and there was another sister, Johnson, English and sallow, with black stiff eyebrows and hairy arms, who had worked with her in the hospitals of India and the forward dressing-stations of Burma and who shared her lovelessness and her impatient hatred, really a pretence, of all the men they nursed with devotion and fortitude at various comfortless places in jungle and desert and in the hospital Dakotas that flew the wounded out from the battlefields. As if scorning the weaknesses of femininity even in names, they called each other Burke and Johnson, and had taken on, like a hard shell, a covering of the very masculinity they seemed to despise.

'She sent her regards,' Carrington said. 'She'll be in from Comilla tomorrow and will look you up.'

He did not answer. If there was one thing he did not want it was Burke, with her masculine angularity, her medical cleanliness and her whisky. Nor any longer did he want Carrington. That was quite certain.

'You had better look out for a tent for yourself tomorrow,' he said. 'There's simply not room here.'

'It was only for one night, anyway,' Carrington said.

For a moment he did not know what to answer. The whole thing was a ghastly beginning. Simply through pure pig-headedness he had put himself into the most monstrous and ridiculous of situations. He had behaved as a whole class of irresponsible and unfit officers behaved towards people of inferior rank: as if pompously drunk with the small beer of power. Among flying men these distinctions of rank did not count for much. There were a lot of terse, rude, appropriate names for behaviour of that sort and he knew perfectly well that Carrington would be thinking of them. Even the heat, the dust and the general mess of the whole situation were not enough to excuse it. And yet now, realizing it, he could do nothing about it. He knew that Carrington and Blore were simply objects on which he was venting the complicated hatred of something else. They could not understand that and he could not explain it, and so the whole impossible situation would go on until he was calm enough or detached enough or big enough to set it right.

He reached for his towel. He had thrown it down in the dust and now he could not reach it without getting out of the bath. Carrington picked it up, dusted it off on the legs of his bush-trousers, and handed it to him without a word. He snatched it and said 'Thanks.'

Carrington began to walk away.

'All right,' Forrester said. 'We'll go over to the air-strip first thing in the morning. You'll want to have a look at this damn country. How long have you been out here?'

'A bit more than a month,' he said.

He turned and went straight into the tent. With savage rubbings Forrester dried himself with a towel that because of his own carelessness was full of harsh fine dust as raw as pumice stone. The moon was clear of the palms now. Splendidly enormous and orange and warm, without any of the green-white iciness of the north, it shone down on a world so quiet that he could hear the smallest sounds from the corners of the camp: bearers talking to each other among the lights of the tents, the sound of a gramophone playing light piano music, and from somewhere up the road the noise of a harmonium playing hymns with the voices of men trying raggedly to sing in tune with it, the piano and the men and the harmonium fighting in a strange Western discord against each other.

The sound of the hymns reminded him suddenly of Harris. He remembered he had not delivered the message to the corporal at the medical centre. This thought of the message brought back to him in turn the thought of the Burmese girl waiting for him to wake into the strange world of the veranda under the great shady scented tree, the garrulous energetic doctor with his prescriptions, and the sick Burmese child lying on the wooden bed under the green mosquito net, frightened and dazed by the stupor of fever, like a little glass-eyed yellow doll.

He thought of it all as he finished drying himself. It came back to him in vivid waves of recollection, sharpened by the same scent heavily falling now, deeper than the honey-sweetness of lime-flowers, from the many trees about him. And suddenly, together with the coolness after the bath, it calmed him down.

When he went back into the tent Carrington was lying on his bed, under the half-draped mosquito net, as if nothing had happened. But to his great astonishment Blore was standing up.

He looked nervous and upset, and kept rubbing his right hand across the back of his neck scrubbing at the short grey hairs. He stood stiffly and formally by his bed, almost at attention.

'Look, sir,' he said. It was only in the Intelligence office tent, on operational occasions, that Blore ever called him sir. There seemed something curiously unfriendly about it now.

'What's up with you?' he said.

'I'll see the Commandant in the morning and get fresh quarters,' Blore said. 'It's better for you and Carrington to be together.'

'Don't talk cock,' he said.

'No,' Blore said. 'It's better.'

'What are you binding about?' Forrester said. 'You're posted anyway. You'll be gone in a day or two.'

'You see, that's it,' Blore said. 'I'm not posted. All that's been cancelled.'

'Tough tit,' he said.

They sling you about like bags of offal, he thought. He felt suddenly sorry for Blore.

'What wonder have they thought up now?' he said.

'I think there's a flap on,' Blore said.

'There's always a flap on,' he said. 'The whole thing is a flap.'

'You can think what you like,' Blore said. 'But all fighters are grounded and a new outfit moves in from Akyab tomorrow. What does that spell?'

'All sorts of words of one syllable,' he said.

'Mandalay,' Carrington said.

'Mandalay's a name,' he said. 'By the time it falls no one will care.'

'But it will fall,' Blore said. 'And when it falls we move.'

'And until it falls,' Forrester said, 'for God's sake sit where you are. There's a place called Meiktila, where the poor old Regiment holds the air-strip all day and then the Japs come and take it away from them at night. That's a picnic. They might send you there.'

No one spoke again: and after a few moments he buttoned his tunic and picked up his shabby dust-bloomed hat and walked out of the tent. His body was cool for the first time that day as he walked slowly across the camp, in dust as thick as the dry sand of a sea-dune, to deliver the message from the doctor.

4

In the early afternoon of the following day he took off with Carrington, flying eastward. After the downward blinding light of the air-strip, which even the constant spouting clouds of dust could never kill, it became quite cool in the aircraft, the brutal heat of the plain below forgotten. The shadowless plain became something of no more terror than a huge monotonous shore, unbroken except by the pencilling of tiny roads and by scattered groups of dark-green stars that were clumps of palm, stretching away between the river and the mountains. The river became like a bright extended arm of transparent glass, the brown contours of its bed and the blue-green depths of its waters revealed like muscles through a silver skin that had no ripple or movement from so far away, in the glittering bright air. And then in the distance, flowing out of the characterless mass of purple heat haze, the shape of the lower jungle began gradually to come to life like something seen through binoculars. Out of the haze came the dark sun-split fissures that were the valleys: then out of the valleys, more slowly, the rocks that were the lateral spurs; and then out of the rocks the trees, like gigantic masses of encrusted moss, that were the jungle itself. Unbroken except in the extreme edges of tiny veins of roads that looked no more than animal tracks and utterly unbroken by any glint of water, the jungle spread out, dark and barbaric, into limitless distances beyond the plain. The mass of purple mountains that from the ground had seemed like nothing more than a remote thundercloud now became a continent, green and black and sometimes in places a curiously brilliant brown where the sun burned treeless outcrops of rock, viciously and curiously dead in the light of sun.

Sometimes out of the gigantic curtain of moss there appeared small tributaries of blistered sand, white as bone. To Forrester they looked like the dried valleys of smaller water-courses. They would fill with the rains of the monsoon, becoming gushing torrential streams in the steamy heat of July, and would lead down, in time, to the bed of a larger stream, as the stream itself would in turn go down, through the heart of the jungle, to the great river flowing southward out of the plain. Whenever he saw these waterless courses, scorched dead by the long heat of the dry spell, he thought of them instinctively as possible means of escape. This assessment of the earth below him as a possible or impossible place for landing had set up inside him a permanent state of contradiction. It had persisted side by side with his desire for death: so that even when he deliberately sought a way to die he was also instinctively seeking a way of escape from disaster.

And now as he flew on beyond the plain he found himself consciously photographing the mass of rock and jungle below, trying to break the bewildering enormity of it into fragments he could recognize and remember. After a time he gave up trying to record the vast repetitive cushion of green and black below, but the little tributaries of sand persisted in fascinating him. They helped to ease the long boredom of daylight flight. He had heard a rumour lately that the Japs had less than a hundred and fifty aircraft left in the whole of the country north and west of the Irrawaddy, and sometimes he thought it might well be true. He had never seen anything distantly hostile even in his longest trip to the east, and sometimes he had flown for an entire afternoon without seeing more than a little L 5 below him, small as a bird, flying out from some remote jungle post with a wounded man, or perhaps two men, who would otherwise have rotted and died. He knew then that there was really no way out of that roadless and unknown territory except by air; that if ever you got down there and were wounded there could be nothing for you but, quickly or slowly, death in the sun.

In spite of it all the dry tributaries continued to fascinate him. And for a moment he felt half-inclined to talk to Carrington about them. He thought a moment and then changed his mind.

He said instead, quite flatly: 'Everything all right with you?'

'Perfect,' the boy said.

He detected in the voice an answering flatness that he knew quite well belonged to what had happened the night before. 'We can't go on like this,' he thought. 'This is just bloody silly.' All his irritation had evaporated, as it always did, in the serious business of flying with another man. In the air he became impersonal as far as all behaviour was concerned, very calm and quiet, concentrated and yet detached from this self that made of the slightest grievance a cause of irritation.

It was part of the contradiction of the business of flying that as he sat there, talking quietly, looking calmly down on the hostile mass of rock and jungle below, he looked like a man who was never anything but self-possessed. His tiredness, the long deep tiredness of war that he had felt so sharply the night before, had become merely part of the tautness of his face.

As he was about to speak again Carrington gave him an alteration of course. He looked instinctively at his watch. The change had come practically at the correct second. They were flying on a sort of dog's leg and this would be the turn at the elbow. Nothing much wrong, he thought.

He flew on for another twenty minutes before Carrington gave him the second change that would take them back to the air-strip. He looked at his watch again and saw that it was almost four. They would be back by half-past and in another hour the really fierce maddening heat of the afternoon would be gone.

He took the aircraft down in a steady line for about a thousand feet. The heat bumped it heavily for a moment or two. Then as it levelled out and steadied again he looked down, still fascinated, at the veins of sand splitting the dark valleys below and saw that the whiteness of sand had begun to be broken by dark patches. He decided to go a little lower and discover what these dark patches were and in a few moments, going down another thousand feet, he saw that they were patches of scrub. He could see the branches, sage-green in the sunlight, against the brown-grey glitter of boulders strewn like giant shingle about the river bed. It was only here and there that the sand lay quite clear, in stretches two or three hundred yards long and perhaps a hundred wide, where the torrent of the monsoon had

46

smoothed it away as with a vast flat knife, leaving it white as salt and cruel as broken glass in the glare of sun.

In another ten minutes they were over the plain and in another five he could see the air-strip, the dark lane of bitumenized jute like a sear of burning across the yellow dust, the bungalows and bashas of the palm-fringed town like the wooden play-blocks of a child, the tents like clumps of brown sea-shells, the palms fringing the water-holes that dazzled like squares of mirrored glass. As he came in to land they seemed to be flying up to him, until at last the aircraft and the dark dusty landing strip became smoothly one and he was down and all the cool restful remoteness of the sky was gone.

As he took the aircraft from the strip to its dispersal point at the far end he felt the heat concentrate violently in the cabin. It became terrific in the few moments when he taxied in, his two ground crew boys running by the wings, naked to the waist, so dark with sun that they were almost as dark as the Burmese boys still filling in with loads of rubble the bomb craters of the road running between the strip and the town. By the time he brought the aircraft to a stop and cut its engines he was drenched with sweat, and as he climbed down on to the dust the final rush of heat and light rebounding off the glassy particles of dust smashed across his eyes, dazzling him with such violence that he could not see.

'Thanks,' he said. He pulled down the peak of his cap to shade his eyes. 'Very nice do.' He knew that Carrington would deduce from that flat piece of understatement, in words that by themselves said nothing, that he was really very pleased. Perhaps the boy would be pleased too; and this, perhaps, in a cautious way, would be the beginning of the reconciliation that sooner or later would have to come. But to his surprise the boy said nothing. He did not even seem to be listening. And suddenly Forrester, turning abruptly, saw why.

Carrington was standing with his mouth tautly open, staring down the air-strip. Forrester heard him shouting, the words simply a gabble of incoherent horror. At the same moment one of the ground crew boys yelled, 'Jesus Christ! he'll hit it!' and then ran wildly forward, brown arms waving madly.

Forrester turned in time to see a Mosquito, far down the

strip, coming in to land. He knew at once that it was coming much too fast. It hit the dust with great violence, hiding itself momentarily in an explosion of sulphur cloud, then drove on through the cloud of its own making, one wheel still up, very fast, swinging away towards a Dakota that stood parked, propellers slowly turning, two hundred yards away. As it hit the Dakota the dust seemed to darken and then turn to orange as it rose. It became a flame of horrifying beauty and depth, the rich oil smoke shooting upward in crimson and yellow and blackened orange until it was like thunder against the sun. Out of this vast upheaval of smoky flame Forrester presently saw a figure running. It seemed to him like a figure of terrible loneliness. It ran wildly towards the open centre of the air-strip and then it too burst into flame. He saw the flames spring out of it like vicious orange feathers, yellow at the tips, covering it until at last they overcame it and it fell down in the dust, rolling over and over, the flames eating it away.

Forrester saw Carrington begin to run. He had for a single moment an impulse to go after him. Then he checked it. He knew that it was already too late. The air-strip was blotted out from sunlight now by a twilight of smoke-cloud and from everywhere across it, dark and puny and in some way unreal in that tropical thunder-light, figures were running. One of these figures came presently to the man convulsively writhing among feathers of flame in the dust. He began wildly to shovel dust on it with his hands. As the dust was scattered the flames died out and in their place there rose only a gust or two of smoke, feeble against the great smoke-cloud of the burning plane, until at last the body lay still and consumed, smoking slowly, like a dead branch thrown from a fire.

Already Carrington was walking back. The horror of the thing was clear on his face. He looked at Forrester with a glance of fear that was too swift to check, and then grinned, and Forrester saw in the grin the very words that the boy would say.

'Quite a wrap-up,' the boy said. 'Two kites in one go.'

'Careless sod,' Forrester said. 'Means another new kite. And that's probably the last in Burma. We're two short now.' He obeyed instinctively some damnable rule in these things that made the aircraft more precious than the man. And yet out here, vast distances from home, in a country of which he supposed hardly anyone at home knew more than that it produced rice and rubies and was a lump on the map between India and Malay, he knew also that in a way it was true. Life, under the everlasting fatalistic light of sun, had an astonishing cheapness. The sun bred too much of everything except planes. It bred the teeming, useless, corruptible masses of India that for all their vastness had less power than the single machine and the man he saw burning now. It bred too a contempt for life that went far beyond the practised stoicism of the fighting man. It bred the feeling that in the terrific prodigality of life, under the scourge of sun, even the best was replaceable.

He looked at Carrington again and saw by the look in his eyes that he did not know these things. He was not only very fresh to the country; the whole fatalism of the East was still hidden from him in the bewildering heat and glare.

Without another word, he walked slowly away up the strip. The smouldering body in the dust was hidden now by the ambulance, a jeep or two and a crowd of men, mostly gibbering Indian boys, who had collected from every tent on the field. He suddenly saw them like a flock of vultures feeding, as he saw them feeding on the roadsides of the East wherever a cow or a buffalo or a dog had fallen to die, on the body of a man he had known. And in a moment it was as if he had been hit by something in the face. He forgot the mere exasperation of knowing that he must somehow replace the plane that was lost, he forgot that it meant for him another letter to England, of condolences hard to feel and express, to someone he had never seen, a mother, a wife, a girl, telling of death in an unheroic and futile circumstance. He forgot the shocked face of Carrington trying to show the stoicism that was expected and that he did not feel. He walked through the drifting oil smoke, terribly stifling and oppressive in the already terrible heat of the afternoon, and felt it to be suddenly like a wall of ice.

He knew suddenly, from that moment onwards, that he no longer wanted to die.

5

As he walked across the air-strip, following the ambulance, watching the smoke shadow race in dark running folds over the parched white dust, he heard a voice go past him in a shout: 'Mr Anderson, sir, the Scotsman,' and then, 'Sergeant Watson too.' He was inexpressibly shocked. He felt the heat of the sun clench down on him and stagger him with a wave of sickness that was really the sickness of an immense nausea for the ghastly futility of the thing he had seen. And then as he half-paused to answer vaguely he became aware of the identity of the man who had spoken. It was his own rigger, Brown, the naked upper part of his butter-brown body flaked with the black dust of the fire.

Forrester stopped abruptly, staring at him too as if he had been something running from the dead. 'Brown,' he said. 'Brown. How the hell does this leave us?'

Brown was instinctive in his understanding of the half-expressed fear of his commanding officer and said at once:

'Two, sir.'

'Good Christ,' he said.

'Three grounded, sir. Now this one wrapped up. That leaves your own and Sergeant Philips, sir.'

They had never been much more than half a squadron but this was worse than he had known. Philips was new in from India and, like Carrington, still a little mystified and untried by the vastness, the peculiarity and the intricacy of the terrain. But it was not Philips that troubled him. Once again it was the loss and shortage of planes. He faced once more the fact that men, even the best of them, were replaceable.

'Poor do, sir,' Brown said.

'Bloody,' he said.

'Reminds you of the time when the ants started to eat the Warwicks,' Brown said. 'Remember that?'

'Yes.' He remembered how in the early months of the year huge pale armies of ants had really started to eat the fuselage of the transport Warwicks. 'How they could stomach them I don't know.'

'No future in them,' Brown said. 'I'd rather ride in a bus.'

Forrester moved away and then remembered something.

'Get the damn things flying as soon as you can,' he said 'We're stuck without them.'

Brown stood smiling, shaking his head.

'Not me, sir.'

'Why the hell not?'

'Time expired, sir,' Brown said. He grinned more broadly than ever. 'On my way home from Thursday. Me and Clarke, sir. Home together.'

'Clarke?' he said. 'Who's Clarke?'

'Nobby,' Brown said. 'Your fitter.'

'Good God.'

He stood stunned by the news that Brown and Clarke, his ablest men, were about to be snatched away from him by the irony of a calculation of time. He wondered impatiently if something diabolically deliberate had not suddenly wrecked the entire fabric of things. No sooner had Carrington arrived than Anderson and Watson were gone; no sooner were Anderson and Watson gone than Brown and Clarke were going home. He had no better men than Clarke and Brown; he had grown through all the irritations of dust and heat to have the most steadfast confidence in them. They had treated every defect of his aircraft with surgical confidence and skill, never defeated by all the endless aggravating problems that dust and heat could raise in the body of an engine. They had been the sanest persons in a world driven slightly mad by heat and dust and such small matters as ants feeding on the fabric of planes. And now they were going – and he felt as he might have felt in a hospital crisis and the best of the doctors had suddenly gone away.

'Been together ever since we joined, sir,' Brown was saying. 'All over the shop. Everywhere.'

Forrester was not listening. He began to walk away across the strip, where the smoke-shadow was clearing a little at last, letting in the thundery gold light of sun.

As he moved away Brown called something after him that he did not hear, and it was only after a second or two that he realized that a truck, driven by an Indian boy, had gone close by him, too close and too fast, and that Brown had really been shouting a warning and swearing at the boy at the same time.

He turned for a moment partly to avert his head from the dust of the truck, partly to look at Brown. Brown was looking at him queerly, squinting through the dust and sun. He looked as if he were troubled by something in Forrester's behaviour. He could see in reality something that Forrester could not see: that the truck had almost hit him, wholly because Forrester was walking without direction, like a man blinded and stupefied by thought. 'It gets you like that in the bloody finish,' Brown thought. 'Round the bend. Half-dopey. Christ, I'm glad I'm going home.'

Forrester walked on across the strip without knowing where he was going. The complication of events bewildered him – letters to write to the relations of dead men; Clarke and Brown time-expired; four of his six aircraft grounded – so that he was only half-conscious of thinking or walking. He thought vaguely that it was always like this: that everything went crazy at once, that once in a while everything fell to pieces, leaving the design and purpose of the campaign and your personal part in it wrecked into futility. Aircraft for which he had waited months and which came to him at last by perilous sea-routes, half round the world and infinitely costly in life and time, were wrecked and burned in a second or two by carelessness or accident or by the sheer damnable fate of a thing no larger than the strength of a screw.

He had almost reached the dispersal tent at the edge of the air-strip when the ambulance went past him again, raising dust as heavy as sulphur smoke as it turned. This time he saw it and stepped clear. As the ambulance drove past him he saw a figure of an officer hanging on to the side, but beyond that it was there he did not take much notice of it. It was only when it jumped off and solidified out of the dust that he realized it had an identity.

He stopped dead as Harris came towards him, waving his hand. And with a great shock he realized also that it was the second time in five minutes that he had almost walked past someone he knew.

The cherubic face of the doctor, dark with smuts from the fire, seemed to have a look of ghoulish amusement that was grim too. And then he saw that behind it all Harris was terribly troubled. He started to run forward, giving a smile of pained delight. He stretched out his hands, gripping Forrester by the shoulders.

'For God's sake, man. For God's sake!'

'What's up? What is it?' Forrester said.

'You!' the doctor said. 'You! They said it was you!'

The doctor, beginning to laugh nervously now, licking the dust from his lips, pointed after the ambulance.

'It was you I was driving away in there,' he said.

Forrester stood without answering. From behind the clear fact of his not wanting to die there suddenly shot out at him another, more clear and shocking than the first. It was the fact that he might have died. And it not only shocked him violently and instantly as he stood there looking after the ambulance containing the body of someone that might have been himself. It brought rushing back to him a forgotten sensation. This sensation swept over him and bore him forward in its own flood of thought, out of the long bitter negation of the moment when his wife had been blasted out of his arms through to the dazed and unembittered moment of not wanting to die and out to the very edge of the future. It was the sensation, positive and frightening in its clarity, of wanting to live. It had in it a kind of aching sweetness. It was also mixed with fear. And suddenly he knew that all of his flying life since the bomb had never meant anything because it had never had that fear. It had been dead and he himself had really died with it, numbed and negative, selfish and bounded by selfishness, wherever he went and in whatever he did. All the things he had done in the air were as dead and empty as a seedless husk because in doing them he had never been afraid. And now he was going to be afraid. He was afraid already as he looked after the ambulance containing the body he had seen writhing and flaming in the dust, and with the feeling of his being afraid he was also glad. And he was glad because in a sense the body that was being carried away,

53

charred and burned out of recognition, was really himself. It was the man he had been, broken by catastrophe, negative and selfish and empty and self-consumed.

For some seconds longer he stared after the ambulance as if still believing that he was looking at some ghost of himself being carried away. Then he realized that the doctor was looking at him. And in realizing that he remembered something else. He remembered how Brown too had looked at him, queerly, rather pityingly, as if mentally shaking his head. It was exactly the sort of look people gave you when they thought that at last the sun had got you.

He grinned as he thought of it, and the grin became wider as he realized that for the first time he was laughing at himself. The ambulance had driven away now, out of sight, and the smoke of the fire, with its occasional crack of exploding shells, was thinning out into a vast grey column, away from the sun. But he was still in a daze of thought and it was some moments longer before he realized that he and the doctor had reached the edge of the strip.

The doctor was standing by his jeep and was actually climbing into it before Forrester came fully to himself and heard him say:

'It's a good thing you're all in one piece because tonight you're coming out to dinner.'

'In which of our wonderful messes, doctor? Tell me.'

'You're dining with ladies,' the doctor said.

And who the hell, he thought, can they be? – unless they are a pair of horse-faced twin nurses down from Comilla that the doctor has to amuse officially. Probably much worse, if that were possible, than Johnson and Burke.

'We'll have to take food,' the doctor was saying. 'Scrounge it from somewhere. They've got nothing. They trekked all the way from Rangoon and then the Japs stripped them here.'

He put his foot on the starter of the jeep, and the engine roared.

'Now I think if we got rice and tins of meat and curry powder – '

And then Forrester, suddenly and with immense surprise, realized who the doctor was talking about. He saw once again the cool pale face of the girl as he had seen it on waking in the shade of the veranda. He saw the black deep eyes looking down at him and he recalled the heavy fragrance of the tree. He thought with wonder that it was the first time he had remembered her that day.

6

As he sat on the veranda in a warm darkness broken only by the orange glow of lamps through the glassless windows of the house and from above the tree by a star or two that shone like reddish trembling fires caught at the leaf-tips, he did not feel the heat as he had felt it the previous day. He had bathed early in water as cool as Ali could bring it and had changed out of his green jungle battledress into a khaki bush tunic and long trousers. He sat with the neck of his bush tunic open and now and then he could feel the slightest wind, not really cool but refreshing out of pure movement, coming up from the river. He heard it stir in the great tree above the house and run in dry whispers along the fence of palms beside the compound and die out somewhere in the darkness of the sandy track among the floppy silk leaves of the banana trees. From all the outer expanse of the plain there was no other sound. It was too early yet for the howling of jackals. The roar of planes that went on most of the day across at the air-strip was gone at last, leaving over everything an immense cushion of silence, very beautiful and silky and warm, covering him like a soft insulation against the heat of the day.

As he sat there he presently heard the voice of the doctor laughing inside the house. The doctor was helping in the kitchen with the rice and the tins of meat, and Forrester could smell the sharp rather acrid odour of something cooking. Then in a moment he heard the outer door of the house swing back, as if the doctor were coming, but there was no other sound.

He sat there for a moment or two longer by himself, in the dark silence, before realizing suddenly that someone had come out of the door and was standing by him. He turned sharply to see the girl standing there, perfectly still. He saw her smiling in the light from the windows.

'I thought you might be asleep again,' she said.

'Oh no.' He got up quickly, pulling towards her one of the bamboo chairs, laughing. 'I only sleep in the afternoon. Please sit down,' he said.

She sat down and smoothed the pale green dress over her narrow thighs with a long slow sweep of her hands and said:

'It is very kind of you to come and see us again.'

'Yesterday it was you who were telling me not to say that,' he said.

'Was it?' She was smiling in a way that pressed her eyes more flatly across her face. 'Then we are even now.'

'That's very nice,' he said. He sat with a glass of lime juice in his hands, turning it round and round, the colour of the lime almost exactly the colour of her dress in the thin light from the window. He did not know what else to say to her until he remembered suddenly the child lying in the dispensary across the compound, and said, 'How is the child that was ill?' and she said, turning her face towards the hut, where he could now see a small glimmer of light as if a candle were burning there:

'She ought to be asleep. I am going to look at her to make sure.'

'I will come with you,' he said.

He got up and walked across the compound with her to the bamboo hut where the child lay. As he followed her inside he saw that it was not a candle burning but a hurricane lamp turned low and set on a table by the bed and it occurred to him that it was Harris who had brought it there.

The girl went silently over to the bed and turned up the wick of the lamp very slightly, so that the light fell clear on the face of the child, turning it deeper than normal yellow under the mosquito net. Even from where he stood he could see the sweat pouring down from the forehead and running down like thin oil over the closed lids of the eyes until it spread over the cheeks and ran down into the yellow troubled mouth that lay open and quivering in its struggle for breath.

After a moment he saw the girl take a towel from the table and begin to wipe away the sweat by a series of the gentlest skilled downward strokes across the face. She moved so quietly that she seemed to calm rather than trouble it. He did not speak.

He watched her until she had dried the face completely and then he saw her, now with gentle downward strokes, smooth the cotton sheets across the shoulders and at last close up the mosquito net, leaving the child serene and quiet, like a body embalmed in a little cage.

As she turned down the lamp again he walked out of the hut and waited for her on the steps outside. When she came out he said: 'You've done things like that before. Where did you learn them?'

'In Rangoon. In the mission,' she said. 'I trained in the school there. To be a nurse.'

'You were at the university too?'

'Afterwards. Yes,' she said.

She moved delicately across the compound and as he looked at her level gliding aristocratic way of walking he thought suddenly of Johnson and Burke, also nurses, tough and arid and masculine, smoking too much, drinking bad Indian whisky in their fight against the strain of heat and work.

'When did you come from Rangoon?' he said.

'Three years ago.'

'To here?'

'No. First we went to the town. Then later we came out here.'

'How did you come?'

'By foot,' she said, and he wondered at the same time how far it was from Rangoon.

'Not all the way?' he said.

'All the way: yes,' she said. 'My sister and my mother and I. And Miss McNab.'

'Your mother is here?' he said.

'Yes,' she said, 'she is here. In here. You will see her.'

'And who is Miss McNab?' he said.

'She is the Scottish missionary from the school,' she said. 'She is here too. Yesterday when you came she had gone to the settlement on the other side of the river.'

He sat for a moment trying to work out for himself a clear picture of the two girls, the mother and the missionary trekking up during the months of the dry season through long, bitter, exhausting days of remorseless and unbroken sun. And then no sooner had the picture begun to form in his mind than she destroyed it:

'There were almost five hundred of us,' she said.

He was shocked not so much by the picture as by the calm clear way she spoke of it.

'Almost all of them died.' She spoke on in the same calm dispassionate voice. 'There was malaria and dysentery and bad water and some cholera. There was not much food and many died from that.'

He did not know what to say. He stood in the centre of the compound looking up at the stars, thinking:

'I never knew about this. I never thought of it. It was never in the papers.' And then: 'How the hell could it be in the papers? No one ever came out to tell of it.' In that moment he looked sharply down at the face of the girl, and he was shocked by something else. He saw how very young her face was and thought, 'If she is twenty now she was not more than sixteen or seventeen then. A girl. A child among the horror of five hundred women struggling not to die.'

He was aware as he thought of it of an odd rush of tenderness for her. He tried to think of something to say to her, but the words seemed very small against the huge brutal fact of her experience. And he was glad when suddenly from the door of the house he heard Harris calling her name.

'The meal is ready,' she said, and in another moment the opportunity of saying anything to her was gone. He felt only the tenderness remaining clear and uppermost in his mind.

She led the way into the house a moment later and he held open the door for her as she went in. The door opened straight into a room in which he saw Harris and the elder sister standing by a long table covered with a white cloth incredibly embroidered at the edges. He stared at it in astonishment. Then at the far end of the table he saw the mother: a woman of sixty, small, light coffee-brown in colour, with delicate flattened lips which were pressed wider, without completely opening, to welcome him. She did not speak as he leaned across the table to shake hands. 'My mother cannot speak,' the girl said. 'She has not spoken since the time I was telling you about,' and he knew that there was still more in it than he knew.

'I am sorry,' he said. He waited to sit down.

'Please sit here,' she said. She held a chair for him so that he would sit on the right of Harris, who sat at the top of the table, and on the left of the elder sister, and opposite the girl and her mother.

He sat down and looked at the table. The white cloth was covered with flowers of scarlet and apricot, like large hibiscus blossoms, strewn among wooden dishes of parrot-green bananas and limes. He put his hands on the edge of the table and felt the lace veins of embroidery with his finger tips. And then before he could speak again the door at the other end of the room opened and there came bouncing in, holding a large wooden bowl of brown rice and curry, a little woman of fifty-five or sixty with a bony, bright face and large brown eyes with bluish whites and a mass of startling mahogany hair, and he knew it was the missionary, Miss McNab. She began to talk to him at once with screaming delight.

'Mr Forrester, it's impossible for you to know what an honour and delight this is. Impossible! Don't get up. Sit you down, Mr Forrester, sit you down. Doctor Harris, ye're a shockin', disappointin' man. Ye didna tell me the man was as young as a' that!'

'She's a man-killer,' Harris said.

'Never deny it, never deny it!' she said. She laughed at Forrester in a screaming thin little voice and began with bewildering energy to serve the curry. 'It would be a sin to deny it!' she screamed, and as she leaned forward in the lamplight he saw that she had dyed her hair. There was no mistaking the startling mahogany fire of it, piled up in a high old-fashioned mass on the crown of her small head, so that it sat there like a muff turned up on end, or the way it had begun to grow grey again at the roots beneath the dye.

Suddenly she stood with the spoon poised in mid-air as if she were about to throw it at him. 'I believe it's you that's the wicked, sinful man, after all, Mr Forrester. Ye know that ye've made me forget Grace! Ye have that!'

She put the spoon down on the dish and bowed her head. She said a few words of Grace in a gabble of reverent energy and in the few seconds of her speaking it he looked across the table at the girl. She was sitting rather stiffly, head unbowed, and with eyes closed. She seemed to be staring straight at him through the calm closed lids, and in a moment he felt the wave of tenderness for her return, so that when she opened her eyes again he knew by the startled brightness of them that she became aware of it, fully and unmistakably, for the first time.

In another moment the Grace was over and Miss McNab, waving the curry spoon, was screaming at him again with proud delight.

'Will ye be takking a peg o' something, Mr Forrester? The doctor brought us gin from Calcutta. That foul, benighted, godless city – d'ye know it, Mr Forrester? I'm tellin' ye the only good that came out of it was the gin and rice the doctor brought!'

Harris got up from the table and came to pour gin into Forrester's glass.

'And ye know I will!' she said.

'I know,' Harris said.

'Am I shocking you, Mr Forrester? The drinking missionary? You know what?' She had already served five portions of curry and now brandished the spoon at him before serving her own. 'You know what?' she said. 'I say if Heaven's as hot as Burma then the Lord Himself'll be taking a peg or two sometimes. D'ye fly, Mr Forrester?'

'Yes,' he said.

She sat down with her plate of rice and curry and began to push the food into her mouth with sloppy excitement.

'Of course you do. Anna told me.' He looked up sharply from his plate. 'And ye have your wings. What is it you fly?'

'Mosquitoes,' he said.

'And what are they? Bombers or fighters? I never know.'

'Both,' he said.

'I say damn them all! I say damn them! I say they're wicked, damnable, devilish things!' She spoke with shining vehemence that was almost lovable.

'True,' he said.

'There!' she said. She pushed great spoonfuls of rice into her mouth, sucking the loose brown grains from her chin. 'Ye're very quiet!' she screamed.

He smiled at the girl across the table and with hardly a movement of her lips she smiled back.

'Ye didn't tell me he was such a quiet thoughtful one, doctor, ye didn't tell me!'

'He didn't expect to be overtaken by the McNab monsoon,' the doctor said.

She screamed with laughter, so that the great reddish muff of dyed hair rocked forward and fell down over the keen vivacious eyes. She waved it back.

'What ails ye, Mr Forrester?' she said. 'Don't ye like the curry?'

'It's wonderful.'

'Then what is it? This is no funeral!'

He smiled and put both his hands on the edges of the table.

'It's the tablecloth,' he said.

'Man, ye're a wonder!' she said.

He let his fingers run once again over the ironed pattern of lace, its starched parochial cleanliness, so formal and homely under the flowers of scarlet and apricot and the brilliant green of the fruit, fascinating him deeply.

'Man, ye've a fine eye for things!' Miss McNab screamed at him. 'Ye're no fool!'

'It's a wonderful tablecloth,' he said.

'All the way from Rangoon!' she said. 'Through every inch of the way I kept telling myself, "McNab, whatever else ye may lose ye'll no be losin' the tablecloth the girls worked for you at the Mission".'

'On her twenty-first birthday,' Harris said.

'Tak' no notice, Mr Forrester!' she said. 'I'm no ashamed of my age. For my fiftieth birthday they worked it, Mr Forrester, Two years before we came here.'

He did not speak. Opposite him the girl had finished eating and now was sitting with her hands on the tablecloth too, eyes down, as if remembering.

'Ye can taunt me, Doctor Harris!' Miss McNab said. 'But three hundred women and children died on that journey! That's how old I am!'

'And if you hadn't been with us – ' the elder sister spoke

suddenly, for the first time, her English correct and formal, the tone of her voice falling away at the end.

'Some more curry, Mr Forrester?' Miss McNab waved the spoon, tossing back her dyed hair, screaming at him. 'Ye're no eatin' a thing!'

'Thank you, no,' he said. 'It's wonderful.'

'It's a sign ye've no been without rice for three years!' She began eating again, spilling the tawny-yellow curry down her chin until it hung there like a beard.

'McNab,' Harris said, 'there's one thing I'll do when I get back home or God help me. I'll get you decorated.'

'You will not!' she screamed. 'Tak no notice of him, Mr Forrester.'

'Somehow,' Harris said.

'Give Mr Forrester some more gin and don't grab so much!'

'Somehow I'll get you decorated,' Harris said. 'Somehow.'

' "Somehow, somehow",' she mocked. She suddenly spoke with startling ardour, wiping the curry in a single vehement gesture from her chin. 'And me only the instrument of something! You should decorate the Lord, I tell you! If you'd decorate the Lord and get His name into Honours List somehow then ye'd be talking! Then ye'd be talking!'

'Somehow,' Harris said.

'And what would the citation be?' she said. 'Singing *Onward Christian Soldiers*? And that reminds me! Ye came to help choose the hymns for Easter Sunday and ye're not leaving this house tonight till they're chosen. D'ye know any Easter hymns, Mr Forrester?'

At this moment the girl and her sister got up and began to take away the plates. He thought for a moment, looking at the big scarlet blossoms on the table, and then said:

'Isn't there a hymn called *Allelujah*? Isn't that for Easter?'

'There is! I said ye were no fool, Mr Forrester. I see ye've been well raised.'

'It's a beautiful hymn,' the girls said.

'We'll sing it!' Miss McNab said. 'We'll practise it after supper!' She got up with a flare of energy and began to take away the empty dishes, almost running with them out of the room. He could hear her voice even as she screamed from somewhere in the kitchen.

'Take some fruit, Mr Forrester. I'll be making a cup of tea! Take yourself a nice cool melon!'

'Take yourself a nice cool melon,' Harris said, grinning. 'That was what you wanted.'

He did not answer Harris, but sat looking across the table at the mother. From the kitchen he could hear the voice of Miss McNab screaming, with occasional bursts of 'Allelujah!' at the two girls. He heard the voice of the younger one laughing lightly in answer, a soft and tender laugh that in its rise and fall was like a little song. He found himself listening to it eagerly, almost hungrily, excluding all other sound, even the voice of Miss McNab. Then as he listened to it he watched the face of the mother. It was a face in which there had been no movement, except the movement of eating, a repeated slow unexcited tremor of the brown lips, since he had first come in.

'She can't speak,' Harris said. 'She hasn't spoken since – you know – that.' Forrester did not answer once again. He knew now that what troubled and fascinated and mystified him was the darkness of the face. It was purer and lighter in tone than the faces he had seen in India but it was as remote in colour from the colouring of the girls as it was from the face of Miss McNab. The eyes had under them the curious tragic bruised shadow of yellowish purple-brown that you never saw under the eyes of women in the West unless they were ill or bullied or weak of heart or unhappy. It gave to the eyes, brown and staring and yet lightless, an expression of limitless sorrow, more terrible because it could never be spoken. It made him uneasy not only because it was the remembered sorrow and terror of the journey from the south but because it had something in it also of the sorrow of women as he had seen them in the East, depressed and silent and so often laughterless, with dark downcast eyes bruised into the face of centuries of servility and sun.

He was startled as the girl came back to the room by the likeness to her mother, by the strange similarity of bone structure that could not be mistaken, and by the incredible pure creaminess of skin that only heightened it. He saw in her smile

64

across at him as she went past a moment of swift tenderness. And then in a moment Miss McNab, carrying a large brass tray with very Japanese-looking cups and a big brass tea-pot, came bustling back into the room.

'Ye'll no be saying no to a cuppa tea, Mr Forrester, I'm thinking!' she screamed. 'There's no milk! Will ye have a wee slice o' lime? Even the buffaloes have gone dry!'

'Lime,' he said, 'please.'

'Anna, will ye slice a lime for Mr Forrester, please?'

'No,' he said. 'I can do that.'

'I will do it for you,' the girl said.

She spoke tenderly and quickly, and he thought as she sliced the small green limes and then passed them to him across the table that there was a little excitement in the way she held the dish, so that some of the pale green juice ran over the edge and down on to the bright white cloth. No sooner had it fallen than she set the dish on the cloth, covering it up. He knew that he would have done the same, and for a fraction of a second he saw her eyes light up with a touch of tender mischief that drove through him with the effect of sharp intimacy.

By the time he had put the lime into his tea Miss McNab was screaming again:

'And when d'ye think the war will be over, Mr Forrester? When d'ye think we'll get down to it and gie the Japs what for?'

'Hard to say,' he said. Sometimes he saw the war as going on, in the East at any rate, almost without end. He saw Burma on a sore, pained, outstretched finger-tip trying to scratch the vast body of the Asia occupied by Japan.

'When you go over next time give them hell from me!' Miss McNab screamed at him.

He did not answer. Sometimes, even allowing for the fact that the Japs were withdrawing steadily southward, on the ground and in the air, he thought he had given the Japs or anyone else most of the hell he was going to give. And sometimes again he wondered if the Japs were finished, if it were true that they had less than three hundred planes in the whole country, or if they might not one day, suddenly and savagely, strike out again. He was never sure.

'Drink up, Mr Forrester!' Miss McNab said. 'Drink while it's hot! You know what they say – you've got to sweat it out of you!'

Forrester smiled quietly, half looking at Miss McNab, half at the girl.

'He's a dreamy man, doctor!' she said. 'Always in a dream!'

'Liver,' the doctor said. 'Never takes his mepacrine.'

'He'll no be needin' medicine when we've sung a round of *Allelujah!*' she screamed. 'I'm tellin' ye! That's more of a tonic than a' your damn' tablets!'

'That reminds me,' Harris said. He got up from the table and began to go out of the room, towards the compound. 'Forgetting a patient.'

'She was sleeping,' the girl said.

'Some more tea, Mr Forrester?' Miss McNab screamed as the doctor went out. 'Be cleanin' your pipes out ready!'

'No, thanks,' he said.

'Ah! come on, Mr Forrester, a wee cup! You know you have to drink in this climate.'

'Let me take your cup,' the girl said, and stretched her slim pale arm across the table to take it.

'Tea!' Miss McNab gave an exhausting, piercing sigh. 'That's another thing I'm sure the Lord has in Paradise.'

After a moment or two his filled cup came back, the girl passing it to him and then holding the plate of sliced lime out to him, more steadily this time but still watching him with a half-smile, intimate and tender.

'D'ye know any more Easter hymns, Mr Forrester?' Miss McNab screamed. 'Or is that the one sole blessed memory of your Sunday School?'

'It's my sole blessed memory,' he said.

The doctor came back, greeted by long peals of screaming delight from Miss McNab.

'Everything all right?' Forrester said.

'Fine,' the doctor said. 'Somebody flying up from Akyab way. Gone now. Otherwise not a sound.'

'D'ye sing tenor or bass, Mr Forrester?' Miss McNab shouted.

'Anonymous,' he said.

Everyone laughed, Miss McNab lying back in her chair until the huge dyed mahogany mass of hair fell slowly backward off the small bony face that she had dabbed with bluish powder while making the tea. He could see where some of the powder had fallen on the front of her dress and on her skinny neck and on her shoulders.

'Oh! the dear Lord, doctor, it's the quiet ones you have to watch!' She lay back, shrieking with a fresh shrill gust of laughter. She lay for a moment or two longer and then with a great sigh gave up, her eyes running with tears, the wetness marking the powder under her eyes, her hair settling back into its place, and he knew suddenly that she laughed like that and screamed like that because she was really on the edge of a great nervous wilderness into which one single calm reflective moment would plunge her, hysterically shattered.

No one had time to say anything more before Miss McNab began singing the hymn. With a confident lifting of her head and a strong-grained thin voice she sang boldly and excitedly, smiling because she already felt the glory of it, waving her hands nervously because now she could release her energy through something other than a scream.

Almost instantly the two sisters and Harris joined in.

Forrester felt self-conscious for a moment and then he heard Miss McNab, singing the words as if they were part of the hymn, reprimand him, 'You're no singing, Mr Forrester, you're no singing, Allelujah, Allelujah!' and he saw the girl smiling at him, partly in encouragement, partly delight.

He began singing then, and the words he had known as a child and had not sung for so long and felt that he had forgotten came back to him like a long habit, without an effort of conscious thought. And as he sang he saw beyond the sweating nervously energetic face of the little missionary and the gentle face of the girl and the dark joyous face of the mother listening to the words she could not sing a moment of his childhood, an Easter Day, filled with a great scent of daffodils. It flashed through him in a moment, the scent of the flowers stronger than the hot thick sweetness of the great tree outside the house, more living than the smell of dust and tea and heat and the acrid little fires burning everywhere in the darkness under the palms.

As soon as they had sung the hymn Miss McNab gave a scream of delight and began clapping her hands. 'It was marvellous! It was wonderful! Ye put in some grand spasms o' bass, Mr Forrester!'

'Spasms are what I felt,' he said.

'Ah! d'ye hear him, Anna! What a man!'

She clapped her hands again and then let them fall into her lap, quiet again, out of breath. In the moment or two of silence that followed he could hear the distant sound of an aircraft from somewhere far across the plain, but before he could listen more closely Miss McNab had recovered. She tossed upward her mass of red dyed hair in a movement that was like a paroxysm of excitement and screamed at Harris:

'Now, doctor, you were raised on porridge and Presbyterianism – you choose the next! You! You! – come on!'

'I was never more than half-Scots,' Harris said. 'Born in London. Now let me think –'

'We're no waiting for people to think!' she screamed.

'Let Anna choose,' he said.

'Ah! ye're no half the man Mr Forrester is!'

'Let's have another dose of *Allelujah*!' Harris said.

'If you like *Allelujah* there's *Christ the Lord is risen today*,' the girl said. 'There's *Allelujah* in that.'

'Grand!' Miss McNab screamed and began to strike up at once, waving her arms, shouting down the table, 'Put in your spasms, Mr Forrester, plenty o' spasms!'

And then, even as she spoke, he was not singing. Something queer and painful took hold of him. The past, leaden and bright, divulged suddenly the harsh remembrance he could not bear. All that was happening at the table in the lamplight, all the beating of voices against the cushioned tropical night, all the bright flowers on the embroidery of the tablecloth and the brighter purple and yellow of the women's dresses, had a scrambled grey futility. In a moment the exquisite scents and colours had gone. He could taste nothing but the black burntness of scorched mushrooms. He could feel for a few moments nothing but maddening impulses, to be presently replaced by the idea that Harris was watching him and then by the still odder sensation that from all the unshuttered windows of the room a score of brown-yellow moon-faces were staring in at him, eating up the strange sight of Western man, with three Burmese Christians and a very odd red-haired specimen of Western woman, singing the unintelligible rhythms of worship to a God that had no image.

He looked up like a man unprepared and frightened. Harris was not singing. The faces behind him, yellow and curious at all the windows and now even at the door, were real. From all across the dark compound they were pressing forward into the lamplight, men and woman and children, yellow and solemn, magnetized by the sound of voices. Strange Western man, strange missionary, strange rhythms, strange mad war — he saw it all in the thunderstruck gravity of the silent almond eyes.

Soon the four women and Harris were aware of it. The singing died and Miss McNab, pleased and unsurprised, said: 'Ah, it's nothing. That always happens. Sing four bars in Burma and you have a congregation.' The unblinking eyes stared in, waiting for the singing to go on. 'Three nights of this and we'll have them half-converted. Eh, Mr Forrester?'

He did not answer; and Harris, watching him closely now, said with hurried brightness that only seemed to increase the futility of the whole affair, 'It's the curry that does it. Did you ever eat curry at the Bengal Club, Forrester? Not a patch on this!'

'Ah, the British in India,' Miss McNab said. 'What do they know about curry or any other damn thing? The Scots pray over their porridge and the English pray over their lamb.'

Forrester was oppressed by new and ghastly complexities and could not speak. The faces at the window seemed to be mocking him, and the face of Anna, silent and bright and searching, became lost among them with the flaming head of Miss McNab.

Suddenly it seemed as if he were looking, in a strange way, through a crumpled lens; that he was hearing voices in distorted echo.

'The British in India can be swine,' Harris said.

'The Americans are swine too,' Miss McNab said. 'All they

think of is –' and in a moment words were stampeding through his head, violent and scrambled: meaningless futile words, the British in India, the British in Burma, curry, something about Rangoon and the uncouthness of Americans, the Scots praying over porridge, the English praying over lamb, and then fresh words from Miss McNab, who began excitedly shouting and singing at the same time the words of a new hymn for Easter Day.

He could bear it no longer. He got up under a frenzy of impulses that did not seem to be part of him. Another hymn from the screaming McNab and he knew he would be screaming too. As he jerked up and away from the table a fissure of momentary decency opened up before him in the confusion and he saw the face of Anna, startled and delicate, staring at him with the unsteady surprise of pain. A shadow seemed to go over it in the lamplight and for an awful moment it reappeared, unforgettably frightening, as the face he had loved long ago in England.

It broke the last of his resistance. He rushed out of the room and the light gauze-covered door flapped about as if in a sudden wind and all the bland soft faces were scattered outside it like golden kittens.

He walked across the compound without knowing what he was doing; he leaned against the palm-fronds by the fence and put his head in his hands. Dry whispers of footsteps fluttered about the house as the Burmese moved back to the windows to watch the singing, and in the distance there was still the moan of a plane.

'Were you angry with us? Was it something we did?'

To turn and see the girl standing there, in the half-golden light of the house, was like the shock of self-inflicted pain. He could not answer her. She stood with a kind of gentle supplication as he spread out his hands, mute and helpless. He felt very big and stupid against the small light figure and could not move. She put her hand on his shoulders and then drew his head down to her and held her face against him. He was caught up in a moment of furious self-disgust. He wanted to shout at her 'Don't talk to me! Don't say anything for God's sake!' but she was quiet and did not speak, her face cool and negative as a leaf against him. He felt all the time that if she spoke again he would beat the face away.

And then suddenly he was not listening for her to speak. He forgot the rage that had sent him out of the house. He was listening for something else. He was disturbed by something peculiar about the sound of aircraft coming in from across the plain.

He pressed the girl gently away from him and they stood for a second or two looking up into the sky together. He saw the door of the house flap to and fro in the lamplight and then the figure of Harris on the veranda, startled and arrested as it ran forward and halted to listen too.

He walked fast across the compound.

Harris said, 'For Jesus' sake, it can't possibly be. They've never raided a thing for months.'

They stood together on the steps of the veranda, looking up, hearing the close treble-beat of engines.

'It can be and it is!' Forrester said. 'What do we do?'

'They'll go over. They're heading for the strip.'

'Then we've got to get there.'

'Right. Get the jeep while I tell them in the house,' Harris said.

He walked back across the compound, looking up, trying to see the sky beyond the darkness of the tree. He had reached the dark side of the compound when he saw something light beside him. It was Anna, standing where he had left her by the fence. Before he could speak she said, 'I know what it is. I have heard them before,' and he said, 'No need to be alarmed. Going over. We must go too,' and then in that moment he knew that the planes, three of them now, were too low and too close, and in another second he heard the bombs begin to fall. He thought, 'Christ, how can this happen? Where is everybody? Where are the boys?' and then he heard the increasing drum of the bomb stick as it came up through the village.

The third had already fallen when he flung himself forward on his face. He took the girl with him in a huge instinctive lunge, half-falling on her in the dust. As she fell he tried to put his left arm forward so that he could break the fall but it was too late and he flung it across her face immediately, where she lay. He felt her face held downward in the dust, and said, 'Hold it there, keep it there.' and then the fourth bomb fell, very near and so violent that he felt the shock of it shudder through her. It was as if she had been terribly frightened in the dark. She made no sound at all and he put his other arm right across her body, as far as he could reach. For what seemed an immensely long time he lay waiting for the fifth bomb to fall, the blank space of waiting seeming to go beyond the edges of the earth, and in the heart of it he heard an astonishing defeatless sound from the house: the sound of Miss McNab still singing.

It stopped a second or two later. The sound of the bomb crushed it out, and he thought, 'This is it. This is ours,' and then he felt once again the sensation that had for so long terrified him and made death seem a sweet and preferable thing, the sucking, blackening pull of close blast that seemed as if it would tear the clothes from his body and the skin off his face. The immediate terror of it seemed suddenly to cancel out all his former terror, and in a moment he was doing what he had cursed and blamed himself so long and so often for not doing five years before. He held the girl violently to him, with both arms and with all his strength. In a sort of angry defiance he frenziedly thought, 'It shan't happen. Not again. I won't let it happen. I won't let it,' and then the power of the blast suddenly seemed to extinguish itself and he heard the rain of dust and debris coming down through the trees, striking the brittle fronds of palm and the flat banana leaves like a storm of hail. And then the sixth bomb fell, somewhere beyond the compound, very loud but now only like an echo of the one before it, and he knew that then, with luck, it was all over.

He lay for what seemed to him ten to fifteen minutes before he moved or tried to wake any movement in the girl. Afterwards he knew that it was only a second or two before she turned over her face. Now the light of the house had gone out and he could not see her. He moved one of his hands and ran his fingers over her face and felt it covered with dust. Presently as they lay there he began to wipe the dust away with his hand, feeling her mouth and eyes closed against it, and in the first few seconds of all this he had no time to think of anything except the fact that she was living; relief and anxiety and gladness not crystallizing into one emotion or thought until he heard her speak:

'Are you all right?' she said.

'I am all right,' he said.

'I'm so glad.'

The tenderness and relief in her voice was more for a moment than he could bear. He smoothed his hands upward for the last time across her face, letting them continue with great gentleness through her hair. In the moment of patting his face against her, in the sensation of touching her living flesh and in the reality of knowing that she in turn was glad he was living, he felt the things he had feared and hated go out of him for the last time. He could think of nothing but that he was alive and was glad.

He held his mouth against her face for a few seconds before moving again. The gentleness of his affection brought from her only a very quiet response: the slightest turning of her face, without words, brushing her mouth against him, almost as if sleeping.

And then suddenly he seemed to wake violently. The sound of the singing had stopped. The sound of falling debris in the leaves was like an echo, and in the place of these sounds he could hear another. It was the sound of screaming. As it rose from the village, from the terrified voices of children and women among the trees, it seemed to rush forward in an increasing wave of sound, like the noise of the bomb, until it became a single scream, terribly shrill and repeated, from within the house.

The girl sprang to her feet. He got up and listened with her to the scream coming across the compound. It was repeated regularly and piercingly, curiously like a scream of joy. And suddenly he realized that he did not know the voice. He knew that it was not the scream of Miss McNab, nervous and volatile, to which he was listening any longer.

He knew even before the girl began running towards the dark house that he was listening to the screams of the mother.

7

Some minutes later he stumbled across a wreckage of bamboo
fences and tangled branches and vines back into the compound
from somewhere beyond the other side of the house. He was
carrying in his hands the mutilated and bloody carcase of a
boy, skinned by blast into a mess of raw tissue, like a rabbit,
and the boy moaned as he carried him, with a continuous plead-
ing murmur, conscious but without words.

He carried the child straight across the compound to the little
dispensary. There were more lights in the house now and he met
Harris, stripped to the waist, walking across from the dispensary.

'Not here. In the house,' Harris said.

Forrester turned and followed him carrying the child across
the compound and up the steps of the veranda and into the
room where, it seemed to him a hundred years ago, he had been
singing under the screaming leadership of Miss McNab.

In the first few seconds of going into the room he stood with
the child in his arms and stared at the girl and her sister and her
mother. They seemed to have come to life with cool efficiency
and were tearing strips of cloth, talking together. Then he remembered the scream. He remembered running with the girl
across the compound towards the scream and then suddenly
parting from her, hearing the wild moans of the little boy
beyond the house, and then running across the smashed fences
beyond the trees, as if he were chasing a wounded rabbit. Now
he saw to his astonishment that there were other children there.
Two brown bodies were laid across the table, bare of its tablecloth now, the meal snatched hastily from it. Then as he laid the
boy gently on the floor he saw another there, with a Burmese
woman lying beside it, mute and tired and yellow with shock,
eyes staring upward dumbly, the dark pupils not moving as he

laid the other child beside her. Then even as he laid it down he knew that a change had come over it. It had ceased moaning at last. And as he drew away from it he saw the bloody purplish mass of its smashed intestines bubble out over what remained of the groin and in a moment of horror he tried to push them back with his hands. Then knew that it was no use. He got up hastily and pulled off his bush jacket and covered the child with it, leaving only the face exposed.

When he got up a second time it was to see, coming in from the kitchen, the astonishing figure of Miss McNab. He looked at her as if he were drunk. She was not the volatile, restless, screaming Miss McNab he had known; she had taken off her dress and was wearing nothing but a pale pink underslip, one of the shoulder straps of which had broken and was hanging down. He thought for a moment, wildly, 'She was hit. It blew the clothes off her,' and then he saw that what she had done was quite deliberate. She had stripped herself of the vulgar flowing dress and she was screaming no longer. She had in her eyes the look of calm and efficient resource, cold and steadfast, rather grim in its selfless devotion, that he knew must have been there a long time ago, in the graceful and pleasant days at the mission, before the bitter journey north had begun.

As he stood looking at her she said, in a low, normal voice, all hysteria gone from it, so that it was like the voice of a different woman:

'Will you boil quantities of water, Mr Forrester, please? The fire is just outside. Quantities and quantities of water. God bless you.'

He stood for a second or two trying to collect himself. Then he turned and went through the door from which she had just come. As he turned to go he looked at the child he had placed on the floor. Covered by his bush jacket, its mutilations seemed like the memory of something unbelievably ghastly. He could not believe in their reality. He stood for the smallest moment longer, looking at the small flat yellow face, quiet in death and mercifully dark in the shadow beyond the lamplight. And in that moment he was struck violently by some odd flash of familiarity about it. It afflicted him with haunting pain, as if somewhere in his life he had seen it before. And then in another moment he knew that he had seen it before. It was the face of the smallest of the brown laughing boys who had ridden on the doctor's jeep, with such noisy bouncing joy, only yesterday.

He went through the kitchen and outside to the back of the house to where, in a part of the compound clear of the great tree, the fire was burning under a sort of open oven of rock. Miss McNab had left a large bucket of water on it and he could see it steaming a little in the light from the house. He stood for a minute dazed and trembling. Then he remembered the face of the boy. And now it did more than haunt him. It swept through him a gust of anger. He was overcome by a stupefying sense of fury and sorrow. He felt suddenly that what he had carried in from the jungle of wretched little houses and trees and fences was not simply a single child with its stomach gouged from it like a mess of unspeakable offal, but innumerable millions of children, of all creeds and classes and tongues and colours, everywhere all over the world, born to be skinned and smashed and sacrificed in living mutilation.

The dissolution of his anger into this stabbing sorrow drove him into a sudden frenzy of activity. He began to grope about the dust of the compound, finding lengths of bamboo for the fire and throwing them under the bucket. Then as the fire flamed up afresh he found himself doing a curious thing. He was instinctively holding out his hands, warming them against the flames. And as he did so he realized that it was not a foolish or forgetful thing. He was shuddering violently. For the first time since he had come to a country from which he had never been able to escape the heat he felt great shudders of shock running through him, leaving him icy and weak and quivering.

The worst of this passed off and he pulled himself together just as the girl came out of the house. She came straight towards him and he put out his arms and held her quietly, the last of his shudders almost dying out. He did not say anything but only held her against him, desperately trying to crush the last of his trembling out of himself.

Then she spoke. 'We need the water,' she said.

'It's almost ready,' he said. 'How are things?'

'They are still bringing people in,' she said. 'They are coming because they know the doctor is here.'

'How many?' he said.

'There is a man and four women and three more children now.'

'God,' he said. 'God! God damn them!'

'Oh, please,' she said.

'I'm sorry,' he said. He held her face with his hands. 'I'm truly sorry.' Her skin, very smooth and cool and clean of dust now, was comforting to his hands.

Very calm, she let him hold her face a moment longer. And in that final simple movement of calm intimacy the shuddering went out of him, and he knew that he would be all right. He kissed her face and then, lightly but seriously and with a sort of relieved gladness, her lips, and heard her say a moment later, 'There are a lot of reasons why you shouldn't do that.'

'There are no reasons and there never will be any reasons,' he said.

'You must bring the water,' she said.

Then he remembered the scream. 'Your mother!' he said.

'Yes,' she said. 'She can speak to us. She suddenly began speaking.'

It seemed to him all at once that she did not want to talk of it. She turned away from him, crouching low over the fire, and in the light of it he saw her face troubled and anxious for the first time, its calmness gone. Something about its delicacy, nervous in the light of the fire, troubled him in turn. She seemed to be on the verge of a moment or two of delayed shock.

'Now it's you who are tired,' he said. 'Let me hold you.'

Before he could touch her she stood up again. 'No,' she said. 'No. I'm not tired. I am all right. I'm not tired.'

'There's something wrong,' he said.

'We must go in with the water,' she said.

She tried to lift the bucket from the fire.

'I'll do it,' he said.

'Quickly then.'

Before he could speak again she had turned and gone into the house. He did not try to follow her but stood for a few moments longer, pushing the unburnt lengths of bamboo into the fire. Watching them flare fiercely and brightly he crouched down, listening to a sound he had not consciously heard before. At first he could not identify it. It was like the sound of low wind blowing in beneath the trees from across the plain, the sound of a storm rising and whining and crying in the blistered palms. And then he realized it was not that. He knew that it was the crying and whining of human voices: the excited speechless echoing murmurs of people crying among themselves in trouble, the universal sound of human beings weeping to each other in common grief.

And then as he crouched there listening to it he was troubled by something else. He knew that somewhere he had heard that sound before, pitched on just the same crying murmuring note, rising in just that same way in the darkness. And for a few moments longer he sat trying to remember where it was, tormented by its familiarity and haunted by its awful intangible melancholy until at last he did remember. He knew then where he had heard that same sound, in another language and yet always in the same language. It was the sound you always heard, rising and falling in the street, rebelliously crying in the darkness, a mixture of grief and curiosity and protest and wonder poured out by the voices of countless invisible people in that same low crying murmur in the first moment after the falling of a bomb.

As the remembrance of it swept over him in a wave of impotence and futility he got up and took the bucket and went into the house.

He was confronted immediately there, not by the girl, but by the calm and almost noiseless figure of Miss McNab. He thought perhaps he had been a long time heating the water in the bucket; he seemed to have struggled back through years in order to identify the terrible crying voices. But as Miss McNab took the bucket from him she said: 'Splendid. You've been very quick,' and he felt relieved and glad.

'More, please. Quantities and quantities. More please, Mr Forrester,' she said. 'You'll find another bucket outside.'

Without answering he stood for a moment and took in swiftly what was happening in the room: the girl and her mother still tearing strips of cotton cloth into bandages, Harris bending over the table on which lay a small Burmese girl of eight or nine, the lower half of her left arm blown away, leaving a stump of smashed blue and white bone. On the floor the woman still lay by the covered body of the little boy, and beyond her lay the man of whom the girl had spoken, and beyond him another child. All that was happening seemed to be governed by the strange orderly calm of Miss McNab, skinny and yet unridiculous in her underslip, her small bright eyes passionately calm, even the mass of her dyed untidy hair no longer fantastic. Harris too moved with calm and rather slow but unbroken efficiency about the table. In the light of the lamp all his boyishness had gone, so that he was no longer the man who had regarded the occupation of Burma as a huge fraternal joke. And in all that was happening, except for the whimpering of the child on the table and the heavy gasping breath of the woman on the floor, there was only a single sound of panic. And to Forrester's astonishment it was not the sound of the mother, as he thought at first, unable to stop the fragmentary sound of her voice dribbling through her lips in its first rush of release, but the voice of the sister, who had sat through the meal in repressive silence, gently dignified, almost without a word. The sound of her whimper of hysteria was astonishing and troubling in the little room. The trembling indrawing of her breath was sharply like the echo of the wailing voices outside.

In the few seconds as he stood there watching all this something else happened. He heard Harris say, with abrupt impatience, 'Scissors, please, scissors.' He saw the mother swiftly drop her bandage and move away. Then as she crossed the room, coming towards him, Forrester saw the girl move even more quickly from beyond the table, coming towards him in the same way. In a second she was across the room, going straight between himself and the mother, saying with astonishing violent curtness: 'It's all right. Go back. I'll get them,' so that the mother turned with meek abruptness and went back again.

He watched the girl with absolute astonishment as she went past him but she did not look up. She was breathing very fast, as if she were frightened. And the way she went past him without speaking gave him suddenly the feeling that he was not wanted, the feeling that she might suddenly have regretted all that had happened – that all the gentleness and intimacy between them had been a mistake.

As he saw her go back across the room with the scissors in that same frightened almost wild way, he went outside. The fire of bamboo had burned itself down. He stirred it and the dry husks of bamboo shot into flame, so that he could see. Then by the light of it he found fresh bamboo and piled it on and immediately afterwards Miss McNab came to the door of the house, saying to him:

'Mr Forrester, the water is in the tank. I was forgetting you didn't know. At the end of the veranda there.'

He stopped her before she went back into the house:

'What was the matter with Anna just now?'

'She's a fine wee girl,' Miss McNab said. 'The finest we ever had. She was the youngest ever to go on to the university.'

'She looked frightened,' he said.

'Mr Forrester,' she said, 'it's the first time she's been bombed. It's the first time any of us have been bombed. We're all frightened.'

'I'm sorry,' he said. He was overcome suddenly by the idiocy of his own selfishness.

'She's been very brave,' Miss McNab said. 'Wonderfully brave.'

He could not speak.

'I think she's been brave because you were here,' she said. 'She had to show you that.'

He stood staring at the fire, watching the flames consume the flaming husks of bamboo as his own anger was consuming now, all dry and bitter, his own stupidity and selfishness.

'You've seen all this sort of thing,' Miss McNab said. 'It's not new to you. You're used to it. What she did she had to take from you. And she is very glad of that.'

'I'll get the water,' he said.

As he picked up the bucket to move across to the water tank she said:

'Are you married, Mr Forrester? Excuse my asking a personal question.'

'No,' he said.

'I'm glad,' she said.

She suddenly pointed across to the village, where little fires and lights were burning now among the trees, flickering sharply in the darkness and where the wailing, low and confused, haunting and continuous as before, still went on.

'If it weren't for you she would be doing that,' Miss McNab said. 'She'd be giving way to that awful damn' panic. You saw the sister.'

'Yes,' he said.

'They're not like us,' Miss McNab said. 'Made of ice, God forgive us. I know them. I've lived with them for forty years. I came out here as a young girl. They wail it out of themselves. Ye've heard it in India, Mr Forrester. They wail it out of themselves.'

Once again he did not speak, but stood gripping the bucket hard with both hands, staring at the fire.

'They can't leave it in, Mr Forrester,' Miss McNab said. 'As you and I could. To rot.'

He wanted in that moment to say something to her, to tell her more intimately of some of the things, perhaps all the things, that had troubled him, with awful self-tribulation, for so long. But before he could speak she had gone into the house. She turned only as she went in to say:

'If you think you could be making a cuppa tea after the next bucket we'd all be glad. It's awful hot and thirsty.'

'I will,' he said.

No sooner had she gone than he found the remedy for his own sickness of himself in action: collecting bamboo from the compound, building the fire, finding another large flat tin pannikin under the steps of the veranda and filling it with water. He moved at first savagely, in anger against himself; but gradually he felt the anger spread out in cool distribution through his limbs and finally leave him altogether. He knew that what Miss McNab said was right. And suddenly as he moved about the compound he looked up and listened and knew that the murmur of voices, like a great creeping clot of sound, was in some mysterious way gathering strength. It was beginning to move in an uneasy and mutinous concert of protest. Deepening but also sharpening, it was coming up through the dark trees on all sides of him like a tide of panic. He stood listening to it fascinated and yet troubled, in a sort of wonder touched by consternation. The rising sound of so many voices, murmuring together in a language he did not know, began to have in it a touch of primitive power. And as he became aware of it he remembered how once he had stood in the heart of Calcutta and watched the fluttering armies of Indians, in their white *dhotis* so like nervous white ants, crossing the roads and flooding the pavement and swarming on trams and buses, and how it had suddenly struck him that if they should ever be driven to run in mass escape from the terror of bombing, the sort of bombing that Europe knew, they would trample down in an hour or two, by the sheer power of panic, in a single mad destructive and self-destructive flood, all of that huge, flimsy, brittle, gimcrack city. He knew that the panic of famine had taken them like that: flooding them out of the foul, sun-evil, vulture-ridden slums of the native suburbs to the long roads by which there was no escape, to die there in thousands, hopeless, directionless, self-destroyed by the fury of a primitive fear of death that had driven them on to rot in the sun.

Now as he listened to the sound of voices rising on all sides of him in the darkness he knew that he was listening to the same thing. As he heard it and stood listening more intently something made him pick up a length of bamboo from the compound. He stood trying its weight, almost unconsciously, in his hands. After a moment he began to move towards the house. He did not know quite what he was going to do. He stood still again and listened. The sound of voices clotted itself all about him with a harsher, darker, more powerful note, growing closer all the time. And sometimes among it there was a single shouting voice: the yell of a single word like a shot in the darkness, primitively splendid and frightening and frenzied in declaration, and then a low answering murmur of many people in reply. And then he knew what was happening. He knew that they were going out. Even though it was night they were going out in a single panic exodus to somewhere across the plain. Through the fear of night and out of the fear of bombing they were being driven by a mutinous and terrified power to a new retreat. It was as if the Japs had given a signal that they were coming back.

With the stick in his hands, he went into the house. He met Miss McNab at the door.

'Something is happening,' he said. 'Listen.'

With averted eyes she stood very still, quite calm, listening. Even from inside the room he could hear the deep march of voices. They were so heavy and near now that it seemed they would trample down the house.

'They are going down to the river,' she said.

'I don't like it.'

'This is not India, Mr Forrester,' she said.

As she spoke he looked round the room. Only the doctor, the mother, the sister and the wounded were there. The girl had disappeared, and in a moment some of the panic he heard in the voices outside shot through him swiftly. 'This is not India and you will never understand it while you think it is,' Miss McNab was saying.

'Where's Anna?' he said.

'She's gone across to the dispensary.'

As he turned and went out of the house and down the steps of the veranda and across the compound towards the light in Harris's little dispensary, he knew by the strength of the voices that the crowd, congested and slow on the little track between the houses, was still two or three hundred yards away.

Half way across the compound he saw the girl coming quickly out of the door of the dispensary. And in the exact moment of seeing her he remembered the jeep. It was standing where Harris had left it, in the track, partly barring the way the crowd would come. And suddenly it struck Forrester that, standing there, it was a dangerous thing. It occurred to him that the crowd would smash it.

In the few seconds of thinking all this he reached the girl. She looked at him in surprise, no longer frightened. Then as he said something to her about the crowd moving out to the river he saw her lift her head, startled, as if hearing the panic sound of it for the first time.

'I'm going to move the jeep,' he said. 'Stay there.'

He ran across the compound and out of the gate in the palisade and climbed into the jeep. Between the offside of it and the far fence of the track there was a gap of less than four feet, and he saw that the crowd would never get by. For a few seconds he sat fumbling in the half-darkness for the ignition switch, looking down at the dashboard. Then when he looked up again he saw the beginning of the crowd, a vague barrier of faces between the fences of bamboo along the track, growing paler and clearer in the light of his own fire at the back of the compound. They were less than a hundred yards away. And now in the murmur of voices, sharp and separated, he detected below its terror the thing he had feared. From deep within it there was rising an anger against something and through his mind went something he had said to Harris – that none of them had any right to be there, that all of them, with their aircraft and trucks and their liberation through destruction and the whole senseless upheaval of war, were in some sense trespassers.

The rush of thought left him stiff and petrified, listening to the rising flood of voices. He could not move. Even in the second before he saw the girl come out of the compound and climb up beside him in the jeep, he knew that it was too late to move.

'Nothing will happen,' she said. 'Let them go past.'

'They'll never get past,' he said.

'Let them go,' she said.

Then the clot of three or four hundred voices broke along the track. It split in an explosion of momentary surprise.

'Get out and run,' he said.

She did not move, but said simply: 'Switch on your lights.'

He did what she said almost without thinking. The full light of the jeep passed suddenly, bright and blinding, down the track. He saw the crowded mass of faces advance for a few moments and then stop dead in the glare of light, flat, bewildered, squinting, the murmur from them abruptly dying out. Then as the crowd stopped, women with children on their backs, trucks of bamboo piled with bundles, the magenta waist-strips of the men almost bright violet in the white lamplight above the dust, he heard the murmur break again. It split with anger and became a new fantastic gabble of voices.

'What are they saying?' he said.

'They want to come past,' she said.

'Tell them they can't,' he said. 'Tell them there is no need.'

Even before he had finished speaking she stood up. 'Tell them everything is all right,' he said. He caught hold of her hand as she stood up. He was shocked to find it cold. He stood up too. 'Tell them it is better for them to stay here,' he said. She did not speak. And then after a second or two he knew why she did not speak. Great deep convulsive shudders of fear were going through her so that she could not hold herself still. In this moment he caught hold of her hand and held it with such tightness that he felt the pain of it shoot up through her and calm in a single convulsion all her trembling.

'Tell them,' he said. 'Tell them it is all right.'

He put his arm about her and took one look at her face, so young and frightened and hesitant in the upward cast of light that he felt in that moment all his feeling for her break into a flower of fresh tenderness and then, strong and clear and open, into affection. And then she began speaking.

He did not know at once what she was saying. The barrier of faces was quiet. And then somewhere among them a child began crying, the sound of it exploding the voices of the rest, the faces beginning to surge forward in the light, shouting. Seeing them, he gripped the girl more tightly. And then he saw the confused multitude of faces suddenly become a single face: the face of a man in a light purple waist-cloth and a brown soft felt European hat. It was as if the hands of the crowd had suddenly pushed him forward, ten or fifteen spaces nearer the jeep, so that he could talk to her.

He began at once to talk very rapidly, making large gestures of argument, waving both hands.

The girl could talk no longer.

'What is he saying?' Forrester said.

'He says they are not staying here. He says the Japs are coming back.'

'Tell them they are not coming back.' He thought rapidly and angrily of the sweating, fever-ridden, leech-sucked, dust-choked, rain-swamped infantry, cutting and slushing its way down from the northern hills to fight now, the ultimate battle of the plains. He had helped to prepare the way for them; nothing could stop them now. Mandalay was going. In a week Meiktila would go. The last thread holding the central plains from the south would snap.

'Tell them they will never come back,' he said. 'Tell them never, never. Never.'

Almost before she began speaking, he saw the man in the brown trilby hat make large frenzied gestures to the sky. Even before the girl spoke to him again he knew what it meant.

'He says they have come back,' she said. 'He says they were here. He says everybody knows they are back.'

'Tell them they have no need to fear anything. Tell them,' he said. 'You must tell them.'

She began to speak again but the man in the trilby hat began to shout at her.

'Talk to them, talk to them,' he said. 'Tell them it's almost over. Tell them it's better for them if they stay here. Tell them there is no need to go.'

The girl spoke a few words and the man, waving his arms again, shouted back.

'He says what about the aeroplanes?' she said.

'Tell them there are the wounded,' he said. 'In the house. We need help. Tell them in the morning I will have food and supplies sent out – '

He did not know what else to say. He saw the man begin to wave his arms again and heard the girl begin speaking. In the crowd the white faces seemed to bubble more restlessly in the lamp-light, and the child began to cry again with a thin anguished wail.

Suddenly the girl said to him, 'Stand up.'

'No,' he said. 'You talk to them.'

'Stand up,' she said. 'Please. Please stand up. I want them to see you. Stand up.'

She took hold of his hand and slowly he stood up. Against her he was very tall and felt embarrassed and conspicuous standing there in the strong upward glow of light, looking at the white mass of faces, partly hostile, partly curious and afraid, packed there in the narrow track. But as he stood up heard the crowd grow quiet. The man in the trilby hat no longer waved his hands and somebody began to scold the crying of the child.

As it stopped crying at last the girl began speaking. He knew after a moment or two that she was speaking of himself. But what she was saying he never knew. She talked all the time very rapidly, as if still afraid that the crowd would come back to its protesting mutinous life.

And gradually as he stood there listening to her talking of himself in a language he did not know he felt growing inside himself a deep humility and out of it and because of it a stronger, deeper affection and pride in her. He saw the mass of uncertain turbulent faces begin to calm down in the harsh glare of light. He saw too that what Miss McNab had said was true. He saw that this was not India, with all its eternal and insoluble problems rising out of a worship of fertility that was itself a way of self-destruction, but something he did not know, something much more simple, much more childlike, much more gentle, something uncomplicated by the thousand religions and the racial clash of the other country but as shining and clear, if only he could get it into perspective, as the white and glittering pagoda shining above the dust of the plain.

He held his arm about her until she had finished speaking. It was only when he saw the front of the crowd gradually give way and grow dark, as the flat moon-faces were turned away and replaced by coconuts of hair that glistened with black brilliance in the light, that he could bring himself to speak again. Even then, as the words came up to his lips, she said:

'Don't speak. Let them go, let them go.'

For some moments longer he stood there silently watching them go and listening to the retreating sound of voices. As the last of the violet waist-cloths swung out of the lamp-light, like brilliant petals, he pressed his hands gently on her shoulders, so that at last she sat down.

'They've gone back,' he said. 'All of them have gone back,' but she did not answer. She sat with her hands in her lap, pressing them hard together.

'Why did you talk to them about me?' he said.

Along the track the last echo of voices was dying out slowly in the darkness under the palms. She did not answer.

'Why?' he said. 'Please tell me,' but she did not answer and before he could speak again and before the last sound of voices died completely she began to cry, at first silently, then deeply, with terrible desperation, holding the sobs against her mouth with her hands and letting the fingers close up like a stiff cage against her eyes, trying to stop the long, bitter tears from falling down.

All the time she was crying he did not speak. From out across the plain the voices of jackals, now more than ever like the wailing voices of human beings crying across a wilderness, broke in at intervals on the quietness left by the voices that had died away. He put out the light of the jeep. The fire of bamboo in the compound had died down and now there was no light except the light in the house and the tiny glimmer of light in the dispensary above the sick child. In the glow of the windows he could see Harris and sometimes Miss McNab moving as they worked among the wounded. 'I ought to go back,' he thought, but the girl went on crying and he went on holding her there and did not move. All about him there fell the sweet drenching scent of the tree, but now with it also he could smell the curious dry odour, dead and sour and chemically rotten, that comes from bombing.

When at last the girl gave up she turned suddenly and caught hold of his face. She drew it down and kissed it with terrible strength and he kissed her in return. And as he did so, feeling her grow quiet at last, he could smell the sharp sweet-sour odour of the bomb and the tree together, and could hear the sound of jackals rising and dying, splitting and deepening the silence of the plain.

8

Harris came out of the house, drying his arms on a towel, meeting the girl and Forrester in the compound. In the light from the windows Forrester could see the arms smothered with dark blotches, as if bruised: great smears of red-brown blood, already too dried in the heat of the night to be wiped away.

'You'd better get back,' Harris said. 'I can't cope here. I need help. We've got hospital cases.'

'All right,' he said. 'Tell me what.'

'Listen,' Harris said, 'go over to the Nurses' H.Q., and get hold of Longman. Tell her I need an ambulance and two nurses. If she can't send two nurses tell her to send one and have two more standing by – '

'She'll say it's very irregular.'

'Tell her to let you bring back the stuff on this paper,' Harris said. 'And then to have four beds ready – '

'She'll say it's very irregular.'

'Tell her to go to bloody hell,' Harris said. 'Tell her what happened. Tell her how it is. She's a good scout really. She'll understand.'

The girl started to run into the house. 'I'll get your tunic,' she said.

He remembered how he had thrown his bush jacket over the child that he had brought in from the compound.

'Get back as soon as you can,' Harris said. 'We didn't get far with the hymns, did we?'

'They were good while they lasted,' Forrester said.

He stood for a moment or two without saying anything, and then the girl came out of the house, carrying his jacket.

'See you soon,' Harris said. Wiping the sweat from his face with the blood-stained towel he went back up the steps of the veranda, his voice tired.

Smiling, the girl held out the tunic for Forrester to put on. He saw the blood of the dead child dried brown in a great smear across the chest and the lower part of it. The sight of it embittered him sharply but he did not speak. He put on the tunic and left it undone.

'Will you be long?' the girl said.

'No,' he said. 'An hour or so.'

He stood for a moment looking at her face, not speaking. He could not tell in the half-darkness whether the deep shadow of her eyes came solely from crying or not. The face seemed to him painfully young and beautiful, and he held it with his hands. 'There is no time to talk now,' he said. He smoothed his hands downward over the two sides of her parted hair and said: 'If I kiss you again will you know that I mean it? Will you believe that?'

'Yes,' she said. 'But – '

'Don't talk now,' he said. 'Not now.'

He kissed her again, lightly but seriously, and after holding her face for a moment or two with his hands, feeling the fresh light tenderness of face, relaxed now and no longer tired, he heard her say: 'You must go now,' and he went across the compound and got into the jeep without another word.

He drove out of the village by the way the girl had first taken him, and in a few moments he was out on the harder track of the plain. In the glare of his headlights he could see sometimes under the fantastic mass of glassy emerald leaves on either side of the track, at the western edge of the village, the wreckage of a hut or two that had collapsed under blast or had been blown outward, a mass of splintered cane and palm with sometimes a sheet of corrugated iron, twisted like paper, and among it all a knot of faces, pale as they whisked past him in the light, talking excitedly.

The nurses were billeted in a large bungalow, once the house of the resident manager, attached to the big rice-mill on the far side of the town. In two months of occupation they had converted into more than a tolerably good hospital the main mill, wrecked in the retreat of 1942 and then left by the Japanese to be eaten by the strangling vines and grasses that had sprung up with evil luxuriance, stronger and wilder, each year of the monsoon. As he left the plain and skirted the town by the perimeter road that coolies and Burmese labourers were laying, the moon began to come up across the mountains and in the deep and powerful orange light of it he could see all the broken pagodas of the great monastery shining like towers of sugar cake, and then along the last splintered palm avenue of the town, the tall iron chimney of the rice-mill, like a black funnel in the glowing sky.

It was not until he stopped the jeep by the rice bungalow that he heard the hum of the main electric generator still working at the camp. In that moment he really came to himself. For the first time he was jerked sharply out of the unreal world across the plain. The electric generator stopped working every night at ten o'clock and suddenly he realized that it was still very early; that all that had happened to him had happened in the space of a few minutes, that what had seemed like a huge section of a lifetime, with its deep and shattering experiences, had really all been over in half an hour.

In a dazed way he found himself in the ante-room of the hospital. Screens of split bamboo rising half-way up the walls partitioned it off from the rest of the building, and in some miraculous way there were electric fans slowly turning under the rafters.

The duty nurse was sitting at a table just inside the door. She was very young and she was drinking a cup of tea. He stared incredibly at this civilized act and at her clear brown English face and said:

'I want to see Longman. Urgent, please.'

'Is it an accident?' She stared at the blood on his tunic. 'Longman is in Calcutta on leave.'

Oh! hell, he thought. 'Yes, it's an accident, but not to me. It's from Wing Commander Harris. Who's in charge?'

'Macmillan,' she said.

'Never heard of her,' he said. He thought of all the feminine evils he knew, and the least was Johnson. 'Get Johnson on the buzzer. Tell her Squadron Leader Forrester is here. Tell her it's urgent.'

'Johnson is probably asleep,' the girl said. 'She comes on duty at two o'clock tomorrow morning.'

'Look,' he said, 'a whole bloody village has been bombed. Kids have been blown to hell. Didn't you hear it? It's a shambles. Perhaps you were having tea?'

The large brown eyes of the girl looked very offended and a little frightened. She picked up the telephone. He heard her call an extension number and then wait. She did not look at him. He walked round the room, not realizing how nervous he was or how badly he was behaving until he heard the click of the receiver going back.

'I'm sorry,' he said. 'Just like me. Excitable. I'm terribly sorry. Is she coming?'

'She's coming,' the girl said.

'Good kid,' he said.

He walked about the room again. They were all good kids, he thought. All of them. There were none better in the world. They had no business to be here, any of them, east of Bengal. He looked at her face, brown, fresh, rather friendly now. She looked perhaps nineteen: no more. Back in England and America millions of people living narrow lives of petty ineptitude and selfish complaint did not know of her or think of her, sweating out her youth in a climate not fit for a dog.

'I'm really awfully sorry,' he said. 'This bloody awful country.'

'I love it,' she said, and grinned, dry and ironical, already seared in the experience of battles.

Johnson came into the room a minute later. She looked straight at his tunic.

'What mess have you been getting into?'

She had been washing her hair and had tied it hastily in a wet black screw above her sallow-muddy face. It was a face that had about it the queerest kindly ugliness he had ever seen.

'What's up?' she said. 'You know you'll get me hung.'

He told her what had happened.

'Here's Harris's list,' he said. 'And don't say it's irregular.'

'It is irregular.'

'Get two nurses and the ambulance and tell them to follow me. I'll take them out there.'

'I can spare an ambulance and one nurse but not two nurses,' she said. 'And you're lucky to get that. It's only because Harris is senior M.O.'

'All right, one nurse.'

Johnson turned away to the girl at the desk. 'Ring 38 and get No. 3 Ambulance,' she said. 'Say it's for Wing Commander Harris if they ask. Then ring the bungalow and get Burke.'

'Burke!' he said.

'I know you'd prefer to have someone you had faith in,' Johnson said.

'My faith in Burke is boundless,' he said, mocking her. 'It has no beginning and no end.'

'Anyway, she's the only one I can spare,' she said. 'So you're done, anyway.'

'It's all very irregular,' he mocked.

'Most irregular.'

'I'll be outside,' he said.

'I'm coming that way myself,' she said. 'I'll just get somebody to pack these things.'

While she went back into the hospital with Harris's list he went outside and stood for a few moments on the dusty track running between the hospital ward and the bungalow, with its entire roof still a mass of salmon-scarlet under the moon. After a few moments Johnson came out to him.

'What had you been saying to the orderly nurse?'

'Nothing.'

'You'd got her fairly jumping about on the seat.'

'Oh dear!'

'You know it's very wrong,' she said. 'You just look at these girls and next minute they're breaking their hearts. It's too bad. Considering the future you have.'

'Considering the future any of us have.'

'You men!' she said. 'Thinking of nothing but yourselves.'

A moment later the ambulance came round the corner with the other nurse, Burke, clinging on the side. She was wearing long khaki trousers and had tucked her rather fluffy brown hair under her cap, like a man.

As the ambulance slowed down she jumped off, seeing Forrester and Johnson standing together.

'Well, for God's sake,' she said.

'How's Calcutta?' he said.

'I wouldn't be knowin',' she said fiercely. 'I've been up to Comilla. Where the work's done.'

'Will you ride in the ambulance or come with me?' he said.

'Take the greater privilege,' Johnson said.

'What else would I be doing?' Burke said.

'All right. Come on,' he said.

'For God's sake,' Burke said. 'We're all in a tearing hurry, aren't we?'

'Tell the driver to follow on.'

He climbed into the driving seat and while he started the engine Burke climbed in at the other side. Letting in the clutch, he waved his hand to Johnson, who lifted one hand in reply. Then, at the last moment, he remembered the medical supplies for Harris, and at the same time caught sight of the young orderly nurse, running out of the hospital building with a black tin box in her hands. 'Put it in the ambulance!' he shouted.

Not thinking he was driving fast he drove out along the new perimeter road by the monastery, twice looking back over his shoulder to see that the ambulance was following. The second time the ambulance had not turned the bend from the hospital, and he slowed down. Then as he drove on, past the great monastery, with its two gigantic elephants, white and gilt and scarlet, high and brilliant above the vast branches of the banyan tree that filled with its pendulant root-branches and black shadows all of the great compound in front of the still unfinished greater temple, he saw Burke look at him sharply.

'What has Johnson been saying?' she said.

'Nothing.'

'Sometimes she makes me wild.'

He turned and looked at her, not speaking. The deep Irish upper lip, set and fierce, seemed uglier than ever; the lips, hastily lipsticked, were sloppy and large. Then it struck him suddenly that she was asking about Johnson the very question that Johnson had asked about the orderly nurse.

'Well, what brings you down from Comilla?' he said.

'I wouldn't be knowin' and I wouldn't be tellin' if I did.'

'We'll all be moving soon. Mandalay is going.'

'Where the front moves we move,' she said. 'That's all I know.'

In another three or four minutes he turned off the perimeter road and began to take the track across the plain. The jeep bounced out of his hands in the half-filled shell-holes, throwing Burke across the seat. The dust still rose as it did in the day-time, but now it seemed less fierce and stifling. It was blown up like mist in the golden moonlight that was barred with blacker shadows, under the trees, than even the shadows of day.

'You're travelling miles too fast,' Burke said. 'Are you forgettin' the ambulance is followin'?'

'I was after forgettin',' he said, mocking a little.

'Well then be after rememberin'!'

'I will an' all an' all,' he said, mocking still.

She gave one of her fierce masculine snorts of pretended disgust, and he laughed a little, good-naturedly.

'What in the name o' God's come over you?' Burke said.

'I wouldn't be knowin',' he said. 'Why?'

'The last time you were up at Comilla you were like a bear with a sore head and a sour liver and God knows what. There was no doin' anything with you. We all hated you.'

'You had too much Indian gin,' he said.

'None of your damned English insults either!' she said. 'If y'are feelin' better.'

'I never felt worse,' he said, grinning again.

Presently they were beyond the last of the roadside trees. In the clear empty space of the plain the dust was like golden ash under the moon.

'There's something different about you,' she said. 'You've been doing too much flying or something lately.'

'Hardly any,' he said. 'Been waiting for this thing to blow up. Whatever it is if it ever blows up. Not to speak of a new navigator.'

'Ah!' she said. 'The boy we had in hospital.'

'Yes.'

'He was dreadin' meetin' you.'

What the hell? he thought. He did not speak.

'I'm tellin' you,' she said. 'He was dreadin' meetin' you.'

He slowed down, taking the jeep over the railway track. In the moonlight the narrow gauge stretched like a toy across the vastness of the plain.

'He was fresh out from England,' she said, 'but he'd heard about you.'

'And what he hadn't heard you told him.'

'I did.'

'Trust the Irish,' he said.

'And trust the English,' she said, 'when it comes to conceit and smugness and self-importance and not seeing beyond their noses and all the rest. They make me mad.'

'What brings you to Burma?' he said.

'Sometimes I wouldn't be knowin' myself!' she said. 'You'd better wait for the ambulance, hadn't you?'

He looked over his shoulder and saw the ambulance crawling slowly across the track, three hundred yards away. He stopped the jeep and switched off the engine and waited.

'What was this about Carrington dreading meeting me?' he said.

'And who wouldn't?' she said.

He sat watching the ugly thick-lipped face turned towards him in the full moon. It seemed to regard him with almost affectionate antagonism.

'And who wouldn't?' she said. 'You're enough to put the fear o' God into anybody.'

Looking over his shoulder again, seeing the ambulance less than a hundred yards away, he did not speak.

'Except me,' she said. 'You don't fool me, you know.'

He wondered how it was that he did not fool her and the next moment started up the jeep, roaring the engine hard, so that the sound of it roared explosively across the plain.

'And you needn't be mad, either!' she said.

It took him a moment or two to discover that he was not angry with her at all. He looked at her good-naturedly and quietly and then saw the thick ugly gash of her mouth move itself convulsively, as if repressing itself in a moment of involuntary tenderness, but without a word in reply. She put out her hand and then, looking over her shoulder, withdrew it sharply.

'Oh! why in the name o' God did we have to come in convoy?' she said.

He let in the clutch and drove on, not speaking again. She was quiet too, not saying another word until he had driven some distance out of the plain under the thick trees, where a few fires were burning in the little village compounds, lighting up here and there again the groups of pale flat faces, staring as the jeep went by.

'This is queer,' she said. 'How did you and Harris come to be out in a hole like this in a raid?'

'This is a Christian community,' he said.

'You needn't start blasphemin',' she said.

'No,' he said, 'we came to choose the hymns for Easter Sunday.'

He saw in her face as he turned to look over his shoulder for the last time, a remarkable shock of surprise – of surprise that was almost hostile, as if she resented the fact that she did not know whether he was speaking the truth or not.

Then as he drew up the jeep beyond the fence of the compound, so that the ambulance could come behind him and pull up at the gate, he saw the figure of the girl crossing the compound, a flash of white in the strong moonlight before it darkened under the black shadow of the tree. And seeing her he felt his own shock of surprise – of surprise tender and beautiful and fresh as if he were seeing her for the first time, so that he at once climbed down from the jeep and went to the gate of the compound to meet her, forgetting that Burke was there. And standing there at the gate, greeting her simply by pressing his hands tenderly on her bare arms and looking at her face and not speaking, he forgot also that he had left the engine running and did not become aware of it until, some seconds later, he heard it switched off by Burke as she still sat there.

Presently he saw Burke climb down from the jeep and he took the girl by the arm and went over to her.

'This is Anna,' he said. 'She's from Rangoon really. This is Sister Burke.'

Burke was very quiet. The girl, smiling, said, 'It is good of you to come,' but Burke simply grunted 'Good evening' and went down the track to where the ambulance stood.

'Is everything all right?' he said. Now that Burke had gone he bent down and pressed his face against the girl's face, feeling the softness of it with relief after the harsh, brittle aggressiveness of the nurse. The girl smiled and with the slightest turn of her head put her mouth against his face, not speaking, but telling him in the brief and tender movement all he wanted to know. A second later he heard Burke demand with fierce professional impatience from the ambulance:

'Where are these cases? D'ye think we've got all night to stop here?'

'She's Irish,' he said to the girl. 'You'd think she ought to be fighting on the other side. I'll go and show her the way to the house.'

The girl kept him beside her a moment longer, holding his sleeve.

'There's something I want to tell you,' she said.

Burke yelled from the ambulance: 'Where's Harris? Where's everybody? Is everybody round the damn bend?'

'I must go,' he whispered.

'In a moment will you come back?'

'I must help with the cases,' he said.

'And then will you come?' she said. 'I will wait for you in the dispensary. Over there.'

'Is it important? – what you want to say?'

'Oh! for God's sake!' Burke yelled.

'Yes,' the girl said.

He looked down at her for a moment longer. He saw her eyes almost frightened again as they looked up at him, and then he turned and went down the track to where Burke was standing, yelling now:

'Is that where Harris is? In the house?'

'In there.'

'Well then for God's sake let's get in the damn place.'

Without another word he went across the compound towards the house, Burke following him, muttering as they went, 'How you and Harris came to find this dump I don't know. How the blazes you came to find it I can't think.'

He did not speak but took her straight up the steps of the veranda into the house, opening the door so that she could go in. As she went in he saw her stiffen herself, as if it was necessary to become suddenly the correct and professional person, hardened in battles. With hardened face and short-cut hair tucked severely under her cap she looked extraordinarily like a man. In the lamplight he saw the bright, belligerent offended eyes flash sharply backwards and forwards, taking in the figures of Harris, the mother and Miss McNab and then with cool assessment the wounded lying on the floor.

'This is Sister Burke,' Forrester said. 'The ambulance is outside.'

Harris looked up from the table. A Burmese woman was lying stretched out on it. On the far side of her Miss McNab was holding the oil-lamp, so that the light, deep orange, fell more fully on her face, terribly tired and yellow with shock, the sweat so heavily washed across it that in the lamplight it was like a face of varnished wood.

'Four stretcher cases must be taken, sister,' Harris said. 'And two sitting if you can.'

'Yes, doctor,' Burke said. With partially hostile surprise she looked hard at Miss McNab.

'Miss McNab,' Harris explained. 'From the Nonconformist mission in Rangoon.'

Burke did not speak. Forrester saw that she was looking now not at Miss McNab but still harder and with still sharper surprise at the girl's mother, standing by the side of Miss McNab, holding in her hands a bowl of blood-browned water.

'Did you get the stuff?' Harris said.

'Yes,' Forrester said, 'I – '

'I'll get it from the ambulance, doctor,' Burke said. 'You'll be needin' blankets, too.'

She went straight out of the room.

Harris covered the woman on the table with a length of rusty brown cloth and Miss McNab took away the lamp. Only the mother stood for a second or two longer alone, holding the bowl of blood-stained water, staring down with subdued terror at the sweat-bright face below.

'Thanks for going, Forrester,' Harris said. 'You were bloody quick.'

'I'm sure you could do with a wee cuppa tea, Mr Forrester,'

Miss McNab said. Harris stood with his hands limp and relaxed in momentary exhaustion at his sides. 'And you look as if you couldn't say no yourself, doctor.'

Vaguely, not saying anything, Harris stood in a dream of weariness, staring down. At that moment Burke came back, carrying in her arms a pile of six or seven grey blankets. Without speaking she took one of the blankets from the top of the pile, throwing it with deft lightness over the body of the woman on the table, and then she set the rest of them down by the feet of the woman, spreading and smoothing the edges of the first blanket with her free hands. 'I thought you'd be needin' the blankets first,' she said to Harris, who stood all the time as if he were not listening. 'I'll be gettin' the rest of the stuff.'

'I can get it,' Forrester said.

'No,' she said. 'I'll go. If you're aching to do something, cover those patients.'

She went out again before he could speak and this time she seemed to be gone much longer, so that he had finished covering the wounded and was drinking a cup of tea, talking to Harris and scarcely getting a syllable in answer, when she came back, carrying the black tin box into which the orderly at the hospital had put Harris's list of things. She seemed to move now with aggravated professional calm. The ugly Irish upper lip was no longer loose and sloppy, but hard and aloof, almost contemptuous, and once as she moved about the room, fierce in little passing gestures of attention to the wounded lying on the floor, she brought round her arm and pushed Forrester out of her way with a stab of impatience, almost shouting: 'If you can't be useful you can at least get your big six-foot carcase out of my way. Go on. Do something! Help the orderly with the stretchers.'

Miss McNab and the mother stared. Only Harris seemed neither to care nor know quite what was going on.

Forrester put his cup on the table and went outside. Before he had reached the centre of the compound he heard her running after him.

'The way people stooge about you'd think we'd got all night to stop here!' she said. 'For God's sake!'

Sharply she walked past him, with long awkward mannish

steps to where the ambulance stood by the gate of the compound.

'Get those stretchers out!' she shouted. He saw the figure of the orderly driver stir sharply on the front seat of the ambulance, and then relax suddenly as if pinned back by a fresh order from Burke: 'Don't disturb yourself! Don't put yourself out! I'll get them! What in the name o' God d'you think I'm here for?'

She wrenched open the rear door of the ambulance and began to drag out the stretchers, walking away with two of them on her shoulders before Forrester could say another word. He pulled out the other four and put them on his shoulder and walked slowly after her. Half-way across the compound he stopped. The light was burning low in the little dispensary, and he thought as he stopped of the girl waiting there, sitting in the small light where the sick child lay under the green mosquito cage, and he wondered for a moment if he should go in. Then as he stood wondering he became aware for the first time since coming back with the ambulance of the great silence of the plain. Nothing was happening to break it now, and he stood for a moment or two longer listening to it, wonderfully still and breathless and unbroken even by the turn of a leaf in the tree above the house. He seemed to hear in it a deep vibration all the silence of the East, spreading away into limitless vastness, depthless, without a whisper. Until it was suddenly split by the voice of Burke:

'Is it yourself you're carryin' on the damn stretcher or what? Come on!'

9

By the time he found the girl across the compound it was quiet again. She was standing by the door of the dispensary, leaning her head backwards against the teakwood post of the door. Behind her the hurricane lamp shone through the mosquito net, embalming the yellow face of the child in a cage.

He held her face, feeling it cool and tired in his two hands.

'You were going to tell me something,' he said.

'It wasn't much.'

'Tell me,' he said.

'It was something to give you,' she said.

He felt her draw his two hands down from her face, pressing them together. When he opened them again a small white packet of soft paper was clinging to the sweat of one palm. He stared at it for a moment, not knowing what to do.

'Open it,' she said. 'It's for you.'

He opened the paper slowly, leaning a little nearer the light inside the hut. In a moment he saw the light shining on the pinkish brilliant blood of a ruby, small but clear.

'It's for you,' she said.

He could not answer.

'You have no one to give it to,' she said.

'No.'

'I'm glad,' she said. 'Because now you can keep it for me.'

More than ever he did not know what to say. He stood staring at her face and then at the ruby in his hand. Then suddenly he closed the palm of his hand very tightly, so tightly that he could feel the stone pressing into his flesh like steel, and held the clenched palm with the fiercest tenderness against her face. All he had ever felt about himself seemed small and rotten.

'I can't say anything,' he said. He pressed his face against her in a final second of reproachful bitterness against himself.

'There's nothing to say,' she said.

In a moment of monstrous agony he felt tears spurt into his eyes, salting them with the bitterness of sweat.

'Don't say anything,' she said. 'There's nothing to say. It's a little thing for you to keep for me. That's all.'

Oh! Christ, he thought.

'Don't say anything,' she said again.

He let the last wave of self-reproach rush over him, leaving him dry and steady and skimmed of the remotest dregs of self-pity, so that finally he could speak again.

'It's a lovely stone,' he said.

'Please keep it.'

'I shall keep it.' He grinned. 'I'll carry it with me all the time. My lucky stone for flying.'

'It's wrong to be superstitious,' she said. 'That was the trouble with them tonight. The people. Running away. They were superstitious. When are you coming again?'

'Tomorrow. Every day.'

'Will you fly tomorrow?'

'Yes,' he said. 'I think so.'

'Will you go away?'

'Not yet.'

Before she could speak again he saw the door of the house open. A long bright bar of lamplight pricked across the dust of the compound underneath the tree. A moment later Miss McNab and Miss Burke came out, carrying one of the children on a stretcher.

'We must go,' she said.

'No,' he said. 'Not for a moment.' He held her face again between his two hands, calm now. He watched her dark eyes that in his own shadow were without a glitter of light. 'I had a lot of things to say to you.'

'Tomorrow,' she said.

'Probably they would seem stupid to you,' he said.

'No,' she said. 'I could see the trouble in your face when you came yesterday. Nothing would seem stupid.'

'Listen, please,' he said. 'I want to say this.'

Across the compound Miss Burke and Miss McNab had loaded the first of the stretchers into the ambulance and now were walking back to the house. Miss Burke was carrying the empty stretcher on her shoulder. Half-way to the house they passed Harris and the mother, carrying a second stretcher. The shaft of light cut across the figure of a woman covered with a blanket. He heard Miss Burke in a purposely lifted voice say:

'Always missing when you need them most – ah! for God's sake some people!'

He let her go on across the compound and up the steps of the veranda before he spoke again.

'I shall try to come every day.'

'Yes.'

'But perhaps some days it won't be possible.'

'Yes.'

'But if I don't come one day I shall come the next. And if not that day the next. And if not the next, the next.'

'Yes.'

'Whatever happens,' he said.

'Yes.'

'Take no notice of what anyone says. Take no notice of anything. Rumours. Talk. Anything. I shall come back.'

'Yes.'

She came very close to him and he ran his fingers along her cream-cool smooth arms that were loose across her breasts. It was the first time he had touched her so intimately and he felt her surprise at it leap up and then tremble down and tranquillize itself.

'You said something about never going back to England,' she said. 'What did you mean?'

'I meant that.'

'Would you stay here?'

'I think I would. Yes,' he said.

'After all, many Englishmen lived in Rangoon.'

'Many Englishmen will live there again.'

'It would be very wonderful,' she said.

He heard Burke and Miss McNab emerge for the second time from the house. This time he did not look up. All that was happening and had happened across the compound seemed for a few moments like part of a remote world. It seemed shut off from him by the bar of light under the tree.

In the moment of feeling this he said to the girl, very quietly and very detached, no longer troubled:

'I wanted to die.'

She kept silent, looking straight at his face.

'For a long time,' he said, 'I was trying to die. Every day.' He felt himself speaking with astonishing calm. 'But not now. That's why you thought I was troubled.'

Across the compound Burke said in a loud voice: 'People lugging their guts out for God's sake and nobody givin' a damn.'

He turned his back to the compound, holding the girl in front of him. From the house the light fell with distant softness on her face, and the light in the dispensary, cast upward into the orange-frame of the door below the dark cave of palm, softly and deeply on her black hair. He bent down and kissed her with unhurried tenderness. As she moved her head, the rose-pink flower woven into the scroll of her hair fell away, as he always expected it would, and he caught it with his hands. In the cage of light in the dispensary the child did not stir and over against the gate, by the ambulance, where Burke and Miss McNab were sliding the second stretcher into the vehicle, there was no sound except a babble of voices from a little crowd that had gathered there.

'Your flower,' he said. He held it for her to take from his hands. The stem was milky and he could smell the fragrance of the clustered blossom.

'Thank you,' she said.

'What flower is this?' he said. 'I wanted to ask you.'

'The frangipani. The Life tree. In Burmese Ta-yop-sa gah.'

'It is very beautiful.'

'It is the flower of immortality,' she said. 'Because it can live on and on. Without soil or water. For ever.'

'Now who is being superstitious?'

'Oh! no,' she said. 'Everything is immortal really. We are all immortal if we want to be.'

She put back the flower into the side of her hair and he smelled the drenching scent of it against his face.

'You will see,' she said. 'It will be there when you come again. This blossom will fade and then another will open.'

'I shall look for it,' he said.

'Don't die again,' she said. 'Inside yourself. It isn't good.'

'Never again,' he said. 'Not now.'

'I'm so glad,' she said.

'Some day I will tell you more about it than this.'

'Good-bye,' she said. 'They will be calling for you again.'

It was as if she did not want to trouble him. He looked down for a moment longer at the pale deep-eyed face that now seemed so much older and yet in a way more poignantly and terribly young than when he had first seen it. It was very lovely with the rosy buds of flower clustered in the black hair. After a moment he could hardly bear it and was almost glad of the raucous voice of Burke shouting his name across the compound, slitting the warm darkness. 'Forrester, Forrester! where in the name o'God have you got to? Forrester!' It was so loud at last that in the little cage of light in the dispensary the child turned and woke and put its hands to its hot yellow face and began to cry.

As the girl went inside the little hut he walked across the compound, knowing that there was no more he had to say. Burke's voice, raised harshly again, shouted: 'If you wouldn't mind ridin' in the ambulance, doctor, I'll risk my life with Forrester. Where in the name o' God are you, man?'

Walking across to the gate he saw her going into the house, followed by the orderly, to fetch the last of the stretcher cases. Harris and Miss McNab were walking together across the compound. He met them and said something about being sorry but Harris, slowly peeling off the skin of a small green orange, his arms washed clean again, only grunted something in reply. It was Miss McNab who spoke, saying: 'Mr Forrester, I'd like to talk to ye, but there's no time,' dropping a little behind Harris as they walked. She did not speak again for a moment or two. And half-way across the compound he turned for the last time and looked towards the little dispensary. Through the open door he could see the small light burning and in the glow of it the cage where the child lay, the girl half-kneeling beside it. The child was not crying now and there was no sound, but he saw the lips of the girl moving slightly in the lamplight, as if she were talking the child to sleep again. In that moment Miss McNab said, 'Ah! it'll not matter now.'

He got up into the jeep and she stood leaning against the side of it, her dyed hair flopping and cheap and yet somehow very human as she pushed it back from her forehead in the lamplight. 'Ye've made a great impression on her, Mr Forrester,' she said. 'I can see that. Ah, I've knocked about a bit. I know.'

'I shall be back,' he said.

'I know ye will.'

'Whatever happens. That's a promise,' he said.

'No need to promise. I know.' From the door of the house he heard Burke shouting again. By the gate the crowd of Burmese faces clotted against the palisade, to see the last of the stretchers carried out. 'There's some ye know in two minutes, and some ye don't.'

She did not speak again until the crowd of faces had been pressed back again, to let the stretcher through, and Burke had finished shouting: 'Of all the damn silly clots, these people, pushin' and shovin'. Don't tell me the squadron leader is here at last!'

'Wherever y'are there'll be a bit of prayer being said for you,' Miss McNab said. For a moment some of the old frantic gaiety returned, as if for some reason she were suddenly all nervous again. 'Especially if it's Calcutta. Bring us a little rice if you go over. The doctor gets it from the Army and Navy. And a drop o' gin.'

A few moments later the ambulance was loaded. He saw Burke pushing her way towards him through the crowd of faces. Miss McNab smiled and said, 'Thank you for all you did, Mr Forrester. Ah, it's a terrible damn thing, all of it, an awful thing. It's nice to think of one decent thing coming out of it.' Only half listening, he looked across the compound at the house and then at the little dispensary for the last time. At the door of the house the mother and sister were watching, framed in the light, but the door of the dispensary was empty, as if the girl was too shy even to come and watch him go.

'Ah, get the damn thing started,' Burke said. 'These clots make me sick.'

Not speaking, he started the engine. He switched on the head-lights and saw for a moment, fantastically framed against the brilliant tender green of palm and banana and vine, the fiery mahogany head of Miss McNab, her watery reddish eyes gazing at him for the last time. A curious confident tenderness set them shining brilliantly.

'Ah, God, get crackin',' Burke said.

Without a word he drove away along the track under the trees. He did not look back, but the picture of Miss McNab gazing at him in the headlights and the picture of the girl half-kneeling by the child in Harris's dispensary remained with him for a long time. They almost became, as he drove clear of the last trees out to the clear track across the plain, the same thing. Then all of a sudden he remembered the last words Miss McNab had spoken. 'It's nice to see one decent thing coming out of it,' and he felt that somehow they defined and deepened all the half-defined, half-realized tenderness that he had felt growing in himself and had been unable to say. He had not time to think more of it before Burke spoke again.

'God, what you see in these clots I don't know.'

'Happen to be human,' he said. He kept his eyes straight on the yellow dust of the track ahead. 'Or hadn't you noticed?'

'I noticed,' she said. 'God, I noticed.'

He did not speak.

'You men,' she said. 'Something comes along with a flower in her hair and looks at you and you go as soft as a wet custard.'

Deliberately he turned to see if the ambulance was coming. He saw the lights of it following very slowly, three hundred yards behind. He slowed the jeep down.

'Don't you know that at bottom they all hate you?' she said. 'Indians, Burmese – all of them. Isn't it just like the English? – get stuck with an Empire where everybody hates them and they never know it?'

'They never know it,' he said. He was surprised to find himself not angry with her at all.

'Ah, you're all alike,' she said.

'All alike.'

'Thinking of nothing but yourselves, morning and night.'

'Nothing but ourselves.'

She snorted with abrupt violence. 'Choosin' hymns for Easter Sunday! That's new.'

'Harris's idea.'

'Ah! Harris,' she said. 'He's just as bad.'

He had reached the railway track and now as he looked round and saw the ambulance slowly following, four or five hundred yards away, some devilment made him stop the jeep on the crest of the track. 'Always wanted to do this,' he said. 'Wait for the train.' The track was not yet in use and there was no thrill in sitting there because no train would ever come. 'Down came the engine and broke Paddy's bones,' he said.

'Can't you be serious for a moment? What in the name o' God's the matter with you?'

She turned hastily round and looked back to where the ambulance, churning dust like a pale yellow mist in the moonlight, was still two or three hundred yards away.

'You're all the same, and they're all the same.' She began suddenly to speak with astonishing excited violence, her eyes quite wild. 'These girls. All of them. They're having a good time now. Layin' themselves open to get you. Givin' you what you want. Playin' up to you for what they can get. And half of them nothing but sluts. Cheap little sluts, that's all, touched with the tar-brush – '

He let her go wildly on for a moment or two, not trying to stop her, his hands on the wheel of the jeep, his eyes fixed ahead to where he could see, far off, the pagodas of the town shining in the moon above the black ridge of palms. And then suddenly he turned round at her with an abrupt violence that shocked her heavy ugly mouth wide open.

'If you talk like that again I'll kill you.'

Her mouth began slowly to close, sloppy and quivering.

'I mean it,' he said. 'I'll kill you.'

He let in the clutch and drove the jeep off the narrow track. Turning to see how close the ambulance was he saw for another second the face of the nurse. It could not have been more shocked or terrified if she had suddenly seen a train descending on her like a shrieking ghost out of the empty moonlight. The mouth had been hit in the middle of its loose and petty garrulity and seemed shocked so stiffly open that it could not close.

All the way back to the camp it remained like that, and she did not speak another word.

10

With one aircraft burned, a crew dead and his own ground crew
time-expired he knew there would be little flying for a day; yet
he was surprised, next morning, by a note from Harris, delivered to him by Ali while he breakfasted.

'There is a Mr Pang, or Penang, or Phang, or Prang, or some
such name,' it said, 'over at the river settlement. He is asking for
medical stuff for minor casualties. Could you go over? You'll
find him at the school. The corporal will give you the stuff
and Anna will take you. Aldridge,' it added, 'has been
appeased.'

He put the pleasant jovial note in his trousers pocket. Momentarily it struck him as curious that Aldridge, his commanding officer, should have been informed so early of Harris's
irregular business with the gentleman at the settlement. Then he
forgot it. He left his breakfast of toast that had been thrown on
to a brush-fire by Indian bearers and raked off again, bitterly
charred, and of tea that poured from pots like cream-brown
toffee, and walked away across the dusty trackless mess of palm
and tent and pagoda, thinking lightly of Mr Prang.

He drove out across the plain with the box of medical supplies about ten o'clock. Along the tree-shaded road the heat was
fringed with coolness and in the village there was a gleaming
movement of banana leaves against an exquisite white-blue sky.
In bombed compounds villagers were clearing wreckage and on
roofs were cheerfully laying new thatch of pale brown palm-
fronds. They lifted hands in greeting as he passed and there was
a faint odour of explosive blast in the air.

He saw the girl with a shock of delight as she came out of the
house, in a blouse of pale green and a long-slit almost betel-red
skirt. There was a liquid delicate surprise in her face as she
came and held his hands.

'Only half an hour ago Miss McNab has gone to the settlement!'

He was suddenly glad McNab had gone. 'We can take the jeep,' he said.

'We have the river to get over,' she said.

'And how do we get over?'

'There is a ferry,' she said. 'The school is on the other side.'

Slowly he drove the jeep through the village and beyond the last of the bamboo fences and through the stretch of dusty half-forest, with tall poplar-thin trees and bushes of plumed mauve flower dust-bloomed by the track. Nearer the river came long screens of bamboo, greener from the moisture of the swampy edges, the papery fronds stirring a little in the movement of air that blew quietly in from the yellow-green river, here about half a mile wide with a small shore of whitish sand. A hundred yards out lay the wreck of a river steamer, half-submerged, the white paint above the water-line blistered away in long curls, and half a mile below it Forrester could see the ferry, made of two sampan-like craft lashed together with planks and bamboo and poled by small darkish men naked except for brown-purple waist-cloths, just floating in from the other side.

They left the jeep on the higher track above the shore and in ten minutes were being ferried over with an ox-cart, a dozen peasants and two water buffaloes. The dark little ferrymen lashed at the water with twenty-foot poles of bamboo and ran straining and pushing along the ferry deck, crying incomprehensively, wild-haired and sweating as they struggled against the deep currents of mid-stream. Out on the shadeless water it was already very hot and the little men broke into long swearing songs, fighting to keep the boat from drifting away.

'What do they say?' he said.

'I can't tell. They are strange people. They come from nowhere.'

'Karens?'

'No, not Karens. The Karens are fighting men. These are different. They come from nowhere.'

The little men who came from nowhere ran with their great poles along the deck and chanted with savage murmurs at the yellow-green currents; the water-buffaloes, primitive and dumb,

112

rocking drunkenly, stolidly stared at the sombre green of the far shore, where the palm huts of the settlement were visible behind the fawn-green fringe of bamboo.

'There are strange people in the river,' she said, and he caught for a moment in the wild chantings of the dark little boatmen a touch of the dark heart of a country he did not know. One of the water-buffaloes bellowed in trouble and the sound boomed down the yellow sun-glittering water and out into the shadowy low forest edge. And in the boat the pure cream naked arms of the girl and the stretch of her naked thigh shone with milky cleanness against the Indian brown bodies of the running, chanting men, and her red skirt and pale green blouse were dazzling clean against the iron-dark hide of the buffaloes, bellowing impatiently again for the shore.

On the other bank of the river Forrester and the girl walked up a track of sand made into a tolerable road by laid sheaves of bamboo. Down on the river Forrester heard the final chantings of the boatmen die. The mysterious spell of the thick yellow waters rolling away between narrow edges of silent bamboo was broken.

And then down the bamboo road came a sudden figure. It came as if borne on a parachute bicycle. It wore a bright magenta shirt with brown long trousers and a very green, very civilized homburg hat, and over it all it carried, giving the parachute effect, a black umbrella.

It was Mr Prang.

He leapt off the bicycle with an agile, podgy flourish, grinning brilliantly. The umbrella acted as a kind of airbrake until Mr Prang snapped it neatly shut in the moment of dismounting.

'So long!' Mr Prang said.

'This is the schoolmaster from the settlement,' Anna said. 'Mr Forrester.'

'Mr Fresta! Sir!'

Mr Prang bowed with beautifully elated zeal, taking off his hat. 'Mr Fresta, sir, this is everlasting honour.'

Somehow Mr Prang held the bicycle, the hat, the umbrella and shook hands with Forrester.

'I am seeing you coming!' he explained. 'I am dashing to meet you on the bike!'

'He is from Rangoon too,' the girl said. 'We were great friends there.'

Forrester looked quickly at Mr Prang, who was a man of twenty-eight or thirty, and felt, before he could check or consider it, the oddest start of jealousy.

'Yes, Mr Fresta, sir. I am too from Rangoon. I am student of Far English.'

'Advanced English,' Anna said.

'Far advanced,' Mr Prang said. 'That's me. You are knowing London, Mr Fresta, sir?'

'Yes.'

'There is somewhat of ruin there?'

'Yes.'

'And death and pestilence?'

'Death,' Forrester said, and the word had neither meaning nor terror nor even association at that moment in memory. 'But not pestilence.'

'That I do not get,' Mr Prang said. 'Here with death we had pestilence. Yes, Anna?'

'Yes,' she said, and Mr Prang gazed with quiet thought at the river. 'Now swimming at least is somewhat possible.'

Mr Prang gazed for a moment longer at the river and then turned the bicycle round. In another instant he snapped the umbrella open.

'Mr Fresta, sir. Anna,' he said. 'Partake of the umbrella if you please.'

'It is very kind of you,' Forrester said. 'But it's really not necessary.'

'It is eminently necessary. Please,' Mr Prang said. 'Sir.'

Forrester took the umbrella, holding it over himself and Anna. She looked at him in the sudden dusky shade of it and smiled and he felt the smile cut across the curious spasmodic moment of his jealousy of Mr Prang.

The three of them walked together up the bamboo road, Mr Prang talking with unctuous joviality of Rangoon.

'In Rangoon I have bike-shop. Always I have the possibility to make big money. But no. I say to myself no. I say to myself after the war – London. That's me.'

114

From up the road Forrester heard the voices of children and saw the flash of white and brown and purple dresses in settlement compounds.

'I am on my way,' Mr Prang said. 'I am previously acquainted with all.' He was very determined and very proud. 'Charing Cross, Piccadilly Square, Leicester, Buckingham, Circus. I am well aware of the city. All is manifest to me, Mr Fresta, sir.'

'There is the school,' the girl said.

'One bomb drops here. One in river,' Mr Prang said. Bright butter-brown children were running about the wooden school-hut and the road. 'But no death. Only wounds. That is why I ask Miss McNab for medicines.'

'Has the missionary come?'

'Oh! no, sir. Was she to be expected? She was here yesterday.'

'I think she will be across the river,' the girl said.

'Please to rest in the school,' Mr Prang said. 'This way, Anna. Mr Fresta, sir.'

The dusty compound of the school-hut was shaded by a few pipul trees. Groups of small children came laughing to run by the bicycle and Mr Prang, with a flourish of podgy coppery-cream fingers, rang the bell. All the children laughed and suddenly to Forrester it was as if, walking under the shady umbrella with the girl, in the tree-cooled compound, with the laughing children and the eager ebullient Mr Prang, he was a million miles from war.

They sat for a time on the wooden steps of the school-house, eating pale green slices of melon brought by Mr Prang, the shade of the umbrella breaking the heat of the sun. The children had gone away. 'The children will bring flowers for you,' Mr Prang said.

Below them, through the trees, the river glittered more green than yellow in the sun. The ferry, something like a low house-boat, seemed small as it struggled against the current, and the voices of the small brown men, compressed by trees and then magnified by water, had the soft rise and fall of horns blown quietly far away.

But Mr Prang thought only of London. 'Most Burmese are not so great travellers,' he said. 'We are much surrounded by mountains and we do not get out.'

'So people get in,' Forrester said.

'People get in,' Mr Prang said. 'But me – no, I get out. London – that's me.'

'You must fly to London. Two days.'

'Oh! no, sir,' Mr Prang said. 'No flying for me.'

'He will go by bicycle,' Anna said.

'Yes, sir,' Mr Prang said, 'I shall go by bicycle.' Forrester and the girl laughed together under the umbrella, but the face of Mr Prang was calm, serious and unaffected. 'Oh! yes,' he said. 'Oh! yes. Of course, of course. How else shall I be going except that way?'

'Six thousand miles by bicycle,' Forrester said.

'If you can go six miles you can go six thousand.'

'But the time?'

'Time?' Mr Prang smiled with exquisite blankness. 'Mr Fresta, the meaning of time is somewhat relative, or am I wrong, sir?'

'He will get there,' Anna said.

'Of course,' Mr Prang said, 'of course. That is the idea. If one desires enough to do something one does it, isn't that right, and time is nothing.'

'Nothing,' Forrester said, and remembered how in the East time gave that effect; the effect of slipping away, unreal and too bright and meaningless and fast, the days drowning each other with dazzling fatalistic repetition until all count of them was lost.

'The children are coming back,' the girl said.

Forrester and the girl got up from the steps of the school-house and walked across the compound to meet the children, who were bringing garlands of cream and crimson flowers, with richer stars of brown-eyed marigold. There was suddenly a scent of lime and jasmine in the air, and then the crushed close odour of marigold, rich in the heat of the sun. The girl bent down to her knees, so that the children could place the garland round her neck, and as she bent there, leaning forward, Forrester saw the creaminess of her breasts revealed by the loose pale green blouse falling away. In another moment they were hidden from him by the necklet of cream and crimson and gold; and then she got slowly to her feet, looking up at him, shyly but intimately, knowing what he had seen. Then he too bent down, but he was too tall for the children to reach him, and finally as he knelt on the ground, the hot dust burning his knees, the compound full of the light laughter of children and the shrill ringing of the bell on Mr Prang's bicycle, the children danced about him. The garland went over his neck and then as he got slowly to his feet he looked up and saw the girl still watching him in the same quiet secret way, smiling tenderly.

'Now you will have somewhat of happiness on your journey!' Mr Prang said. 'Now you will have good luck, sir!'

'Thank you,' Forrester said.

He stood with the flowers about his neck, smiling and happy, and then he remembered Mr Prang's umbrella and shut it and handed it back to him.

'Oh! no, sir, Mr Fresta,' he said. 'The umbrella may be lent. Please take it now. It is very essential for the heat.'

'It really isn't necessary – '

'Mr Fresta! Sir!'

'Let us take it,' Anna said.

'It is of the greatest simplicity,' Mr Prang said. 'You may leave it with Anna and then tomorrow or the next day I have the possibility to get it back.'

'It is very kind,' Forrester said.

'Mr Fresta, sir!' Mr Prang said, 'it is everlasting honour!'

The two men shook hands in good-bye. Children began to wave their hands and Mr Prang said good-bye to Anna, first in English and then, once again waking in Forrester's mind the absurd sharp stab of jealousy that half-fretted, half-amused him now, in Burmese. When the girl answered in Burmese too he felt the jealousy sharpen and become a pain, the centralized heart of all his feeling for her suddenly hot and possessive, the reality of it so clear that for a moment he was almost angry with her, saying farewell to the absurd Mr Prang in a language he could not understand, so that he could not bear even the tiny formal air of secrecy the moment gave.

In another moment it was all over. The children were waving,

Mr Prang was waving, and someone was joyously ringing the bell on the bicycle. Anna and himself were walking down the bamboo road under the umbrella and Mr Prang was shouting 'Thanks for the medicines!'

'It is nothing!' they called back. 'A pleasure.'

'Farewell!' Mr Prang shouted. 'Farewell, Mr Fresta, sir!'

Standing on the boat under the umbrella the girl and Forrester were ferried back. In the heat the glitter of sunlight leapt glassily sharp from the green-yellow water, flashing up beneath the umbrella, meeting there the stab of sun piercing the thin black fabric from overhead. The breath of wind had died on the water; the sombre mutterings of the dark ferrymen running nakedly with their poles were like groans and had lost the sound of distant horns. Sweat ran down their Indian-dark bodies and saturated their dirty loin-cloths like spent oil until Forrester, watching them, felt his own body grow clammy and musty with the prickling, running rash of new sweat.

It seemed no cooler in the jeep as they drove away, churning out from deep hollows of yellow river-sand, on the other side.

At last he felt sweat pouring from under his cap, running into his eyes, so that he could not see. There was nothing to do but stop and wipe his face.

Sitting there, drying his face with his handkerchief and then the saturated rim of his hat, he looked at the girl, cool and pale beside him, and then at the river, greenish as if with a touch of water from very distant snows, beyond the sparse fringe of bamboo. It too looked wonderfully cool, and the girl spoke as if suddenly she knew what was in his mind.

'You could swim,' she said. 'The river is good now.'

The thought of swimming drained through his mind with delicious freshness, and he said:

'Will you swim too?'

'I have nothing to wear.'

'Swimming with nothing on is very wonderful,' he said.

She did not answer.

'You could undress behind the umbrella and I would not look,' he said.

'You would look.'

'It would be very lovely to look,' he said.

'You said you would not look and now you say it would be very lovely.'

'I would try not to look.'

'How hard would you try?'

'Not very hard.'

'You see it's just as I said.'

'Did you expect that I would not look?' he said.

'How could it be otherwise?' she said.

He looked at her with a moment of tenderness that left him faint and quivering and there was a scent of jasmine and the dark odour of marigold in the air as he pressed his mouth against the cool skin of her neck.

'Please swim,' she said.

'And you?'

'Tonight I will make something to wear,' she said. 'Tomorrow we can swim together.'

They got out of the jeep and she walked through the fringe of bamboo to the river-edge while he undressed himself. As she walked away he took off his own garland of flowers and threw it over her head, so that she wore a double rope of cream and crimson and browny gold.

He left his underpants on and then went into the water at a run. As he went in carving under through cool fast water, he remembered some regulation about bathing in unauthorized places but in the same moment it did not matter and he did not care. He seemed to go down to the depth of all the coolness in the world, and then up again, with exquisite relief, into the high dazzle of sun. He treaded water for a moment or two and brushed the water out of his eyes and then looked back at her, where she lay on the sand, one of her thighs naked where the slit in the red skirt had fallen back, and all the upper part of her breast drowned in flowers.

'Wonderful!' he called.

He went under again, washing away all the sweat, the tedium, the heat and the irritation he had known. Coming up again, he called:

'Please come in!'

'Tomorrow.'

'Now. Please.'

'Tomorrow.'

He swam nearer, paddling water, smiling.

'You could wear the flowers.'

'Mr Fresta, sir!' she said, laughing too.

He turned and took one long good swim towards the wreck of the river steamer lying out in the stream and then on a long easy back stroke into shore and then out at last to lie beside her on the small shore of monsoon-silted sand.

'Was it good?' she said.

'Wonderful.'

'You looked so happy.'

He lay and let the sun burn the moisture from his body. Water ran down from his hair as sweat had done only a few minutes before and into his eyes, so that for a moment he could not see. She leaned forward and wiped away the wetness from his eyes with the fringe of her skirt and he pressed his wet mouth against her naked thigh.

'Come and swim with me now.'

'Tomorrow.'

'There may be no tomorrow.'

'You are like a boy who wants sugar,' she said.

Down across the river the sound of ferrymen's voices began again, like wild, faint horns and the boom of a buffalo faded through the forest fringe. Far off too in the clear hot silence Forrester heard the ringing of a bicycle bell. He wondered for a moment what tomorrow would bring – odd to think that perhaps Mr Prang would go to London and he, English and for ever exiled, to Rangoon. Odd to think that now, after the long complication of living death, he could ask for something as simple as that.

Across on the other bank the bicycle bell rang shrilly again and he said:

'There goes Mr Prang.'

'His name is Mr Phang.'

'I call him Prang. It's better.'

'It doesn't mean anything.'

'Oh! yes,' he said, 'it means something. It's an important word with us. It's a kind of comic word.'

'How is it comic?'

'It means to crash,' he said. 'An aeroplane – blow up, an accident. That's prang.'

She did not speak and Forrester, looking up, saw her staring dark-eyed and troubled across the water and beyond it to the bright green of the forest fringe. From down the stream came again the sound of ferrymen's voices, incomprehensible and wild and faint as the sound of dying horns. Mr Prang's bicycle bell rang shrilly somewhere among the palms of the settlement. The boom of a frightened buffalo died on the sunlit water and Forrester felt for a moment all the life he wanted hang on the echoes of ephemeral sound.

He moved and lay with his face pressed into the double necklet of flowers, breathing the scent of jasmine and marigold that seemed to lie caught like a nest of fragrance between her breasts. He heard her say 'We will swim tomorrow' and knew that now she had begun to understand, too sharply and too finely, with both love and terror, the language he spoke and the kind of life it gave.

11

He woke in the morning to the ring of the field telephone that stood on the table by his bed. Before he could lift the mosquito net Blore, who was standing shaving himself on the other side of the table, picked up the receiver and listened.

'For you,' Blore said.

Forrester took the receiver and half lay with it under the mosquito net, looking at the watch on his wrist at the same time. It was not quite seven o'clock and he wondered for a moment why anyone should call him so early, and then heard the voice, rather too cheerful and precise, of Aldridge, his commanding officer. Aldridge talked with an affectation of immense boredom that was highly deceptive. It had about it an accent of finer flippancy. 'Want to see you, old boy. Awful bind. Minor flap from Group. Munch on an egg or something and then come over.'

'Right, sir,' Forrester said. 'No trouble at all. Good-bye.'

'Oh! I say,' Aldridge said. 'Has Blore surfaced? Want to have the odd word with him if I may.'

'Certainly,' Forrester said.

He stretched up and pushed the telephone receiver under the loose mosquito net to Blore, who stood with one half of his face still covered with lather. Blore took the receiver and spoke formally into it and then listened. He listened for a long time. In the receiver the high drawling voice of Aldridge seemed to make curiously comic splutters of alarm, and on Blore's face there grew an odd look of surprised tension, heightened by the white lather, which clung there like half a beard. 'Yes, sir. Yes, sir,' Blore said several times. On his lower lip a lump of soap trembled like a feather and then dropped down to his chest. 'Yes, sir. Yes, sir,' he said. He put the receiver down.

Swinging out of bed, Forrester said cheerfully: 'What's up

with the old man?' Blore did not answer. He stood with his razor in his hand, staring in thought. Forrester slipped his feet into his canvas shoes and went out of the hut into the cool fresh sunlight, hearing Blore say rather vacantly, 'Something about my posting. It's on again.'

When he came back into the hut seven or eight minutes later Blore had still not taken all of the lather off his face. He seemed to move about the hut like a man looking for something. Still in a daze, he looked clumsy and messy, the wet white lather dropping down on to his chest and trousers and the floor of the hut. For two months Forrester had watched him dress like that, slow and finicky and stupid, angered each morning by the big helpless man moving about the hut like a fat purblind mole trying to grope his way to daylight. But now he was not angry. He felt suddenly rather sorry for Blore. He wanted to say something to him, in a friendly and decent sort of way, but it did not come. He had long employed a kind of oblique bitterness when talking to him and now the habit was hard to change; he felt that Blore would, perhaps very naturally, think of a sudden gesture of friendly decency as a new and refined sort of sarcasm. The preoccupation on his face was so deep that at last Forrester gave up the thought and went out to breakfast without another word.

Half an hour later, when he came back from the mess-tent to get his jeep, Blore had gone. He got into his jeep and drove out through the wreckage of tindered jungle to the bombed dust track that had once been the central avenue of the town. Half-way along it he caught up with Blore, walking in the sun. He stopped the jeep and said, 'Hop in if you're going to H.Q.,' but Blore shook his head.

'I am going to H.Q.,' he said, 'but it's not far. I can walk. I'd rather walk.'

'See you there,' Forrester said. He tried to put into his voice some of the kindliness that had been too difficult to display in the tent, but it did not seem very successful. His voice seemed strained and hard.

He drove on and five minutes later was standing in Aldridge's large cool tent at headquarters by the end of the road. Aldridge was already at work at his table: a tall man, rather lean and sallow, with black hair and a large sprouting flippant black moustache which he kept caressing with the back of his left hand.

Forrester saluted and said good morning.

'I say,' Aldridge said. 'Very quick.' He looked up from the mass of papers on his desk and began to smooth the moustaches with immense sweep of his hand. 'Take a perch.'

Forrester sat down. A little breeze came in at the open tent flaps and fluttered very slightly the huge purple map on the wall.

'Afternoon ride for you,' Aldridge said.

'Good.'

'Seems an Intelligence type down at somewhere or other got his head cut off by a propeller. Loud cries for new body. Seems there are no bodies in the whole of the bloody country. Except here.'

'So here I am,' Forrester said.

'Here you are. And here,' Alridge said, 'is where you're going – '

Aldridge turned his head and began to point at the map. The great purple horseshoe of mountains, the lighter purple of the plain and the green fingers of jungle had, on the map, a strangely fascinating effect. The country of mountains and dust, robbed of its vast fatalistic haze of light, seemed through its reduction to contour to be extraordinarily complicated; so much so that Aldridge for a moment or two was lost, unable to find the place he was looking for. He gave it up with brief curses and began again to smooth the moustaches.

'Can't find the bloody thing. Anyway, no matter. Parker has the stuff and will tell you all. Nothing for you to do but collect the body and take it down.'

'And who are you sending?' Forrester said.

'Hell, forgot,' Aldridge said. 'Blore.'

'Good Christ.'

'Really? Don't like him?'

'Live with him,' Forrester said.

'Makes just that difference. Good bloke, all the same.'

Forrester did not speak. Aldridge said:

'Cambridge degree. Physics or something.'

'Hell.'

'Didn't know?'

'No.'

'Only goes to show,' Aldridge said. 'Live with a bloke months and don't get the first thing about him.'

Aldridge got up. Behind the lackadaisical twiddling of moustaches the dark eyes were extraordinarily shrewd.

'Nothing wrong with old Blore. Just like the rest of us. Some-times needs a change of air.'

He began to walk to the door with Forrester, very casual and friendly.

'Been for a trip with Harris, I hear.'

'Yes.'

'Interest you?'

'Very much.'

'Natives not hostile?'

'Very much otherwise.'

'Good,' Aldridge said. 'Must keep them on our side.'

Forrester said good morning and saluted and Aldridge, grin-ning, gave a sort of half-salute in reply, waving his hand and then bringing it down on his moustaches. It all seemed very informal and casual and it was not until long afterwards that Forrester remembered Aldridge standing there by the tent door, grinning and watching him go.

He walked across the dusty stretch of broken jungle to where, fifty yards away, the large Intelligence tent stood under a group of palms. Inside, Blore and the duty officer, Parker, were bend-ing over a map.

'Well,' he said, 'my passenger.'

'Yes, sir,' Blore said.

'Where is this place?'

'Here,' Parker said. He pointed with a pencil down to the map. 'Just north of the bend in the river. Where my pencil is now.'

'Not far.'

'How long will it take?' Blore said.

'Can't tell.' He could see where Blore had left little patches of shaving soap under his ears. 'Carrington will work it out. Going over to the crew-tent to find him now.'

He walked across to the open tent flap and then turned.

'How long before you're ready?'

'I've got all my stuff to pack,' Blore said.

'No hurry.'

'I'd like to get it properly packed.'

Forrester looked at his watch; it was not quite nine o'clock.

'Give you till two,' he said. 'Have some lunch first. How's that?'

Blore, not speaking, nodded his head in reply.

Outside, Forrester got into the jeep and drove across the town to the air-strip, to where, in the crew-tent, he would find Carrington. The wheel of the jeep was fiercely hot to his hands and already on the low banana fronds and on the scrubby wiry little bushes growing with mauve feathers of flower by the track the little dew of the night had completely dried. All across the plain the sun was already defeating the first sweet coolness, the dust rising in high sulphur columns, the haze hiding the far purple line of mountains. In another hour the full heat of day would clash down like a frightening hammer-blow.

In the crew-tent he found Carrington reading a two-months' old English newspaper, full of optimistic headlines, bold in prophecy about the war in Europe coming to an end. Forrester knew that somewhere on the back page there would be a much-pruned ten-line dispatch giving in flat dead phrases the un-terrifying news of the war in which he was fighting. The news-papers from England never failed to make him very angry. But now he did not feel any anger as he came into the tent and saw Carrington, with bright almost ivory hair smoothly brushed, absorbed in the paper, and he determined suddenly not to let the slightest echo of impatience or anger find its way into any-thing he had to say.

'Hullo,' he said. He said something about reading the comics and Carrington got up, saying, 'Good morning,' formal and friendly, and then:

'Funny. I read this newspaper in England. Just caught up with me.'

Forrester was surprised; it seemed to him that he had not heard before, or had perhaps already forgotten, about Car-rington being fresh out from England. For some reason it shocked him a little, making him say:

'Newspapers won't tell you much about this war.'

His voice, in spite of himself, was hard. He saw some of the old fear, with a flash of bright resentment, come into the eyes of the boy and then die out, leaving them defensive and cool.

'There's a job for us,' Forrester said. He began to tell the details as he knew them. The navigator folded the newspaper and put it in his pocket. His eyes had become excited. Forrester said, 'I'll take you over to Intelligence and you can work out your stuff.'

He drove rather fast along the road back to headquarters. Driving straight into the sun, he was blinded by it into a desire not to talk again. Carrington, shading his pale blue eyes, did not speak either, and Forrester felt uneasy. He knew that a state of simple and mutual trust had to be established and kept and fostered between them until the remotest edges of all distrust had been smoothed away, leaving them both bound by easy and instinctive faith in each other. He saw suddenly that it would not be easy, and then for some reason he remembered the girl. He recalled the fear growing and dying in her face in the lamp-light after the bombing. It made him say:

'Quite a small trip, this. But interesting. Sort of thing you need.'

'Yes,' Carrington said.

He took Carrington into the larger Intelligence tent and introduced him to Parker, and then through the tent to where, at one end, there was a section that purported to be a separate navigation room. He noticed that Blore had gone.

'Meet Dykes and Porter,' he said. The two officers, both older than himself, got up from the tables at which they had been writing. He thought they seemed very stiff, as if, like Carrington, they felt it necessary to be on the defensive, ready for anything he had to say. He began suddenly to wonder if he had that sort of reputation. The thought shocked him. It had not occurred to him that he might have become a notorious sort of legend. He suddenly wanted to get outside. 'These blokes will fit you up. Be over at my tent with the flight-plan at eleven-thirty,' he said. 'Fair enough?'

'Fair enough,' Carrington said.

He drove slowly back to the air-strip, thinking hard. A

succession of curious events began to slip into place into his mind: the three weeks spell of no flying, Harris's sudden interest in him, the casual catechism about his health, his mepacrine, his glasses; then Aldridge and his knowledge of it all, his off-hand way of bringing it up; and then the stiffness in the faces of the two navigation men, Dykes and Porter. All of it began slowly to mean the same thing. Then he remembered something else. It was a joke of Harris's: 'Remind me to give you something new. Over from Calcutta yesterday. A temperament killer.' At the time it had not occurred to him that it was any more than one of Harris's jocular remarks, a rather slick answer to his own bitterness. He remembered how, that first afternoon of going out to the village, he had not really been able to see straight. He had not cared or understood very much about where they were going. Neither that nor anything else had really mattered. Now the remark of Harris's, a joke no longer, seemed to light up the whole affair. It seemed to flash on the most trivial events and give them the greatest significance, the light rebounding sharply on himself, so that it was as if he were seeing himself for the first time.

By the time he had reached the air-strip the simplicity of it all staggered him. He wondered how it had not been possible for him to be aware of it before. He drove over to where his air-craft, creamed over with dust, stood parked at the far end of the line. The skeleton of the burned-out Mosquito, a heap of black and white like the bones of a bird already picked clean and blistered by sun, reminded him of yesterday. The sight of it threw an unmistakable flash of light on all his thought. He knew now that both Harris and Aldridge had been watching him. He had been under the kind of observation that preceded a ground-ing, a change: a posting: sometimes the end of a man. The trip to the village was not a casual affair. It was not a pleasant joke of Harris's; it was not irregular. It was something Harris and Aldridge had planned together to meet a crisis, an evident and perhaps deadly crisis in his affairs. In a way it was the tempera-ment killer.

Going to his aircraft he saw that Brown and Clarke, his former ground crew, were no longer there. A strange fitter, a young man brown as leather and stripped to the waist, was working on the port engine of the plane. As he saw him and remembered Brown, something else fell into the pattern of his realization about himself, almost completing it. He remembered how queerly Brown had looked at him; he remembered the strange moment of almost being knocked down by the ambulance. He saw again that queer look of Brown's, pitying and stoical, against the smoky sun. And he knew then that Brown was another one, with the doctor and Aldridge and Blore and Burke and God knew how many others, who had seen in him the signs of fibre disintegration, the moral break-up, the end. And again for some reason he was not angry, but only a little hurt that Brown, at the last moment, had not come to say good-bye.

He looked up at the mechanic working on the engine, like a golden-bronze figurehead against the cream-grey fuselage.

'Morning,' he said. 'What's your name?'

'Martin, sir.' He gave an unexpectedly stiff salute. At the same moment the rigger emerged from under the body of the plane and stood stiffly by the wing. Forrester saw in the attitudes of both of them the same thing. They, like the rest, were scared to death of him.

At the same moment he recalled the fitter's face. 'You were with Mr Anderson, weren't you?'

'That's right, sir.'

'Something wrong up there?'

'Not much, sir. Oil feed. It'll be all right.'

'I want it all right. I need the kite for twelve.' He spoke quietly and calmly, but the tenseness in the face of the boy did not go.

He turned to the rigger. 'What's your name?'

The rigger at once saluted. 'Cartwright, sir.'

'London?'

'Yessir.'

'Up the cockneys.'

Both the fitter and the rigger laughed, the tension easing for a moment or two.

'All right,' he said. 'Get it fixed. I mean fixed too.'

'Yessir.'

He felt the tension as he walked away. Then the rigger called after him:

'Sergeant Brown was looking for you, sir.'

'Oh! yes?' he said. 'Thanks.'

He walked away to the jeep and in the moment before he started the engine the mechanic, from the wing of the aircraft, waved his hand, shouting:

'Looks like the Sergeant coming down the strip now, sir.'

'Right,' he said.

He started the jeep and drove it slowly along the dispersal line. Brown was coming towards him and Forrester, seeing him, felt very glad. He stopped the jeep and switched off the engine as Brown came on.

'Been looking for you everywhere,' Brown said.

Forrester noticed that he did not salute and did not say sir. He was not displeased and said:

'Well, on your way?'

'Getting a lift in a Beechcraft at two o'clock.'

Brown's eyes looked wrinkled and tired.

'On the beer last night?'

'With two bottles a month!' Brown said. 'Indian gin, that's all. Gut-rot. Well, it was something.'

'I'm sorry you're going,' Forrester said.

'I'm sorry too.'

'What?' Forrester said. 'You? Time-expired.'

'Well, you. know. Half sorry. Something about the bloody show gets you.'

Forrester got ready to press the starter. He disliked the long farewell. But Brown said:

'Look, sir.'

Brown put his hand into the pocket of his shorts and took it out again.

'Something I knocked up for you.'

He held out a fairly large double-bladed, cork-screw knife.

'Made it out of bits and pieces. My trade. Just a souvenir.'

Forrester did not know what to say. He took the knife and looked at it. Engraved on the side was his name, 'S-Ldr For-rester from Sgt Brown, Burma, 1945.' He looked up at Brown and said, simply:

'It's damn nice. It's about the nicest gift I ever had. I can never keep 'em, though. Always lost them ever since I was a kid.'

'You keep it,' Brown said. 'It's got a cork-screw.'

Forrester laughed and then, as he put the knife in his pocket, felt that he had something more to say. He felt suddenly very close to Brown.

'Look,' he said. 'Tell me something.'

Brown did not speak.

'Have I been round the bend?'

'Yes,' Brown said.

'Much?'

'Pretty much sometimes.'

'How much?'

'About as much as we could bloody well bear.'

'I'm sorry,' he said.

'It gets you like that,' Brown said.

Forrester laughed again and seeing it Brown laughed too. Then he put out his hand and Forrester took it and gripped it hard. They did not speak again, but it seemed to Forrester in that moment that they knew each other very well. And as he started the jeep and began driving away, simply lifting his hand in farewell, he was glad he had spoken.

Driving back across the town he felt the positive touching moment of that farewell join itself to the recollection of all that had happened the night before. He became aware that out of a long negative shadow there had begun to grow positive moments, tender and decent and calm and touching, which he found it pleasant to remember. He sat half-smiling to himself in the sun.

An hour later, in his tent, he found Blore packing his things. The two beds, the bath and the floor were littered with the careful paraphernalia of the man. The boy Ali stood outside; there was no room to enter; and standing at the open flap Forrester watched all the familiar maddening things, the Thermos flask, the writing tablet, the mirror, the bottle of mepacrine, being carefully arranged and packed away. Among it all Blore moved with a kind of anxious reverence; the old unctuous irritating carefulness had broken into unsteady bewilderment. And

131

for a moment or two Forrester was sorry for him and forgot what had once been an insane desire to possess the tent alone.

'Something I can do to help surely?' he said.

'Don't touch anything. I want to be sure everything is there.'

'Anything I can fit you up with? You'll need all the comfort you can.'

'I don't think that very funny,' Blore said.

He did not say anything. It was no use saying anything. He walked away from the tent and remembered the savage after-noon, only two days before, when he had felt that if he didn't get out of the tent he would murder Blore, when he felt that he had to have the tent alone, when the tent had to be moved before he could get the anger and irritation out of his mind. Now he felt sorry about Blore. There was an enmity between them that seemed viciously rooted.

He walked over to the mess-tent on the chance that the new beer ration would be in, but there was no beer and he sat down at one of the empty mess-tables and thought for a moment of the day before him: the flight down beyond the river, the flight back that would defeat the full fierce heat of the afternoon, the bath that Ali would bring before the fall of dusk, the tent alone, the drive out in the cool scented evening to the village by the river. Nothing of what he thought was complicated now by irritation. In the evening he would talk to the girl again. He would tell her of everything that had troubled him and then, strengthened by that, he would talk to the doctor. Very soon things would grow straight and right again. He was keen to fly and glad to be alive, and it seemed very simple now.

When he went back to the tent again Blore had almost finished packing, and Carrington had arrived with the flight plan.

12

He was airborne by half past two, steeped in sweat from the few moments of waiting for his clearance from the strip. The sun was vicious in its downward hammer stab of his eyeballs, where it met the upward crystalline glare coming from the dust below. Then as he climbed rapidly and cooler air began to rush in on him like strong draughts of water, almost icy on his drenched chest and shoulders, all the harsh shocking heat slipped away with the shell-like tents, the toy bamboo-cream blocks of bashas, the dark rosettes of palm fringing glassy squares of water, the sugar-smooth fantasy of pagodas white as snow along the black road that cut away to the villages down the river.

As he climbed and set course south-eastward he thought of Blore, lying somewhere back in the body of the aircraft like a bag of mail. Blore had boarded the aircraft with something of the appearance of an explorer bound for trackless and primitive deserts. He walked submerged by the apparatus of comfort: water-bottle and sling-bag across his shoulders and gas-mask in regulation style across his chest, bush hat strapped under his chin, and then girded across his waist, too tight on the fat body, his webbing and revolver. He was pale and wet, with large black patches of sweat under the bulging breast-pocket of his green bush shirt.

It amused Forrester to think of Blore; and yet now, on the last day of their being together, he was almost sorry to see him go. With him was going the last of his own intolerance. Now, if Blore had remained, it would have been easy to bear with him, even to like him, and at last to discover, perhaps pleasantly, the humanity of the man. It was still not too late, he thought, to make the gesture of decency; and he determined that when they landed, in little over half an hour, he would not only say good-bye. He would go farther. He would shake hands and try with a few words to go beyond the detached and off-hand farewell.

By the time he had finished thinking this, he had flown beyond the edge of the plain. The muscular arm of the river, green and translucent from the long dry season, curved below him, and then eastward, beyond it, the dark-spurred terrain of hills began to shape itself, the little arid yellow valleys like veins in a mass of green-black stone. As he began to fly over it he saw forest and rock welded together into harsh masses, green and green-shadowed with sometimes a gash of torrid brown where great fissures of sand-rock had been violently split away.

When he had flown over this for some time the great mass of forest and rock lay undivided wherever he looked. After another minute or two he saw the river again. Then he saw its tributary coming from the north-west, on an almost parallel line, so that as they bent together and joined they were like the branches of a silver tuning fork glittering in the sun. And then in another moment or two both rivers were gone. There was nothing below him again but the hostile mass of barbaric rock with folds of forest that were like dense crustings of vicious moss.

He spoke to Carrington: 'Mandalay over there. Where the dawn comes up like something or other. Like to look when we've delivered the body?'

The boy grinned and nodded, and for the first time Forrester felt between them a sense of adjustment and decency.

'Everything O.K.?' he said.

'O.K.,' Carrington said.

At five thousand feet the aircraft was bumping a little in the heat, with occasional upward sickening thumps, but his sweat was cool and dry now and he felt a delight in the comfort and detachment of flying and did not mind. Staring at the endless mass of green below he flew forward into a dream of cool serenity.

He came out of it sometime later to hear the boy shouting wildly about the oil. He was waving his arms like a frantic puppet.

From under the cowling of the port engine a spew of oil was pouring across the wing, flattened out by the force of the slip-stream into something of the look of thinned treacle. It widened

134

and thickened as Forrester saw it. It seemed then to congeal to a thickness of brown jelly, about a foot wide, flattening out fanwise. He saw this change in it simultaneously with the pressure on the dial. The two facts met and ignited in his mind. They blew up into a moment of explosive panic. This panic rushed through his brain like a hot flare and then became extinguished by anger, and then he felt suddenly cold and thought of Blore. He saw him in a flash of most comic irony lying somewhere back in the plane, surrounded by his comforts, unaware. He had a paradoxical and insane desire to laugh. Out of this complication of panic and anger and laughter he gave a shout. 'Going back!' It roused Carrington to frantic action on the radio telephone. He saw his mouth opening and shutting more than ever like the mouth of a terribly surprised puppet. And then in that same moment he pulled the aircraft over. The mass of forest and rock tilted up and away and straightened out, striking him with an effect of blazing distortion in the moment when he crossed into and out of the sun. It left him with the feeling that the flash of it had set fire to his eyeballs. He could not see. There was nothing before him but a coagulation of fantastic flame.

This flame leapt out of fantasy into the most ghastly reality a moment later. The entire cowl of the port engine was orange-scarlet. It suddenly trailed expanding and horrible creepers of flame. He thought again of Blore. In that instant he became two persons: the person of conscious and leaping thought, thinking of Blore and himself and wanting to die and now not wanting to die and shouting within himself madly, 'This is it, it can't be, it can't be, after all this time, oh! Christ, it can't be!' and thinking once of the girl serene and lovely and frightened; and then the person of trained reaction, thinking and yet not thinking, framing instinctively the action he must take: watching the flame of the burning engine, putting down the wheels, watching a long dusty pale fissure breaking the hills below, remembering the dried water-courses as means of escape, repeating in his mind the things he would find down there, scrub, rocks, trees, all of it in a race of calculation against the flame now whipped upward like a torch as he took the plane farther and farther down.

From below, the earth seemed to rush up in a mass of barbaric obstacles. He saw the long dead valley waterless and white in the sun. It was as if skimmed by an avalanche. He tried to fix between the mass of vast rock fragments and clumps of grey bush an empty strip of sand.

He came down as if in the thick of a bombardment. From all along the valley there rushed at him a wild rain of dark rock. It seemed to leap up at him out of the white sand. Out of this mass he saw a single boulder, about the height of a crouching man, coming straight towards the plane, and then a second later he felt the wheel hit it and the plane leap in a half-loop, beyond his control, tearing away from the central mass of rock and scrub towards the fringe of jungle, the wheel smashed, the flaming wing projected upward and the flame with the dart of an orange bird suddenly flying downward at the body of the plane.

In the moment before the flame flew towards him he looked at Carrington. He was calling messages into the telephone with incomprehensible calm. He was rigid and staring, as if hypnotized by the glare of flame and sun and sand. It did not seem to Forrester that he could ever move again, and as the plane smashed to a standstill, in a final moment of flaring and explosive terror, he remembered seizing him violently by the shirt, pulling him to his feet, shouting.

Somewhere behind, above the roar of flame, Blore was swearing in a scream.

Forrester rolled over and over on the white hot dust like a man doing a trick fall in a circus. As he got up he saw the astonishing figure of Blore. It stood upright, complete with every accoutrement. It had the surprising incongruity of a wrapped parcel. Something protective in the mass of kit strapped about him like a lifebelt had kept him unhurt, and now he stood like a piece of luggage, violently but safely delivered.

Almost in the same moment Forrester saw all that was left of the figure of Carrington. It was like the terrible reflection of something from the past. It was running, like a torch of flame, into the open part of valley. It ran, burning as it ran, like the figure he had seen on the air-strip. He heard the boy screaming in a wail like a child. He gave a great leap forward, running after him, but the boy fell down, burning, even before he reached him. As he fell down Forrester fell with him, thrusting his hands with frantic power into the dust, throwing it in a solid cloud across the body that was now alight from the loins down. He threw this frantic powerful cloud several times. Each time it fell across Carrington's burning body he saw the flame suffocated and the smoke rise more thickly, until there was no more flame but only the legs of the boy smouldering under the ridge of piled white sand.

He stood for a second or so dazed and panting. Somewhere behind him, at the jungle edge, the plane was burning itself out in a black cloud. He knelt down by Carrington. He lay starkly conscious, staring upward. A whip of flame had gone over the face, singeing the brows and the forward roots of the fine oiled hair, but the flesh was untouched and the eyes and mouth were clean. Seeing Forrester, he tried to say something but the mouth only opened to a grey-red gap and the words did not come.

Blore arrived, running flatly, on flat feet. The boy began to writhe a little under the mound of dust, rolling his face from side to side. In that moment Forrester felt the first savage stab of sun. It seemed to collect above him in the narrow confined strip of valley and then clash with naked and awful power on his neck.

'Blore!' he said. 'Blore!' Staring at him, he got uncertainly and half-blindly to his feet. The comic and parcelled officer, overburdened and too fat, seemed suddenly a wonderful person. Forrester touched his shoulders: he felt the fat flesh of the upper arms in a gesture of relieved gladness. Blore said with curious calm, 'All right. You? Better get the kid out of the sun.'

'Yes,' he said.

'Over there. Some shade.'

Forrester took the shoulders of the boy and pulled him gently out of the ridge of sand. Carrington was conscious enough to wave his hands feebly in little protests of pain. The legs came out of the sand fire-blackened, horrible in the sun. Forrester began to take off his shirt, obsessed with the thought of covering the boy. And then he heard Blore say, 'No. No need.' He spoke in laconic phrases of astonishing calm, using words that were a deliberate ironic joke. They astonished Forrester into a calm of

137

his own: 'Keep your shirt on,' Blore said, and actually smiled.

A moment later he began to strip himself of the webbing, the gas-mask and the bags he carried across his shoulders. He stepped out of them so that they fell about his feet in a heap in the dust. Relieved of them, the bush tunic creased and puffed about him, he seemed to look plumper than ever. He gave the impression of being a person of suave solidity against a wilderness of barbaric light. Then out of the sling-bag he took a towel. It was very large and in colour exactly the grey-green of the bush tunic he wore and much of the colour of the stiff scrub-bush growing about the valley. He folded it gently over and then under Carrington's legs, lifting him tenderly. 'Now,' he said, looking up at Forrester, 'we can carry him now.'

Together, Forrester at the head, Blore with his arms outstretched under the burned legs and walking sideways like a puffed green crab, they carried him a hundred yards or so across the space of sand and rock and bush to the place where low jungle came down to dried stream edge, away from the plane. Forrester had lost his cap. And now as he walked he felt the sun boring like a hot glass gimlet, in a curious spiral splintering motion, down through the back of his neck. For some reason he did not feel the weight of Carrington. He felt only the sun, callous and splintering and jabbing him along across the shadeless dust. Once or twice Blore, walking sideways, trampled blindly into spreading bushes, prickled with white-grey leaf and thorn as if they were glazed with salt, but his short black jungle boots stabbed them down and he went on without stumbling, always with the imponderable solid motions of a monster crab. He called once to Forrester between puffs of his fat lips something about wanting to stop, but Forrester shook his head and like this they staggered on, carrying the burned body across the low fissures bored through sand and rock by the torrents of monsoons and so at last into the broken tree-shade farthest away from the cloud of fire.

When they had laid Carrington down in the thickest of the shade Forrester saw to his astonishment that Blore had also brought the bag. Half-exhausted, Forrester knelt on the ground, head forward over his knees, the sweat running down from it like the drips from a roof-gutter, and watched dumbly as Blore opened it and laid the contents of it on the sand. His body deflated and puffed itself out again and deflated itself in a slow struggle for breath; the flesh seemed to rise and fall under the dusty bush jacket in desperate swollen waves. And then he lifted his hands from the boy. It was to make a gesture, a vague dumb swing of both hands out towards the sun. He took off his hat. And a moment later Forrester found himself wearing the hat, thrust down on his head by Blore in what seemed almost to be a gesture of command.

Staggering about, he walked quite quickly out into the sun. From under the wide brim of the hat it seemed suddenly that the burning plane, the great columns of smoke and the paraphernalia left by Blore seemed very far away. The shock of light and exhaustion seemed to take away his power of perspective. He was seized with the awful and shocking impression that what lay before him was not the narrow valley shut in by its low banks of forest scrub and creeper, but the entire plain, blank under the insufferable afternoon light and rimmed far away by the purple haze of its mountains.

This impression was gone in a second or two. As he walked he wiped the sweat out of his eyes. Dust on his hands, mixed with sweat, became momentarily a kind of thin mud, which dried even as he smeared it over his face and then was wetted again as new sweat poured out of him. By the time he had repeated all this once or twice he knew that it was useless, and he let the sweat fall at last, streaming as it would. By this time too he had focused the valley. It was perhaps a hundred and fifty yards wide. The aircraft had ground-looped almost into the jungle-edge and now, caught by the great heat, some of the trees were flaring too. They burned with clean arrows of flame that darted among the rocks in leaps of scarlet and orange. All the time he could feel heat and oil-stench streaming across like a furnace breath and black smuts of fire pouring into his face like hot dry rain.

He reached the heap of Blore's belongings and began to gather them up. He clipped the webbing and its revolver round his waist. The grip bag had been left in the plane. There remained now only the gas-mask and the water-bottle. He shook the bottle gently once or twice, judging it to be three-quarters full, and then took up the gas-mask. Its case had burst open. To his astonishment there was no mask inside, but only a new mass of trivial common things: scissors, handkerchiefs, nail-file, a bottle of hair cream, a bottle of aspirin, some letters. He shoved them hastily back inside and clipped down the flap and slung the case over his shoulder.

Walking back, carrying the things, he felt a stab of panic. In the glaring light, now re-charged with finer violence as it struck the crystalline dust and flashed upwards, he could see neither Carrington nor Blore. They seemed to have vanished from where he had left them. He looked wildly round and felt himself to be alone in the empty valley. A swift and awful feeling of loneliness went over him like a shadow. He wanted violently to run. And then out of the moment of dazzling terror he saw Blore's head. It was splendidly bald. It seemed to lift itself from the ground only fifty or sixty yards away. So real that it was almost idiotic, it hung suspended against the grey-green jungle like fat ripe fruit on a tree.

When he reached it a minute later he had forgotten the terror, the loneliness, and the dazzle of light. In the shade Blore had taken off his bush jacket and had made a pillow of it for Carrington's head. The boy lay rigid, with closed eyes. Forrester slipped the bag, the revolver and the water-bottle from his shoulders and then took off his shirt. It was soaked with sweat and he let it fall loosely to the ground.

'Fold it up,' Blore said. 'You'll need it sooner or later.'

Automatically he picked up his shirt, folding it slowly, too surprised to speak.

'Got to take care of everything,' Blore said.

He nodded.

'That was a bloody magnificent landing,' Blore said.

Forrester was surprised into his first recollection of it. He had not thought of it, either as good or bad. It seemed simply a terribly shapeless and wild affair.

'How's Carrington?' he said.

'Somehow we've got to get these socks off,' Blore said. 'Hand the bag. Scissors in it somewhere.'

Forrester was about to put his hand into the gas-mask case and take out the scissors, when Blore almost at the same moment took the bag and searched in it himself. 'A couple of aspirins won't do him any harm. Four aspirins. I'm an aspirin addict. There should be two bottles. Get the water.'

He bent over Carrington, who opened his eyes.

'All right. Don't panic. An aspirin or two, that's all. Can you sit up?'

'I'll hold him,' Forrester said.

With his right arm he held Carrington upright. Blore took the water-bottle from him and uncorked it and Carrington wetted his lips. 'Now,' Blore said. 'Swallow.' He gave four aspirins to the boy, who held them weakly against his mouth on the flat of his hand and then sucked them in. 'Swallow like hell,' Blore said. 'Now the water.'

The aspirins broke like chalk in the boy's mouth and then the water washed them back. He made a great effort and swallowed, grinning faintly at the same time. 'Take it easy,' Blore said. 'Lie quiet.'

Forrester let Carrington lie slowly backwards on the pillow of the bush jacket.

'We're going to see what we can do with these legs,' Blore said. 'Lie quiet if you can.'

Blore's head, bending over Carrington's legs, had the surprising coolness of an egg. Smooth and shining, it actually reflected the sharp shadow of the tree above them. Forrester saw the eyes of Carrington fixed on it, watching it grimly. Every now and then his mouth leapt open, the lips white-grey with shock, his eyes withered with pain. 'It's really not bad, it's really not bad,' he said once. 'Really not bad.' Towards the end he rolled his head from side to side with feeble swings of quiet protest.

At last the legs were clear. They had the terribly ruckled appearance of sticks savagely peeled. Blore covered the ghastly blistered lacerations with the towel.

'All right?' he said to Carrington.

'I'm sorry about this,' the boy said. 'Awful bloody nuisance.'

'You bet,' Forrester said.

'Just shut your eyes and lie still and keep quiet,' Blore said, 'while we take stock of my stuff.'

'That'll take a year,' Forrester said, 'and by that time you'll be on crutches.'

He saw the boy smile and was glad. There seemed to pass between them the first spark of friendliness. It remained vivid in the tired pupils for a second or two before he closed his eyes.

Blore had begun to unpack his belongings. Miraculously there was a second towel. He laid it in the dust and then began to spread out on it, methodically, rather slowly, in neat rows, the things from the two bags.

'Chemist's shop,' Forrester said.

'Why not? Give me comfort.'

'There's something in that.'

'There should be a bottle of antiseptic,' Blore said. 'Probably in the flap of the gas-mask.'

Eight bottles, three cigarette tins, four packets and a roll of toilet paper lay on the towel, with a cake of pink soap, a Thermos flask, two books, three white handkerchiefs, a hair-brush and a folded piece of buckram canvas to form a house-wife, with needles and thread.

Forrester marvelled quietly. 'Even a bottle of my favourite mepacrine,' he said.

Blore, insusceptible it now seemed to any touch of irony, so that Forrester suddenly felt cheap and wished he had not spoken, looked over the belongings almost as if counting them and then said:

'Now let's see what you've got.'

'Damn all,' Forrester said. 'I was just flying.'

'Turn your pockets out,' Blore said. 'Even the smallest thing may be important.'

In the pocket of his bush trousers Forrester found a handker-chief, some money in loose change and the knife that Brown had given him. 'Try your shirt,' Blore said, and in the breast pockets of it Forrester found his papers, an old leave pass that had taken him to Calcutta in February, and a packet of tissue paper. He remembered putting the packet into his shirt pocket that morning as he changed his papers from the tunic he had worn the night before, and now he held it in his hands, slowly unfolding it, with incredulous delight.

'A ruby,' Blore said. 'Don't tell me you've been buying those things. They're all synthetic.'

'Synthetic is the only word you don't use about this one,' he said.

He looked at Blore quite savagely for a moment, and then repented. But he saw in the same moment that Blore noticed it, and he felt as if suddenly all the maladjustment between them, so oddly inverted since the crash, came into proper balance and that now, for the first time, they began to understand each other.

The shock of the crash had stiffened Blore into an extraordinary state of clear-headed calm. Now for a moment it seemed to break. As Forrester folded up the ruby and put it back into his pocket Blore held his face for a moment in his hands, as if trying to keep back a wave of delayed shock. Forrester saw him shudder. And all at once felt sorry for the fat bald-headed man squatting in front of his dispersed belongings like a big green frog, sick and panting.

He was moved to put his arms on his shoulders, and said, 'Better lie down yourself. Come on.'

'Quite all right,' Blore said. 'It's just my hand.'

He saw Blore's left hand a mass of heat-dried blood, matted with dust in the palm.

'Better lie down,' he said. 'When did this happen?'

'Can't remember.'

Blore stretched himself slowly out in the dust. Forrester held his left hand. The palm had a laceration diagonally across the hollow of it, as if it had violently clutched a lump of glass.

'I'll wash it,' he said.

'Christ!' Blore said. 'What the hell are you talking about!'

He was sitting bolt upright.

'There's no water for washing!' Blore said. 'The Thermos and the water-bottle – how long do you think it'll last if we start washing.'

'That wound ought to be cleaned.'

'Well, then I'll spit on it,' Blore said. 'What's clean enough for my inside is clean enough for my outside.'

Forrester felt there was nothing he could say.

'You'd better lie down a minute yourself,' Blore said. 'It'll do us all good.'

143

Forrester knelt where he was, looking at the two officers, who lay side by side. He saw Blore shut his eyes. He felt a rush of heat, partly sun, partly the fire of the burning plane, come scorching across the dust like a solid blow, suffocating the three of them with its dry blast. With it came the beginnings of thirst. He heard Carrington coughing harshly and saw Blore retch frantically without being sick. He licked his own lips with his tongue and then regretted it instantly, feeling the lips and the tongue dry immediately in the burning air.

Slowly Blore got up.

'Sorry about that,' he said.

He gave a whitish grin, and then knelt by Forrester.

'What do you know about burns?'

'Saline solution.'

'One small bottle of salt,' Blore said, 'and no spare water.'

'Mix it with antiseptic?'

'Get the handkerchiefs,' Blore said.

Forrester unfolded Blore's three handkerchiefs and his own and laid them out on the towel. Blore poured salt on to each of them and then refolded them into the shape of an oblong pad and over them poured a little of the antiseptic. As he did so Forrester tried desperately to think of all he had ever heard about burns and the treatment of them, but his mind seemed cut off from the remote circumstantial world he had left less than an hour before and he could think of nothing practical or right. Then he knew that they could do no more than the thing they thought was best and right, and he reached over and held the damp salt pads for Blore, who laid them gently over the burnt knees and legs of the young officer, who was silent and did not stir. Then Blore took off his bush jacket and laid it over the legs, and then the larger of the two towels and laid that over the thighs and the loins. It seemed to Forrester all the time that there was an astonishing softness about the fat puffy figure. He saw it give to the boy a feeling of gentleness and succour. By the time Blore had finished covering him Carrington was easier in his way of lying and had stopped coughing and was smiling with dry lips on which were white fragments of aspirin that he could not swallow.

'Nothing you can do but shut your eyes,' Blore said.

'We were on course,' Carrington said.

'Never mind about course,' Forrester said. 'Just shut your eyes.'

'I can talk with my eyes shut.'

'All right,' he said. 'Did you give them positions?'

'Best I could,' Carrington said. 'It was a bit confused. Anyway, they could work it out by time alone, I should say. Parker saw the flight plan.'

'What time is it?' he said.

'Four minutes past two,' Blore said.

'Not quite four hours to dark,' Forrester said. 'Say three. They're bound to see the fire if they don't send a bunch of complete clots.'

Blore was silent. Forrester suddenly had the impression that he did not approve of what he was saying, but he felt neither resentment nor antagonism and went on to say to Carrington:

'If they got any sort of fix it's a piece of cake. Can't go wrong. Have you out of here in no time.'

Then he knew why Blore, staring across at the burning plane, did not speak. All that he himself was saying had the foolish emptiness of something said by a parrot. He knew that Blore did not believe a word of it. And soon, as he sat there looking into the blinding white heat separating them from the black pyre of the burning plane and the dry bushes flickering into flame with little brilliant explosions as they were caught by the heat of the main fire, he knew that he did not believe a word of it himself. All that he saw was there, the fire, the sun, the waterless sand, the barrier of rock and jungle cutting him off on all sides, mocked him cruelly into the most impotent littleness he had ever known.

13

The heat kept them for long intervals from talking in the thin shade. Forrester lay with his hands across his eyeballs, away from the sun. Even then the glare crept along the ground, almost salt-like in its crystal whiteness, and stung like a vicious snake-whip on his face.

Across the valley the plane burned itself down to a white skeleton with furious little angles of flames. The smoke changed its colour from black to grey. Except for the occasional crack of heat-shot metal there was no sound in the afternoon and he was numbed by the oppressive heat, still partly charged from the fire. He had been careful already to wind his watch and when by four o'clock there had been no sound of anything flying he began to try to reconstruct in his mind the country over which they had been flying before the crash, but he saw it only as a mass of encrusted green, roadless and without landmarks, with no fixing point except the river, miles away. And then by concentration he began to remember the river more clearly; and then how there had been two rivers, joining in the shape of a tuning fork, and he remembered flying south-east away from them. He tried to recall even the roughest details of a map. It was not very difficult to remember the shape of the plain. The Irrawaddy came down the eastern side of it; the Chindwin came in from the west and the two of them met below Mandalay. So that if we saw them but did not cross them, he thought, we are somewhere between them. We may be twenty or thirty miles from either of them, perhaps less. But this valley, in the monsoon season, is a river. It becomes a mountain tributary. It joins one or other of them somewhere.

He got up and walked out into the sun. It was now twenty minutes past four and in another hour and a half the day would be gone. Even if they see us now, he thought, it will be too dark, by the time the report is made, to pick us off today. We shall be here at least until tomorrow noon.

Standing out in the sun, he looked up and down the valley. It seemed to run roughly east to west. About five or six hundred yards to the west a heavy knoll of rock, shining like iron in the sun, so that it had a silvery granitic glare with it even at that distance, pushed out from forest escarpment and turned the stream bed away.

He was so absorbed in considering the terrain and in wondering what lay beyond the granite boulder where the valley turned that he became oblivious for a moment or two of the savagery of the sun. Nor did he hear the approach of Blore, who startled him violently by saying, 'You ought not to be out here. What are you looking at, anyway?'

'How's Carrington?' Forrester said.

'It's pretty painful for him. I said what are you looking at?'

'Just looking. They'll possibly not find us tonight.'

'No.'

'And possibly not even tomorrow.'

'You think so?' Blore said. 'Then what are you surveying this stream-bed for?'

'It goes somewhere.'

'That's a wonderful deduction.'

'We may have to go with it.'

'How?' Blore said. 'On bicycles?' His irony had a peculiar precise thinness. His voice squeaked with impatient falsetto.

'Walk.'

'With Carrington? Even with every treatment he couldn't walk.'

'We're as strong as bloody horses,' Forrester said. 'We can carry him.'

Blore did not speak.

'How long will the water last?' Forrester said.

'Three days. Perhaps four. Perhaps longer.'

'Say five.' He stood looking down the valley, in a daze of calculation. 'If we carried him four miles a day that would be twenty. We can't be that from the river.'

'It's possible.'

'It's got to be possible. I don't know how you feel, but I'm going to get out of this place if it kills me.'

The joke did not seem to amuse Blore. He stood with one hand pressed against another, as if in pain.

'What's up?' Forrester said.

'Can't get my hand to stop bleeding.'

'I'll dress it.'

'No, – it's just my blood got so confoundedly thin – '

'I said I'll dress it!' Forrester said.

He walked slowly out of the sun into the shade where Carrington lay. Bending over him, seeing the boy tired with shock, the pupils of his eyes yellow and the blood drained from his face, leaving it grey as putty, the sweat oozing from it like oil, he very gently wiped the face with the towel and Carrington gave a short smile, quite strengthless, without speaking. This smile seemed to Forrester suddenly to have enormous trust. It gave him, almost entirely because it was without words, a new confidence in himself. He felt that the boy understood perfectly what the situation was, but that also, because of Forrester, he was neither troubled nor afraid. He went back to where Blore sat holding his hand.

'Hold it up.' he said. 'Across your chest.'

He saw that Blore, hit by a second wave of delayed shock, was tired too. He lifted his hand mechanically, and the thin blood streamed back down the arm. Forrester picked up the shirt that, only a short time before, Blore had rather curtly told him to fold, but now as he ripped it down from the neck, Blore made no protest. Forrester searched in the gas-mask case and found the bottle of antiseptic and poured a little across the wound and then wiped it clean, as gently as he could. The wound passed diagonally, not very deep, across the palm, above the ball of the thumb; and over it Forrester tied the shirt, then tying it again, more tightly above the wrist, and then knotting the sleeves of it together, so that it formed a sling. He put the sling over Blore's head and then tightened it up, so that the hand could be held upwards, under the shoulder.

'All I ever learned from a nurse,' he said. He grinned and was glad to see Blore grinning in reply.

'You'd better have a drink of water too.'

148

'I'm all right,' Blore said.

'Just wet your lips and do as you're told and lie down.'

'Sounds like orders,' Blore said.

'You know how dominant nurses are.'

He grinned again and held the water-bottle for Blore to drink. Afterwards he corked it carefully and wrapped it, with the Thermos flask, in the towel. What he had said about nurses reminded him, for some reason, of Burke, and he sat for some time thinking of her, amused. He wondered what she would say when she heard he was missing: if she would say it served him damn well right or that it was just like the English or that it was only like a man. She would rampage wildly about it in the nurses' mess to Johnson and take it out, with Irish fury, on the younger girls. He remembered too how he had threatened to kill her and how he had meant it, and this thought brought rushing back to him in tender and unbearably clear waves, the memory of the girl as he had watched her from the jeep, framed alone in the light of the little dispensary.

No longer aware of the sun or the plane burning itself out in the dust or of Carrington and Blore lying down in the shade beside him, he sat staring and thinking of her. For a few moments he seemed to go clean through the harsh and bitter curtain of white light that hung beyond the shade where they lay, and far beyond it to the small dark fragrant world, intensely brighter and more living in recollection, of the raised bamboo house under the tree. He lived so completely within it and about it for some moments, seeing Miss McNab screaming about the hymns in the lamplight, the parrot-green bananas and papaias on the lace tablecloth, Harris drinking gin, the girl smiling at him and then lying in the dust of the verandah as the bomb fell, that when finally he heard a shout and saw Blore leaping about as if the hot sand were scorching his feet he could not believe that the fat and suddenly excited officer was not part of all that had happened the night before.

'It's a plane!' Blore said. 'A Dak! Can't you hear the damn thing?'

Blore ran out into the sun, shouting.

Forrester could hear the engines of the Dakota clearly as he walked after him. The plane was coming from the south-east.

As he heard it he suppressed his own excitement, knowing at once that nothing from that direction could possibly have come for rescue. He heard Blore shout again, 'Must see us! Can't possibly miss us!' and saw him run, with surprisingly fat agility, waving both arms. In his excitement the wounded hand had shot out of the sling, ripping itself free.

Forrester waited for the plane to come into sight over the hills. It suddenly appeared at about five thousand feet, greenish-dusty in the heat haze. The thought of rescue did not worry him. He sat down in a clear space of sand and took a dead stump of scrub in his hands and waited for the plane to cross the sun. Somewhere far out in the open valley he heard Blore shouting in thin squalls as he madly waved his hands. Then as the Dakota crossed the valley, not changing its course, he drew the line of its course in the sand, in relation to the sun.

He was still sitting there, staring hard at the beginnings of his diagram in the sand, thinking hard, when Blore came back. He was walking slowly and disconsolately, both hands at his sides, his face terribly drenched with sweat under the bush-hat that now, more than ever, seemed too large for him.

'For God's sake keep your hand in the sling,' Forrester said. Blood was streaming down again from the cut in the palm.

'Never looked at us,' Blore said. He clenched his hand so that the blood flowed slowly between the fingers, and then wrapped it roughly back in the sling.

Forrester, not answering, stared at the diagram in the sand.

'Never started to see us,' Blore said.

'It's just a mail.'

'What are you up to?' Blore said.

'Supposing the mail came from Mandalay – '

'Are we by some chance expecting letters?'

'Mandalay to Monywa – Monywa to Comilla – that's roughly a line north-west. If we can find the way the stream runs – ' Forrester sat staring again, in deeper thought.

'You seem awfully anxious about this walking. Why don't you start?'

'Look,' Forrester said. He sat back on his legs, curling them underneath him. 'Let's face it. The country is damn difficult. The whole of this mountain jungle stuff looks the same – miles and miles of it – it's hellish to find anything from the air. You've seen it. You know as well as I do.'

'There's the fire. Surely to God that can be seen.'

'The Dak didn't see it.'

'No.'

'Heat haze, angle of light, odd forest fires, a valley going the wrong way – Good God, man, you know how it is. This strip looks like a vein in the trees.'

It seemed to Forrester that it was better to face the truth now, quite simply and plainly, and then prepare for the worst it might bring, rather than later; but now as he spoke of it he could see that Blore was infinitely depressed.

'You'd better rest,' he said.

'I'm all right.'

'That hand's bleeding a lot. Let me bind it up again.' Forrester got slowly to his feet, trying to move and speak carelessly. 'And don't go waving the damn thing again. You'd think the Dak was full of nurses.'

Blore took the joke very well, smiling a little as they walked back together into the shade. Even the shadow of the jungle edge had now no relief for them. The sun beat in beneath the thin outer branches and brought up from the sand a harder, steelier glare. Forrester felt it flat and blinding in his eyes like the dazzle from a mirror, and he lay for some moments stupidly dazed by the ferocity of it, gasping for breath.

Carrington spoke at last. 'That Dak,' he said. 'It's the one that gets in just before five.'

Forrester lay listening carefully, and yet determined now not to show more than the faintest interest.

'I wouldn't worry about it.'

He sat up and began to re-bandage Blore's hand. He tied the shirt more tightly above the wrist and hoisted the sling a little higher at the shoulder. 'Now take an aspirin and rest,' he said. 'It's the best you can do.'

Blore, astonishingly obedient, took two aspirins at once, his big teeth very white against his dry lips, so that he had something of the eagerness of a horse taking a piece of sugar. Then he lay down and put the bush hat over his face and sometimes in the next ten minutes or so Forrester saw it moving regularly up and down, as if he were still trying to get the taste of dry aspirin out of his mouth.

While he lay there Forrester sat with his arms across his knees, thinking of what Carrington said. The sun was beginning to drop fiercely down towards the edge of the valley, and from the horizon the broad purple band of evening haze, pink at the edges, like a fire itself, was growing upwards, already turning the western sky from the whitish-blue of the day's heat to tender green. In a little over half an hour it would be dark. As he thought of it, he gave up the thought of rescue: at first only temporarily, until the morning, and then permanently. Almost as an experiment he began to calculate from the speed of the Dakota and from its time of arrival how far it could possibly be, south-eastward, to the river valley. In a straight line he reckoned that it could not be more than twenty miles; but he knew that the line would not be straight and he began to think of it as thirty miles. Then it occurred to him that they could travel by night; he remembered that the moon would be up by nine. It would be cooler then and there would be none of the exhausting glare of day and he could divide the night into easy marches: of an hour each perhaps, or even of half an hour, with a corresponding rest between. He was strong enough to carry Carrington on his back, alone. Blore, even with his damaged hand, would be able to carry the things, and the moon would give them light enough to see. From that too they would get all night a single bearing on direction, and he thought that if they travelled only half a mile in half an hour they would walk several miles by dawn. Somewhere too on the western side of the river there would be hope of a road.

He sat considering this for twenty minutes or so, turning it over and over in his mind, cautiously at first, as an experiment with an idea, then firmly, with increasing conviction. It seemed to him altogether better to travel at once, while they still had water, relying on their own endurance and strength, rather than to remain and drink the water, relying on the chance of being seen from the air. There are two evils, he thought, and both may be hell; but give me a travelling hell rather than a standing hell any time.

By the time he had come to this simple decision the sun was

already going down. He got up once again and walked out into the valley. The glare of sun was now strong with a strange light of pinkish copper. The sand was a thunderous orange under the western glow.

He walked out into the centre of the valley, where in the rainy season or after sudden torrential storms the stream would flood down on its course. He was still not quite sure which way it ran. Everywhere he could see where water had muscled and ridged the sand into sharp clefts, cutting between dark glinting rock, and down on the central stream-bed the rock had been smoothed by water until it had the glassiness of polished quartz. Here and there he saw long folds of grass and strips of young bamboo massed against the soil-stripped roots of the low scrub, and sometimes the sun-white skeleton of an animal washed down by the flood of rain.

He bent down and looked at the long ribs of sand and then at the wreckage of grass and bamboo, sun-bleached as the bones themselves now, piled up against the withered roots of dead scrub. It was easy to see now which way the stream ran.

To his absolute astonishment he saw that it ran directly west-wards. The sheaves of bamboo caught in the tree-roots seemed to be flowing down in the liquid coppery light towards the thickening purple rim of sunset.

Seeing it, he was worried. For some reason he had based his plan on the idea that the stream would go eastward, entirely the opposite way. The unexpected discovery baffled him for a moment. Then he heard Blore coming across to him, his boots crackling on the debris of dry bamboo and branches. Blore was wearing jungle boots. They were short and squat, power-fully built of black leather, and they seemed suddenly to For-rester very wonderful things. They gave the fat, floppy Blore a sense of strength. And looking at them Forrester felt his own shoes, made of brown suède by a Chinese shoemaker in Cal-cutta on his last leave there, to be flimsy and stupid for what was required of them now.

The boots filled him with a certain respect for Blore, who said: 'And now what?'

'Have a look at the stream-bed,' Forrester said, 'and see which way you think it runs.'

'West,' Blore said. 'I'd looked at that already.'

'It seems odd,' Forrester said.

'I don't think so.'

'No? The Irrawaddy must be east from here.'

'This is a monsoon stream that forces its way between rock,' Blore said. 'It runs where it can. It's breaking through the weak places. It'll end up east, no doubt. But it'll go north, west, south, and every point of the compass before it does.'

'I'm sorry. Of course. I'm a bloody fool.'

For a moment Blore did not speak. Far beyond the valley sun and horizon were meeting in savage clash of purple and blood and copper, the sky above them the tenderest glowing heavenly green.

'If you're planning to walk out of here I think it's mad.'

As he spoke, Blore gave an impatient swing of his wounded arm, only remembering it with the flick of pain.

'I do think of walking out of here.'

'It's completely mad.'

'Tell me something better.'

'They have a fix on us. Sooner or later they're bound to pick us up.'

'You think they have a fix on us,' Forrester said. 'But you don't know. And how soon is sooner and how late is later?'

Blore in impatience tried once again to throw up both hands, and Forrester saw the bandaged hand jerk angrily and painfully in the sling.

'Look,' he said. 'Consider it. Think. We've enough water for three days – perhaps four, even five. We've got bags of dope, but no food. Either we sit here and drink the water and hope, or we drink the water and travel. Does that make sense?'

'It would make sense if it weren't for Carrington.'

'I'm going to carry Carrington.'

'In this heat?' Blore said. 'Under this sun?'

'We don't go under the sun. We go tonight.'

Blore made noises of protest that Forrester did not stay to hear. He was already half-way across the valley to where Carrington lay before Blore caught up with him again.

'Carrington ought to be consulted in this.'

'Carrington has no option.'

'It's entirely your responsibility,' Blore said.

'Responsibility – hell. I'm going to tell him now.'

They walked together, not speaking again, to the place where Carrington lay. In the short twilight, strong with the golden-bronze afterglow of sunset, the face of the navigator seemed as if carved from yellow bone. He grinned up, eyes unamused and dark, as Forrester came and squatted beside him.

'How now?'

'Cooler. Not bad.'

'Listen,' Forrester said. 'We're walking. Tonight.'

Carrington did not speak.

'It's quite simple. Marches of half an hour – then rests of half an hour. I'm going to carry you.'

'It's completely mad,' Blore said.

'Blore says it's mad. What do you say?'

'I don't know,' the boy said. 'You can't carry another bloke as easy as all that.'

'Look,' Forrester said. 'I'm the champion bloke-carrier of all England.'

He saw Carrington smile, and was glad.

'All you have to do is try to sleep from now till nine.'

'I still say it's completely mad,' Blore said.

Across the valley now the sun had completely gone and from the horizon of low scrub, already colourless, the deep rim of purple haze had swollen upward, pale rose at the expanding edges, like a flowering cloud. Between the men and the burning plane, smouldering with scarlet angles of startling fire against the dark slopes of dwarf forest, the grey sand had more than ever the look of a small dead sea.

'And think up some good stories,' Forrester said. 'We can tell them as we hop along.'

14

They began to walk westward down the valley that night about half past nine. In the yellowish-rose light of a moon that burst ripely above the black cutch trees covering the low hills behind them the sand had fantastic brilliance, the rocks all about it like humps of ebony, the scattered stiff scrub like bushes of dusty steel. Forrester and Blore had tied the bush towels like loose pads about Carrington's legs, making the ties with handkerchiefs and spare boot-laces from Blore's belongings. Then Forrester slung the bag, the water-bottle and the gas-mask case across Blore's shoulders and helped him fix the webbing and the revolver about his waist. After that they got Carrington into a sitting position, with his legs apart, and Forrester knelt down between them, on one knee, like a runner getting set for a race. Then Carrington put both arms over Forrester's neck and Forrester stood up, Blore holding Carrington from behind so that he did not fall. By moving deftly and quickly Forrester kept the balance of the two of them well forward and in another second he was upright and holding Carrington's legs about the knees, lightly and strongly. 'Sit upright,' he said. 'As high as you can. Imagine I'm a camel or some damn thing.' Carrington did not answer or make a sound.

'I'll walk in front,' Blore said.

'It's exactly nine-thirty-five,' Forrester called after him. 'We'll stop in half an hour.'

As he walked forward after the figure of Blore, more floppy and ponderous than ever in the moonlight, he saw the shadow of himself and Carrington elongated and queer in the bright creamy sand, like the silhouette of a bat. Blore was about twenty yards ahead. He decided to watch the space before Blore and the black edge of the shadow as a guide, keeping it always at the same distance. Carrington was not heavy. There was some awkwardness in the heavily bandaged legs, but after a time he locked his hands across his waist, so that his arms were angled into greater stiffness and strength. And as he did so he decided not to think of walking or carrying Carrington or of anything connected with these things. He decided to force his mind completely beyond the world of the valley and the physical action that would take him across it. He would deny himself, and so justify himself, by the trick of living in memory. And in this way he began to think of Harris and Miss McNab and the girl as he had known them for the past three days, going back to the moment when Harris had found him by the pagoda, watching the lizard. In a few minutes the journey he was making was not the journey across the barren yellow valley in the moonlight with Carrington on his back, but the journey in the jeep with Harris, along the dusty bullock tracks and out to the plain where small brown laughing boys fell from the jeep in the dust, shrieking under the shade of palms, banana and tamarind trees, fat, creamy, trouserless bellies quivering with joy.

He must have gone on like this for ten minutes or so, walking in a half-dream, not conscious of the weight of the man on his back, when he heard Blore in front of him shouting. Forrester saw his fat face turned round, white in the moon.

'Sort of gully here! Look out! I'd better help you.'

Forrester came to where Blore was standing on the edge of a low ravine that sank to a depth of ten or twelve feet down steep banks of shale that were reddish-black in the now stronger, whiter light. This ravine had been carved by the fury of monsoon water almost diagonally across from the valley-side. It met the main stream bed at a sharp angle under long muscles of ribbed shale and sand.

'Doubt if we'll get across,' Blore said.

'Walk behind me.'

'This is mad. You're liable to fall and then you'll both be hurt.'

'Don't keep saying it's mad. Get behind me. Steady me.'

'Much of this,' Blore said, 'and you'll be mad.'

'Shut up!'

He went slowly down the short slope of the ravine, digging the heels of his shoes into the crumbling strata of loose sand and shale. He heard Blore floundering behind him, jungle boots slipping. The far side of the ravine came down at a shallower angle; and carried by the impetus of coming down the steeper side he went straight up it, driving his feet hard into loose sand, Blore pushing him from behind. At the top of the slope he felt the first edge of his strength break; against the weight of Carrington and the gravity of the slope his knees seemed suddenly like sponge. The weight of Carrington became very dead, pulling him back, and then at the crest of the ravine he pushed his head forward as if there was an invisible cord just in front of his face. He made a frantic effort and pushed against it; and it was as if the cord, bearing the weight of Carrington, bit itself across his mouth, so that he could grip it with his teeth and pull himself free to the level sand.

For some seconds he staggered wildly about the edge of the ravine, his balance gone, his breath coming very fast. The rocks and scrub seemed to hurl themselves darkly together down the valley in a sickening avalanche. His strength seemed to have oozed through his mouth, leaving it scorched and dry, and he felt for a moment that if he stood still for only the fraction of a second he would fall down.

He pulled himself straight with a tremendous effort that drew the cords of his neck painfully rigid, like wire; and then he began to walk forward again. Sweat had begun to run down his forehead and into his eyes in a bitter stream and he could not wipe it away. Behind him he heard Blore muttering long protests that he had not the strength to answer.

All the time Carrington did not speak a word. He clung silently to Forrester like a child being carried half asleep to bed, too tired to protest any longer. And as he realized it Forrester felt a return of strength. The fact that he needed strength for two persons suddenly seemed to give him fresh confidence and resource. He shut his mouth. By sucking at his tongue he drew a little moisture into it. He wetted his lips and for a second, even in the warm tropical night air, they felt cool and comforted. Behind him he heard Blore calling, in the same rather pompously aggrieved voice that had once told him the heat of the Burma summer had not begun, that he ought to rest. He did not answer.

He felt glad now that Blore was behind him. Nothing moved in front of him except the bat-shaped shadow. It gave him a sense of freedom, almost as if he and Carrington were alone. Soon his breath and strength came back to normal and the sweat was almost cool on his face. After the long dry season the sand was very hard, and sometimes extended in broad rock-less stretches for fifty yards or more, so that he found it as easy as walking on a seaside shore. Across these stretches he found a stumbling sort of rhythm coming into his stride. He rolled a little as he walked, keeping Carrington's weight forward, trying at the same time to step lightly. And all the time his determination grew. It hardened into conviction that he was never going to give up. He was not going to be beaten by heat or dust or thirst or weakness. The fanatical pig-headedness that had sent him out over and over again in an effort to get himself killed was now going to keep him walking on and on in an effort to keep himself alive.

In this way he walked on for the rest of the first half-hour. For the last five minutes of it he was a little troubled as to how he would get Carrington down. Blore was thirty or forty yards behind. Rocks were strewn everywhere more thickly now. Here and there in the moonlight they lay with the curious contortions of dead men.

He was struck then by a sudden idea and spoke to the boy. 'We land in two minutes,' he said. 'I'm going to find a rock and let you down on it. O.K.?'

There was no answer.

'Carrington!'

He felt himself startled by the awful fear that the boy had died.

'Sir?' the boy said.

Forrester felt a sense of something greater than relief after fear. He touched one of Carrington's hands. It was warm and living.

'Are you all right up there?'

'Yes.'

'Hear what I say?'

'Yes. I was half asleep though.'

'As soon as I see a rock I'll set you down.'

'Fair enough,' the boy said.

Rocks of more violently contorted shapes now stretched thickly across the valley, which had become narrower by forty or fifty yards.

'Going into reverse,' Forrester said. He stopped in front of a rock about three feet high and then, backing gently on to it, set Carrington down, stooping under until he could slide gently back to the rock.

'O.K.?' he said.

'Fine.' Carrington swung his legs gently over until the rock supported them.

Forrester stood upright. His shoulders were stiff. He eased them by working them up and down, like a boxer. Blore was still twenty or thirty yards away, looking more than ever like an overburdened crab against the moon.

'I'm an awful bloody nuisance,' Carrington said.

'Wrap up,' he said. 'I've just got my second wind.'

'God!' Blore said.

He lay on the sand with the clatter of a soldier piling arms. He began rubbing his right foot.

'What's wrong?'

'Confounded rock. Twisted it over.'

'Painful?'

'Not too bad. Awkward, really.'

'Take your boot off.'

Blore, fat and encumbered, tried to bend forward to his feet.

'I'll do it,' Forrester said. 'Lie back and rest.'

Forrester began to unbuckle the jungle boot.

'Lie right back.'

Blore slowly lay back, his face upturned to the moon. Forrester took off the boot and rolled the sock below the ankle, feeling the bone tenderly with his fingers.

'No swelling there,' he said. 'Just corns.'

Blore, unamused, lay looking at the moon.

'A little support won't hurt it,' Forrester said. 'Better bandage it now.'

He took out his handkerchief and folded it into a triangle and bound it tightly over Blore's ankle. There was hardly enough

160

support, but it was the best he could do. He rolled back the sock and then rested on his haunches, wiping his face with his sleeve.

Suddenly, looking at Blore's face in the moonlight, he was surprised to see that the moon lay over on his left hand. It meant that they had changed direction and were going a little southward. He felt excited. And then as he realized it he decided to keep silent about it. If, in an hour or two, the change held good it would mean very much more to men who were tired.

He got up and walked over to Carrington. The boy, sitting listlessly, still seemed to be gripped by the numbness of delayed shock. And looking at him and thinking of Blore, almost as fanatically opposed to the idea of walking as he himself was fanatically in favour of it, Forrester saw that his own strength was not important now. He had no illusions about his own strength. Somewhere deep inside himself there was contained an unexpendable core of endurance, linked in his mind with the thought of four or five hundred women marching up the typhus-ridden Irrawaddy road from Rangoon, spurred on in stinking heat and dust by the fiery fanaticism of Miss McNab with her mahogany dyed hair and the emblem of a crocheted table-cloth. What he himself had to do now seemed, beside that journey, very simple.

Thinking it better not to speak to Carrington, he sat down under the rock. He rested his back against it, his legs out stretched. The stiffness of his shoulders had eased and he shut his eyes. In the night air there was no movement and from all down the valley and across the low stunted forest there was no sound. An immense silence covered a continent racked in all its latitudes by war. Fifty miles away men were fighting for river crossings that would open the way to the south and yet there was no echo of it in the warm, soft, windless tropical air. It was as if he and Carrington and Blore had become the final survivors of it all, cast up in the heart of a dusty and barren continent, with nothing but their wits and devotion and resource, their water and their aspirins, as the ultimate means of living.

Opening his eyes, he looked at his watch. They had been resting twenty minutes. He turned over the idea of asking

Carrington and Blore if they needed a drink of water, and then decided against it. His own mouth was dry, but not terribly dry, with the heat of afternoon, the taste of fire and the exertion of walking. He could still squeeze saliva on to his tongue.

Then as he sat there he had something like an inspiration. He remembered how, as a boy, he had gone to stay with an uncle, on a Suffolk farm, in harvest-time; and how in the August heat, in the dry eastern fields, the labourers had taught him to suck a pebble, to quench his thirst.

He crawled about on his knees in the sand. In places the rock, thin in its contorted strata, flaked off in wafers of blackish brown, and sometimes the action of water had smoothed it down to flattish tablets about the size of pennies. He put one of them in his mouth. Its neutral dryness, without taste, brought back to him in a split second the Suffolk field where he had played and worked in a summer between the wars, sucking his pebble and making straw bonds for the wheat sheaves mown at the edge of the field.

'Ready to go in three minutes,' he said. The inside of his mouth was quite wet.

Blore did not answer; and Forrester felt a renewal of antagonism in the silence.

'How's my passenger?' he said.

'Fit,' Carrington said.

Forrester moved closer to the boy.

'You're doing all right,' he said. 'This thing will get your weight down and after the war you can be a jockey.'

'Tomorrow I can walk.'

'Think so?'

'Nothing to it.'

'All right. Tomorrow you walk,' Forrester said, 'and I'll ride.'

He knew that the boy would never walk. His face, almost shell-like in the moon under the still smoothed oiled hair, seemed fantastically young. He remembered all at once how he had first seen it and how, because it represented something else, he had blazed at it with stupid hatred.

Now in a curious way he began to feel attached to it. Already it had begun to be close to him. He stood upright, stretching himself. He measured an inch or two over six feet and beside him, sitting on the rock, Carrington seemed light and shrunken. He called to Blore that they were ready to go and there was an absurd clatter of accoutrements as he got to his feet and came over to help Carrington on to Forrester's back.

'Jockey up,' Forrester said. 'All set?'

'All set,' Carrington said.

'With Carrington up the Burma Derby starts with a splendid rush out in the bushes.' He heard Carrington laugh.

'I may as well say again that I think this is mad,' Blore said.

'You may as well. But it'll make damn-all difference.'

Forrester began to walk away, carrying Carrington.

'You slip on a rock and break your ankle and then where are you?'

'Ah! then where? Tell him, Carrington.'

'Giddup!' Carrington said.

'The horse is a domestic quadruped,' Forrester said. 'Sometimes given to kicking with its back legs. It can't talk.'

Walking ahead of Blore he let his mind wander once again into a state of dreamy obsession. Once more he was travelling with Harris, in the shady bullock tracks. He was dashing past the laden bullock carts, cumbersome and primeval, splashed with scarlet-purple waist-cloths and the occasional yellow jacket of a child huddled against the dust as it crouched high on the bundled belongings of the cart. All over the East the same bullocks, the same bundles and the same child were starting on their journeys. They were primeval and timeless and did not give the impression of going out on journeys that would never end, but the impression of going on journeys to nowhere at all. They seemed to be wandering nomadically into space. At night the face of the child riding on the bundles or crouched on the shafts beside the little swinging lantern would be caught in the lights of traffic passing at high speed, and for a moment the half-stoical, half-frightened eyes would have in them all the mute and wonderful fatalism of the East, deeper and older than time. And now as he thought of it he began to feel that he understood why time was of no account in a journey. All that mattered was to go on. Speed, of which he had been an exponent at something over four hundred miles an hour, had no meaning any longer.

He was the bullock, ageless and lumbering and primeval and without destination, and Carrington was the child in the cart, older than time.

He lumbered forward for ten or fifteen minutes in this way, not speaking, simply sucking the pebble in his mouth. He felt fresh and strong and Carrington did not seem very heavy. The rock was more contorted but more scattered now, and there were long stretches of scrubless sand.

Then he became aware of the moon glaring full into his face.

'Carrington,' he said. 'Jockey.'

'Sir?' the boy said. 'Horse?'

'Do some navigating for your living. Look at the moon. What do you make the course?'

He felt Carrington turning a little on his back.

'South south-east. Roughly.'

'South south-east it is.'

'That's good.'

'Good as can be. What's the odds, jockey?'

'Depends on the horse.'

'The horse is going bloody good. It depends on the jockey.'

'Evens?' the boy said.

'The horse can do better. Call it two to one.'

The few moments of banter refreshed him. They kept him from thinking and helped him forward. After them he was aware also of being much closer to Carrington. They had begun to talk the same language. He had already succeeded in filling the boy with some of his own lightheartedness.

There was not the same feeling with Blore. Once he turned and stopped for a second and looked back. Forty or fifty yards behind, Blore was dragging one foot in the sand. As he saw it Forrester had suddenly the feeling that it was not quite real. It was part of the argument against the folly, as Blore saw it, of trying to save themselves by walking. It was a piece of unspoken antagonism against him.

Looking ahead he could see by the fringe of trees how the valley, four or five hundred yards ahead, made a further turn south-eastward. He decided to walk closer to the inner edge of the trees. Presently he was walking only fifteen or twenty feet from the forest, by the fringe of stunted bamboo, the after-crop of the rains, withered and yellow and brittle now, that the floods of the monsoon would smash and sweep away. Against the darker background of the cutch-trees they looked like a palisade of ghostly spears.

He turned to look for Blore, and saw, to his astonishment, that Blore had not followed him. He was still walking alone, out in the middle of the valley, dragging his foot.

Out of the corner of his eye Forrester watched him. They were walking parallel to each other now, and almost on the same line across. He did not stop or call to Blore, and Blore in turn did not change his course. They continued in this way, separated by forty or fifty yards. Something about it struck him as extraordinarily stupid. For the first time he was unpleasantly conscious of physical uneasiness. He wanted to put Carrington down; it was not easy to go on. The buoyancy he had built up for himself suddenly became deflated and limp, his limbs watery and dull. He was not angry against Blore, but he knew that it was something that could not go on. It had to be spoken about when they rested.

Five or six minutes later he lowered Carrington down, as he had done before, slowly letting him slide from his back into a sitting position on a rock. He walked round for a few moments, working his shoulders, and then looked across the valley for Blore.

Blore did not stop. After standing for a few seconds Forrester waved his hand. It had no effect on Blore. Then it occurred to Forrester that at that distance, in the moonlight, it was impossible to see, and he shouted:

'Blore!'

Blore walked on, heavily dragging his foot.

'Blore! What the hell!'

Blore did not make a sign that he had heard. He continued walking down the centre of the valley, now more than ever crab-like with his dragged foot. He was swinging his bush-hat in his hand and Forrester could see his bald head shining in the moonlight. It gradually floated away.

Astonished, not speaking and a little troubled, he sat down under the rock, by Carrington.

'The silly bastard's walking on by himself,' the boy said.

'Can't have heard. He'll stop.'

He looked up at Carrington, who seemed quite cheerful.

'Nothing to worry about. How's the jockey?'

'Good. How's the horse?'

'Could do with a feed of cold beer. Otherwise champing the pebble,' Forrester said. 'How are the legs?'

'I'd swop them for something useful.'

'I'll see what I've got to spare in my play-box. Brown gave me a knife this morning. That's useful. Or a picture of a blonde?'

'Thanks,' Carrington said. 'I always keep a spare one handy.'

He began unbuttoning the breast pocket of his bush jacket. Forrester knew what was coming: the note-case, the wad of photographs carefully preserved.

'There she is,' Carrington said. There was only one photograph after all. Forrester saw a picture, head and shoulders, of a girl of nineteen or twenty, dark-eyed, with an expression decent, candid and tender. Masses of lovely medium dark hair fell softly and loosely about her shoulders.

'This must be the other girl,' Forrester said. 'The dark one.'

Teasing and cheerful again, he forgot Blore.

'Terribly nice,' he said.

'You're married, aren't you?' the boy said.

'No.' He suddenly found himself talking about it for the first time. 'I was.' He began by telling the boy how his wife had died. It seemed very simple now. The boy did not answer.

'All linked up with that bloody awful reception I gave you when you first came,' Forrester said. 'It's over now.' He gave Carrington the photograph back and said, 'What's her name?'

'Sonia.'

'Sorry I've got nothing better in my play-box.' He looked at his watch; there were ten minutes still to go; already he felt rested. 'What will she feel about marrying a jockey?'

'She'll love it. Every Saturday night we'll invite the horse for dinner.'

Forrester lay back on the sand. He spent the rest of the ten minutes looking at the moon. He knew now that whatever happened to them the feeling of understanding, simple and already deep and already in a sense devoted, built up by the absurd cross-banter of talk as they sat there alone, would never be broken.

He got up at last and stared down the valley for Blore. He had completely disappeared. Irritated and slightly perturbed, he remembered that Blore had with him the entire stock of water and comforts, such as they were. He conceived the unpleasant notion that Blore, stupidly driven by some sort of doubly delayed shock, might go on alone or that somehow he might get lost.

Thinking of it, unable to get the whole half-stupid notion entirely out of his head, he manoeuvred Carrington on to his back, staggering with a little more difficulty than before because Blore was not there to steady Carrington's weight behind him. Carrington said something about 'Jockeying up!' but he was really not listening and did not answer.

In the moment of starting off he looked at his watch; the time was a few minutes to eleven. If Blore had walked on, travelling at a faster pace than himself, he might have gone for more than a mile.

The moon was full on his face as he walked on, keeping a line four or five yards from the shadow of stunted bamboo. Ahead of him the valley was empty; there was no sign of Blore. Now and then an odd-shaped rock, fantastically contorted and with a glint of moonlight making deceptive highlights on the quartz-grained face, would seem like a man standing motionless, waiting for him, but after a time he gave up looking ahead and being deceived. It was all he could do now to slog his way through the finer dust, littered with bleached bamboo husk that set up light rustling echoes in the thin moon-broken forest as he walked, but he liked the sound of his feet so much that for some time he did not move outward towards the firmer, smoother sand. And when at last he did so, forced by tiring dust that swamped his feet like light sullen flour, he missed the sound and hated the vast moon-dead silence of the valley in which he and Carrington were the only moving things.

They did not speak much during the whole of that third march and it did not occur to him until they rested again that it was Carrington and not himself who was getting tired. Even then he did not realize it fully. He began to be very worried about Blore. While Carrington rested he walked out into the middle of the mainstream bed, from where he could see clearly, under a moon that was now very high, four or five hundred yards along the valley. But nothing moved there and he began suddenly to think that Blore had fallen down.

He began to walk about, shouting Blore's name. He made a trumpet with his hands and the sound of his voice had a curious rolling shell-like boom as it went down the narrow valley between the double line of forest trees.

'Blore! Blore!'

There was no answer to his shouts and no echo, and God, he thought, where is the fool? He shouted several times again, but there was no sound except his own rolling hollow voice in the emptiness and after one more prolonged deep shout he gave it up and walked slowly back to Carrington.

He saw at once that the boy was tired. He sat hunched-up and weak, his buoyancy and cheerfulness gone. Miserable, partly with pain, partly from tiredness and futility, he did not smile at Forrester, who thought bitterly now that Blore had with him all the things that would have eased that tiredness. Above all he had the water.

Not tired himself, but confronted suddenly with the stupidly unnecessary problem of it all, he lay down on the sand. Thinking first of Carrington, then of Blore, he became oppressed by the idea that perhaps he had asked too much of both of them. It occurred to him that it might after all have been better to wait, to have relied on the chances of being seen through the smoke of the fire. But gradually the conviction that it was right to travel came back. It was right because of the water. They had to beat the water. It was water that settled all his convictions in favour of walking, and now, ironically, he had no water. If Blore had disappeared, if he had fallen down and broken the Thermos flask and shaken the cork out of the water-bottle, this was the beginning of the end.

He sat up sharply. 'How fit do you feel?'

'Not too bad.'

'Could you go on? I mean now. At once. I've got a feeling we ought.'

'Blore?'

'Can't think where the hell he's got to.'

'I'm always fit if you are,' Carrington said. 'If you can do it I can.'

The words, which he was to remember several times later on, brought back his own conviction and faith in himself and what he had set out to do. To the single idea of walking was now added the single idea of finding Blore.

As he walked on, carrying Carrington, he found the moon immense and very dazzling on his face. He blundered once or twice as he walked. And then at the back of his mind there began to revolve the thought, vague and partly realized, that it was possible for a man to get moon-crazy under that brilliant light rather as he got sun-crazy in the heat of the day. There formed in his mind the picture of Blore wandering madly out of the moonlight, seeking relief and shade, until he was crazily lost in the low jungle, stupidly to die there without a chance of being found.

It infuriated him impotently to think that Blore could lie anywhere beyond the fringe of bamboo and never be seen. The structure of a plan for marching all night in fixed relays, originally so simple, was now broken. It began to seem remotely possible that Blore would never be found. The whole thing was maddening and grotesque in its dangerous stupidity.

It even began to seem to him that he was a little moon-daft himself. He had eaten no food since the few pieces of beef stewed with tomatoes that had been called lunch, and now he began to feel the emptiness of his stomach floating upwards, having a curious light-headed effect on his brain.

In his preoccupation with water, hunger was something he had not thought about. In the heat of the East he had never felt like eating much. Now he began to feel not only physically hungry, but brain-hungry. His brain began to grope round, alert and voracious, for things to feed on. His head felt vacuous and large and his brain was a small animal waking inside, famished and greedy and wandering about, fretting for food.

He experienced this curious sensation of light-headed brain hunger for the entire relay of walking. It passed when he sat down. There was still no sign of Blore and the only thing that comforted him was the moon. It had swung well over to his right hand.

After ten minutes' rest he got Carrington on to his back and began to go forward again. This time he locked his hands hard over his stomach. It seemed to compress and then destroy the feeling of emptiness. He was able to pull himself together again, to forget the sensation that his brain was a little animal, strange and ravenous, wandering in turbulent hunger. He was able to talk to Carrington once more, in the old bantering way.

'How are the odds?' he said.

'Two to one. Two for us and one for Blore.'

'Convalescence is doing you good.'

'Say convalescence again.'

Because of the pebble he spoke as if with a mouthful of ripe plums.

'Convasch – convasch – ' he began, and both of them began laughing.

'Shut up for God's sake,' Forrester said, 'I shall swallow my pebble.'

Carrington sat up a little, coughing the last gust of laughter out of himself, and then was silent. He remained silent for perhaps half a minute and then gave a violent exclamation.

'For Christ's sake, for Christ's sake – look!'

Forrester stopped, staring ahead. The boy was frantically pointing with his two hands. And Forrester saw not Blore, as he half expected, but something else. He understood why the boy was so frantic and why he was using both hands.

Two hundred yards ahead of them the valley split into a fork. Two valleys branched out now like the arms of a catapult, the forest a dark triangle between.

'This is something they didn't brief us about,' he said.

Gently and in astonishment he lowered Carrington down.

15

He made Carrington comfortable under a rock, propped up, facing the two valleys. Then he tied a handkerchief to a rod of bamboo, like a flag, and stuck it in the sand. It would mark the place for him. Blore had to be found.

'I'm going to search each valley for an hour,' he said. He reasoned that Blore could not be more than half an hour ahead. 'Get some sleep if you can.'

'No,' the boy said. 'I think I'll have a cup of coffee and watch the crowds go by.'

'Fair enough. Two nice streets here.'

'So long,' the boy said. 'I'll call them Regent Street and Piccadilly.'

Forrester walked away, looking at his watch: it was twenty minutes to twelve. A hundred yards ahead years of flood water had piled up, at the junction of the valleys, a mass of bamboo and branches and bone and rock. This sun-scorched and bleached mass extended up the main valley like a white arrowhead. He decided to take the valley to the left. Long reaches of flat white sand smoothed by the torrent of monsoons spread out for three or four hundred yards, clear of rock, and it was not until he had walked a hundred yards or so along it that it suddenly came to him that he was behaving like a fool. Anxiety had made him forget that Blore would leave some mark of himself in the sand.

He began to explore the left-hand valley for tracks, going crossways over to the outer edge, by the short fringe of bamboo, then back again, then over to the centre, by the piled barrier of flood wreckage that lay like a breakwater of skeletons dividing the valleys. Then he walked for some distance under the barrier itself. There was no sign of Blore's footmarks and finally he climbed up the barrier, pulling himself up by tree roots that broke dustily in his grasp and so over the mass of debris pressed by the force of water into a solid promontory twenty or thirty feet high.

At the top of it he stood and looked down the valleys, then back, in the direction where Carrington lay. He could see no sign of Blore. He could not see the handkerchief he had tied to the bamboo rod to mark the place where Carrington was; and for a moment he felt uneasily and awfully alone. He felt himself shocked and stupefied by the enormous solitude and silence of the place, the starkness of it under the moon, the terrible deadness, the breathless white air, in its own way as dazzling and harsh as sunlight. He hated the glitter of sand against the dark body of forest and on the outcrops of massive sandy shale that was like the dead glare of salt, and the fact that everywhere there was no breath of sound.

And suddenly also he hated Blore. He gave up the idea of the man being moon-struck and wandering off half-crazily alone. The whole thing became a monstrously idiotic folly.

The anger of it drove him down the other side of the barrier and out on to the level sand at the bottom and forty or fifty yards across it at a run. All his earlier anger against Blore, blind and ferocious and madly irritating, came back. He wanted suddenly once again to hit out at the stubborn and stupid smugness of the man. He wanted to hammer him into a cold sense of the reality of what they were up against, the selfish idiocy of their not sticking together, the colossal folly of playing the fool by going off alone with the water. And in his anger he began yelling, 'Blore! Blore! You poor silly bloody clot! Where are you? Blore!' His voice had an unreal and pantomimic sound in the empty valley as he repeated Blore's name. 'Blore! Blore!'

And then across the line where he was running he saw Blore's footmarks. The sight of them stopped him dead. He stood panting deeply. There was something wet in the palm of his hand. It was the pebble, wet with spit. He could not remember taking it out of his mouth as he ran. He put it back into his mouth and stood looking down at the tracks. He could see where Blore had dragged his foot, making a furrow, and then the direction of the tracks, going away up the valley.

He began to walk after them. He was sweating after running.

172

Now he felt tired too, not tired from hunger or exertion or from wandering about the depressing dead solitude of the place, but from the simple frustration of anger. He was angry and yet he knew that it was no use being angry. All the folly of Blore could not be cured or defeated or washed out by anger. It was not so simple as that.

'Blore!' he shouted. 'Blore!' He cupped his hands and let the sound swing out, trumpet-wise, up the valley.

The silence was so deep and breathless and deadly still that he could have heard a whisper in answer. After waiting a second or two he went on. The tracks showed no sign of changing course. They continued straight up the centre of the valley, which had widened twenty or thirty yards from the fork. Its level seemed too to be falling now and soon it began to be broken cross-wise by shallow declivities of dark shale. One of these dropped like a black-red shelf, two or three feet deep, smooth at the water-edge, crustily jagged like rusty steel underneath, across the entire width of the stream-bed, and he could see where Blore had jumped down from it, leaving the mark of his fall bludgeoned in the sand.

He stood for a moment or two on the edge of it and looked round. He shouted several times, but there was no answer and once more he was caught up, half-petrified, by the deadness, the shocking whiteness of harsh moonlight on blistered rock, the grotesque skinned branches like ash-grey skeletons dammed into pyres, the vast moon-silence in which his voice bounded about, puny and tinny and mocking itself, like a celluloid ball that could find no rest. All the time he pressed back his anger. And then, unreleased, it gradually hardened into determination: determination to find Blore, to put things right, to go on, to make a fresh plan, to keep to it, to defeat the things they were up against, so that now as he went on again, mechanically shouting at intervals and stopping and listening for the answer that did not come, he found energy and strength and faith once again hardening over his discouragement like a fanatical thin light shell.

About a quarter of a mile farther on he reached a new shelf of rock. The undershelf was hollowed out by water until the upper edge hung out like a slate cave. Stretching right across the

173

falling valley, it could form a waterfall of six or seven feet in the monsoon.

He stood where Blore's tracks came to the edge of it, and then called. The dark shelf of rock gave him a new feeling of isolation. It seemed to threaten to cut him off, to pitch him forward into more awful solitude. He remembered Carrington. And now he became worried by the fact that the three of them were separated, Carrington helpless, Blore lost, and himself alone between. And against the thought of it he let out a terrific yell.

'Blore!'

His voice splintered about him in determined blasphemy.

'Blore, for Christ Jesus' sake where are you? Blore! Where in hell are you? Where are you? Where are you? You poor half-sharp clot, where are you?'

His voice leapt futilely up the valley, again like a small celluloid ball bouncing about in the vast silence. And once more he pressed his anger back and waited for an answer.

To his astonishment it seemed to come from almost under his feet. Fifteen or twenty yards under the shelf of rock, half in and half out of the shadow of it, he suddenly saw Blore lying on his face. It was as if the weight of his fantastic accoutrements had overbalanced him and pinned him down.

Forrester jumped off the ledge. As he went over he felt his foot splinter the brittle shaly edge of it like the crown of a rotten tooth, and as he went forward, half-balanced, on his knees and face, he knew how Blore had got there.

He picked himself up and knelt by Blore.

'Blore,' he said. 'Blore. God, man, what the hell?'

Blore lay twisted on the sand, like a fat spill of paper, his legs one way, his body the other, his face in the sand.

'Blore, old boy,' Forrester said. 'Blore.' He spoke quietly now and tried to turn him over.

And as he did so Blore began to scream.

It was a short scream, abrupt and fierce, like the screech of a bird. It stopped as Forrester ceased touching him. It died down into a series of sharp deflating gasps.

Forrester's immediate thought then was of the water-bottle

and the flask. Incongruously it occurred to him that Blore had something of the tragic-comic look of a recruit just issued with a mass of accoutrements for service and that somehow the grotesque entanglement had been altogether too much for him and by sheer weight had knocked him down. He discovered the water-bottle intact. The case containing the flask had somehow twisted and fallen on top of Blore and now lay across the nape of his neck. Somewhere underneath was the ammunition belt and the revolver. It was only when he tried to turn Blore over a second time that he could see how the revolver had been twisted and crushed by impact up against his ribs, crushing through the thin bush jacket under the heart. Unbalanced by the arm wrapped in the sling Blore had fallen flatly, like a plank, with heavy force, on his chest and face.

Forrester unbuckled the strap of the water-bottle and slipped it from under Blore. He unhooked the sling of the gas-mask case and slipped that out too.

'Over,' he said. 'Roll over. Gently.'

Blore did not speak, and now Forrester could see him biting his lips together, fiercely, trying not to scream. He pushed against the weight of his shoulders until Blore lay on his back. Then he was able to unhook the clasp of the webbing belt, so that the revolver too came free.

The revolver made him intensely angry. Its use by people who wore it about the camp under regulation orders had always struck him as half stupid, half comic. Blore had never had any need for a revolver. No Jap had ever come nearer to him than sixty or seventy miles. It was unlikely that he would ever be able to fire it successfully or lethally even if one had and the only harm he had ever done with it at all had been to crush his own ribs. Forrester threw it angrily on the ground.

'Now let's look at you.'

Blore's hat had fallen off and lay on the sand. Forrester picked it up and tucked it under Blore's head, lifting it up a little. The big fat face, white in the downward glare of moonlight, was lathered with bubbles of sweat.

'Give you a drink,' Forrester said. He uncorked the water-bottle and tilted it against Blore's mouth. Blore took the neck of it between his loose dry lips and sucked hard, his cheeks working fatly like a man blowing a bugle. Finally he gave a great gulp, as if the water were choking him, and half-blew the bottle out.

He began at once talking with violent incoherence of what had happened. Forrester let him go on. It did not seem to him that he had any help coming from explanations. He was not interested in explanations. He simply sat there, listening, a little tired, partially exasperated, partially depressed by the collapse of a plan that had seemed by sheer simplicity to be right. And in a final flare of exasperation he cut Blore short.

'Don't talk!' He bent over him, moving sharply. 'Now.' Action suddenly crushed his impatience, making him feel intensely and almost ferociously practical. 'Where's the pain? Tell me.' He began to unbutton Blore's tunic. The arm had fallen out of the sling and he pushed the sling away. He pulled Blore's undershirt, drenched with sweat, out of the top of his trousers and up over his stomach and chest. All the time Blore did not speak and then as the undershirt came clear of the ribs Forrester could see why he did not speak. There was no need to speak. Close up under the heart a rib had buckled up, like a hinge.

'All right,' he said. 'Lie still. There's nothing there that a good sharp walk won't cure.'

He tried to put into his voice some of the light banter which he and Carrington used. The beautifully crazy and fictitious arrangement of horse and jockey had given them hope together. It had become their way of looking at things philosophically. But with Blore it did not work. The impression was always that Blore was against him; even that he was against Carrington; even that he liked that triangular antagonism, with himself on one side and they on the other.

He got up curtly. 'Lie where you are. Don't try to move,' he said. 'I'll be back.' He walked away without waiting for an answer.

He walked slowly along under the shelf of rock. At its lowest point it was a little over five feet high. He could reach comfortably over the crumbly brittle edge of it, to firmer rock, with his hands.

And now he was faced with two courses of action, themselves

terribly simple: either to take Blore to Carrington or to bring Carrington to Blore. He walked slowly by the bar of rock-shadow and tried to reason it out. Whichever had to be done must be done, he thought, before the sun rose; it would be a mad business in the heat of the day. Arguing it out with himself, one side against another, he set the job of lifting Carrington down the ledges of rock against the job of getting Blore up and over them. He set one valley against another. He hated the valley where Blore lay and it strengthened tremendously his conviction that the other was right. Then he thought of Carrington's legs, the pain, the shock after burning, the possibility of some sort of fresh disaster, and he set that against all that had happened to Blore, and in another minute, weighing one thing against another and looking at his watch and finding it already nearly half past one, he decided to take Blore to Carrington.

He spent another three or four minutes following the rock shelf as far as the edge of the stream-bed. There the shelf gradually ran out and low scrub grew beyond the fringe of short forest bamboo among flatter outcrops of grey shale. All of it, under the moonlight, had the dead greyness of something dipped in salt, the life blistered out of it by centuries of sun; and once again, as he looked, trying to see some sort of life in the impenetrable mass of forest broken only at the edges by crisp bars of light, he felt renewal of his curious impalpable terror of it, his fear at the rigid and hateful silence, his haunting uneasiness at the too brilliant and shadowy solitude.

He had a sudden longing for the sun. Back with Blore, he felt almost cold under the rock.

'Got to get you back,' he said.

'Back where?'

'We'll pack this stuff together and get you back to Carrington.'

'God alive,' Blore said. He began to moan gently, rocking his head in protest. 'God, no, what do you think I am?'

Forrester turned fiercely from collecting bag and water-bottle and revolver together.

'I think you're a bloody clot! That's what!'

'Start reviling me again. I heard you calling that all down the valley.'

'I meant you to hear.'

'All the names you could lay your tongue to. I was listening–'

'Shut up!' Forrester said. 'And sit up!'

'I can't get up.'

'You got down,' Forrester said. 'And you're going to get up. Even if you stay here and rot something has to be done with that rib.'

He put his arms round Blore's shoulders and lifted him slowly, until he was sitting upright. As Blore sat there, gasping, unable to say a word, his face wet with sweat, he unknotted the shirt that had formed the sling for Blore's hand and tied it for support about his chest.

'Now come on. Get up.'

'I can't get up. I always said it was mad. This walking.'

'Get up!' he said. 'We started walking and we're going to finish walking.'

'God – '

'Get up, for Christ's sake, can't you! Get up!'

His words seemed to give a sort of frightening impulse to Blore, who fell forward on his knees. He remained there for a second or two and then with a curious shocked jerk levered himself first on one foot and then on another. He stood for a moment dazed, hunched forward, holding his chest.

'All right?' Forrester said. 'Hang on. I'll get the kit.'

He slung the bottle and case over his shoulders and then buckled the webbing round his waist. For a second he hesitated, wanting to throw the whole stupid and useless contraption of revolver and ammunition to the ground and leave it there. Then something made him decide against it and he buckled it on.

'Now, ' he said. 'Hang on to me.'

It was four o'clock before he saw, in the first half-light of dawn and the waning moon, the handkerchief he had tied on the bamboo rod where Carrington lay. But when he called from a hundred yards away there was no answer. He was supporting Blore with his left arm as they walked, and holding Blore's right arm about his neck; and hobbling slowly together, out of step, they had something of the look of two cripples left over from a forgotten battlefield. At every third or fourth step Blore would

178

give a curious whistling gasp and stop suddenly, the pain of the rib violently sharpening, so that he could not get his breath. In these pauses Forrester called again, but there was no answer and it was not until he was forty or fifty yards away that he could see how Carrington had fallen asleep under the rock. He stopped calling then, glad he had not woken the boy. But a few moments later Blore let out a higher sharpened screech, like a scared bird, and in the same instant the boy's eyes were open, alight with shock, then a fuzzy sort of bewilderment, then joy.

It gave Forrester great hope and strength and a queer excited amusement to see him there. In a way there was, he thought, something oddly comic about the three of them. With Carrington dozily propped up under the rock, the handkerchief tied to the bamboo, and himself and Blore shuffling through the sand, the picture was of some holiday scene, with slightly distorted difference, taken at the seaside.

He halted ten or twelve yards from Carrington. Blore, heavy and shocked, was very tired.

'How's the horse?' he said. 'Good sleep?'

'Ready for breakfast. How's the marathon race? Thought you were never coming back.'

'Blore's busted a rib. I'll get him over there under the trees and come back for you.'

'Fair enough,' the boy said. 'I'll have two fried eggs and bacon, coffee and a slice of papaia with sugar.'

'Certainly, sir,' Forrester said. 'I'll have the same. With a feed of oats thrown in.'

He walked on with Blore, taking him over to the outskirts of the forest. Thinking now of the sun coming up and the need for shade, he felt pleased and wanted to laugh, and a sort of half-conscious chuckle spluttered up through his dry lips.

'I don't think it's very funny,' Blore said.

'No?'

'You know we've got no food and you talk about food.'

'That's why we talk about it,' he said.

He took Blore ten or fifteen paces under the trees, where the shade would be thick enough to break the sun. He let him slide gently down to the ground, and then propped him against the tree. He laid the water-bottle, the revolver and the bags beside him.

'I'll be back with Carrington.'

He knew that the boy would ask questions. And in the few moments of going back to him he decided what to say in answer. He would try to break down the state of antagonism, old and aggravated now by shock, that had made Blore go ahead alone in the conviction that he would be better by himself; he would tell the opposite of what he felt to be the truth about him.

'How's old Blore?' the boy said. 'Where did you find him?'

'Fallen off a ledge.' He was carrying Carrington now and down the valley, directly east, he could see the upper edge of forest fringed with an expanding crest of tender mauve grey light. 'Up the wrong valley.'

'Bats? or what?' the boy said.

'No. Nothing like that.' He searched and found refuge in the trite protective language of service. 'Good show, really. The old boy had an idea he could walk on and get help in Mandalay or somewhere. Thought it might be quicker by himself.'

'Odd,' the boy said. 'I can smell fried eggs.'

The thought crossed Forrester's mind that the boy did not believe him. He was not quite sure and did not speak again. Under the tree he let him slide gently down until, like Blore, he was propped up, legs stiffly out, by the bole of it.

Blore sat resentful of the allusion to fried eggs. His eyes were half closed. The immediate thought of banter went out of Forrester's mind. He began thinking once again, as he unpacked the two bags of Blore's belongings, of plans for going on. Every moment now the day was growing brighter. Over the forest edge the light rim of mauve, at first tender and fragile as lace, was now smokily thickening, purple and smouldering at the base, pinkish-orange at the fiery upper edge. In an hour the sun would flame clear and begin to stab down, mercilessly white and shocking, blinding them with intolerably savage and evil glitter.

He was ready for that. But before ten o'clock there were nearly five hours of comparative coolness, before the air became like furnace breath and the light like a ferocious glassy hammer, banging down. Somehow in that five hours they must get on. If they moved only a mile, even half a mile, even a hundred yards, he did not care. He saw miraculous virtues in movement. There were peculiar terrors in sitting still.

'All right,' he said. 'Breakfast and then shave.'

'Really,' Blore said. 'Shave. And what with?'

'You've got all the kit. Mirror, cream, razor, towel.'

'And water?' Blore said. 'I take it we shave first and die of thirst afterwards.'

'Use antiseptic instead of water. It's good enough. No explorers' beards on this trip.'

'Coffee smells good,' the boy said.

Blore did not speak again. He sat back against the tree, eyes sunken with tiredness, the lids brownish-yellow, half closed. Forrester unscrewed the lid of the vacuum flask and poured out half a cup of water. It was fairly cool and he gave it to Blore.

'And take two aspirins.'

Drinking slowly, Blore obediently took the aspirins without speaking. He seemed very far away and did not resent the fresh banter of the boy, who stared with mock horror at the two aspirins, white in the palm of his hand.

'Pretty rotten eggs these. No yolks.'

'Hell,' Forrester said. 'I turned them over. Didn't you see?'

'That's how I love them,' the boy said.

He slipped the aspirins into his mouth and sat sipping his ration of water.

'We had a wonderful charlady,' the boy said, with bright suddenness as if apropos of nothing at all. 'Her name was Bass. We called her Basso Profundo. She cried a lot. Her husband hit her over the head with a frying-pan.'

'Perhaps he liked his eggs turned over.'

'Eat yours. Come on. Be a good boy and eat those eggs.'

'I don't like eggs. They don't like me.'

'All right. Drink your coffee.'

Forrester took a sip of the water, leaving it in his mouth a moment, washing away the dryness. Blore was not listening.

Forrester screwed on the lid of the vacuum flask and then, cushioning his head against his two hands, lay down to rest. For about five minutes he lay there, not moving or speaking, letting his body relax flat on the sand. In that five minutes the sun came up from under a vast rim of sublime and gorgeous haze. It sprang up from behind cloudy purple hills indistinguishable until that moment from a deep band of dusky purple, consuming them with wonderful masses of salmon fire that feathered off and upward into tender orange flakes against an even more tender misty blueness of sky. He watched for a few moments in wonder tempered by awe, cruelly fascinated by the splendour of the naked scarlet ball that in three or four hours would blister his brain. It had on him already a sort of hypnotic effect, slightly fatalistic. It convinced him more than ever that they must move, that there was nothing but death in lying there, passively letting the sun burn them where they lay.

It was the first time the thought of death had crossed his mind. It did not frighten him. For about thirty seconds he let it remain in his conscious thought, unheated and quiet and in a curious way impersonal. Then he lifted it out. He took hold of it as you take hold of a silent cat that sits in a chair and is unwanted there and is firmly put beyond the door. It was replaced by the thought of the girl: not so much the thought as the direct presence of her, as if in a simple way a conception of her had sprung up with the sun. He became in a wonderful way physically aware of her young, cool, undarkened face. The frangipani blossom which she always wore in her black hair like a rosy-crimson rosette and which he remembered had fallen out on his hands as he kissed her good-bye under the cool sweet margosa tree in the dark compound, became for a few moments more living than the scarlet ball of sun. He remembered too that it stood for immortality and this image of her linked all his thoughts, for the first time since the crash, with the outside world. It restored a perspective that reached beyond the white sand, the grey scrub, the line of scorched bamboo fringing the jungle on either side of the valley. It made him think with astonishing sharpness of material things: his tent, his mosquito net, his green bath by the white pagoda where the child had killed the lizard. And suddenly, through the image of her, he was violently shaken into knowing of the essential and terrific wonder of such things. He had to get back to them. Out of the recollection of a life that had seemed three days ago fairly and hatefully intolerable there rose a panorama of things simply and cruelly beautiful. He thought also of Harris and Miss McNab. It had, of course, been Harris's idea to take him there, out to the village, with the deliberate purpose of watching him, and now he wondered what they were thinking. They too were bound up with what he had to do. Miss McNab was no fool. She had seen what was happening between himself and the girl, and perhaps Harris had seen too and had been glad. In a final clear image he saw them trying to comfort her and not succeeding and once more the thought of death was back in his mind, not as something menacing himself but menacing the young, tender, frightened heart that did not know if he was coming back. He saw her standing where he himself had stood, only four days ago.

Abruptly he got up.

'Barber open,' he said. 'Who's first?'

'I prefer not to shave,' Blore said.

He spoke with eyes still closed, rather defeatedly, as if he had half given up.

'All right,' Forrester said. 'Mister Carrington.'

'I think I'll grow a moustache,' the boy said. 'One of those. You know. Like two ears of barley.'

'Very becoming too. It'll suit you.'

'Always thought so.'

'I'll hold the mirror for you,' Forrester said.

And while the boy rubbed his face with antiseptic and then with brushless cream from Blore's glass pot, Forrester held the mirror so that he could shave. 'Very good light in this shop,' the boy said. He looked like a half-white comic clown with the cream on his chin and his sunburnt upper lip blackish-brown with dirt and sun. He fingered the upper lip lovingly. 'It'll grow fast in this heat,' he said and away behind him, in the forest shadow not touched by sun, the flash of the sun's reflection in the oblong of polished steel danced like a bird.

After Carrington had finished drying his face with the towel, Forrester began to shave, the boy holding the mirror. It was very civilized and comforting to feel wet perfumed cream on a face he had not realized was so black with sun and dust until he saw it reflected now. He too saw himself as a clown, half-black and half-white, and this in turn made the figure of Blore, sitting silent and in depressive pain against the tree, as incongruous as it could be.

Drying his face on the towel, he said, quietly and simply, without fooling or buoyancy:

'We can do one of two things. We can push on for three hours before it gets too hot. Or we can stew here.'

'Did you say stew or stay?' Carrington said.

'Stew.'

'I hate stew,' the boy said.

Blore did not speak.

'What's it to be, Blore?'

'Oh! I don't know. What's the good?'

'You'd feel better if you shaved.'

'Try our beauty treatment,' the boy said. 'Look at me. You too can be beautiful. Remove that superfluous hair. Don't let those whiskers win.'

'Come on, Blore,' Forrester said. He spoke kindly and decently, worried a little.

Blore spoke with bitterness, opening his eyes. 'My ribs ache. Perhaps they've had too many jokes to listen to.'

'This is no joke,' Forrester said. 'We've got to get on.'

'Exactly how? My rib has punctured something.'

'I don't think so.'

'It isn't your rib.'

Not speaking, Forrester began to pack up the bags. He checked the articles as he put them in. He corked the Thermos flask tightly and wrapped it very carefully in a towel. It seemed about two-thirds full.

To his astonishment Blore staggered up on his feet. He looked gaunt and a little crazy, his beard scruffy and black, his face dust-grey and tired.

'Well: I'm ready if you are.'

He stood swaying about, aggrieved, licking his lips.

'Hang on a minute. If you're travelling, travel in comfort.'

'That's the motto of this outfit,' the boy said. 'Comfort.'

Forrester took off his under-shirt. It was fairly dry now and he rolled it into a pad. Then he untied the bush jacket he had wrapped about Blore's ribs, put the shirt-pad on the rib and strapped the jacket tightly across it. 'Now put your gammy hand in your shirt and hold the whole thing in place.'

'Oh! nurse,' the boy said, 'you're so wonderful.'

'The one we really need here is Burke,' Forrester said. 'She'd give you both hell.'

'That's something we shan't be short of, thank you,' Blore said.

Blore swayed about for another second or two and then staggered forward. Forrester did not speak. He saw that Blore was determined to make a desperately brave effort to walk alone; and suddenly he saw in Blore's desire to be independent, to show himself level in resistance and courage to two younger men, who were flyers too, the entire reason for his behaviour in the night. It seemed to him that Blore was depressed by a complex that made him feel he was less in quality than men who flew.

'You're going great stuff, Blore!' he called. 'How's the old rib?'

Blore waved his free hand as he walked ahead by the curling line of low bamboo.

The sun was clear now of the distant fringe of purple hills and had lost its reddish orange fire, and by the time Forrester, with Carrington on his back, was walking after Blore the hills were no longer purple but a tender smoky-grey, more distant than ever, the sky above them hazily blue with the first lovely morning languor. He was now wearing nothing but his trousers and shoes and he could feel the sun warm on his naked chest as he walked eastwards towards it. Driving straight down the valley, catching the crystalline sand at a low angle between the shelves of glittering rock, the sun had the dazzling whiteness of the headlamp of a car flashed horizontally in his face. The small dew that had condensed like bloom on the rock face had already dried. He could see the prickles of low scrub like needles in the sun. And always, all down the river-like desert between its banks of forest, there was no sound. It had the uncanniness of a forgotten place. He remembered that he had not seen in it a single bird. And thinking of that, he recalled the great dark crows that planed above the mess-tents at the camp between the palms, waiting to swoop down and steal the dinner of some careless airman turning away out of the food-line with his plate; the vultures of the roadside, the delicate white egrets stepping like dream birds about the paddy-fields, giving life to the blistered plain, and the small green parrots, touched with yellow or blue, with their shy sprinkling flight in the pipul trees.

This absence of birds troubled him. A scorched valley bounded by stunted forest that seemed to support not much more than one kind of tree or one kind of bamboo could only lack birds because it lacked water. Birds, man, and water went together, and now when he looked at the sky, empty as far as he could see, he began to be vaguely troubled.

He decided not to speak of it, and came out of his few minutes of thinking to ask Carrington how the jockey was.

'Fine,' the boy said. 'But what the hell's up with the horse? Look where Blore's got to.'

'He's carrying less weight.'

Blore was almost a hundred yards ahead. He was dragging his foot a little but travelling quite fast.

'He's an old war-horse really,' Forrester said. 'He'll get there.'

Already he could feel the sun burning his chest. He had no hat to wear and incessant streams of sweat began to break out of his forehead and run down his face and neck and join the sweat of his naked chest and shoulders. As he went on the streams joined and ran down by the hollow of his navel and warmly and stickily down to join the sweat of his lower body.

Apart from this he felt strong and capable of carrying Carrington for half an hour. He was not thirsty. He knew that it was good to sweat. Gradually he began to get into the rhythm of walking and carrying the weight of Carrington correctly. He walked with his knees flexing, lightly, like a coolie. He even began to keep the example, the image of the coolies, in his mind. He saw them running with long flat feet, naked except for a filthy *dhoti*, along white-hot streets, thin bodies golden-pink with great sweat, and he felt he understood them now.

It was more than half an hour before he saw Blore stop walking and sit down under an overhanging tree. He felt that Blore's performance was fine. With a sort of anxious admiration he had watched him pounding and hobbling ahead, and now he was glad of the chance of rest.

Under the tree, lying flat on his back, too breathless for a moment or two to speak, he remembered he had not wound his watch.

Hearing him wind it, Blore said:

'How long do we walk?'

'I thought perhaps ten o'clock. How do you feel?'

'I've stopped thinking about it.'

'Good show. You'll beat us yet.'

They lay for some time without talking in the shade. The sun had come up with frightening speed, turning the valley into a dazzling channel of light. After some time Forrester sat up and stared ahead. About a mile ahead the valley seemed to make a turn. A shaggy lump of granitic-looking rock lay out in the stream bed like the image of a gigantic dog.

By the time they walked on again, with Blore going ahead as before, he had given up thinking of how he felt. His mind took on something of the hunger-ravaged emptiness of the day before, his brain prowling about like a greedy and fretful parasite, hunting for things on which to feed. Its hurrying and wandering fretfulness made him uneasy at first, and then he discovered the trick of watching the rock that lay ahead. It began to look more than ever like a shaggy dog lying there guarding the entrance to an opening in the forest. It encouraged him to think that it was something like a street corner and that beyond the corner the street of rock and sand and forest would change. He saw the first touch of heat haze gather like pearl-mauve mist beyond it, dissolving into one opaque band the hills and the lower sky. It began to be impossible to reckon distances. He became the victim of an illusion about the rock. It had seemed at first about a mile ahead; he felt it possible to reach it in half an hour. And then after he had carried Carrington for thirty-five minutes the rock was still ahead. He did not seem to have advanced against it at all. The illusion of being permanently distant from it sprang up and began to torment him.

Under a tree that now had something of the protection of a torn lace curtain, the three of them rested without talking, panting in short dry gasps against the rising heat. Forrester longed for the sweet thick shade of the margosa tree. Along the valley a rock glittered like a pile of minutely shattered glass and the glitter crept about it and ran up the valley like an army of silver ants. The sweat pumped out of him and would not dry on his chest, and when he looked at Carrington he no longer saw in the haggardness the beginnings of the cheerful ironic smile. Blore lay flat on his face, his head completely covered by the hat. He seemed to be pressing himself down on the sand, as if it were easier for his damaged rib. His legs were stretched wide, the toes of his jungle boots tightly turned into the sand, in the attitude of a man about to fire a rifle.

And as he sat there watching him, Forrester remembered the revolver. He had a new and splendid idea about it. With it he could kill birds. The fact that there were no birds to kill seemed of temporary unimportance against his rediscovery of the revolver as something important in the scheme of survival. He remembered reading somewhere in a magazine, in the reading-room of a Calcutta club, that in the whole of Burma there were more than eighty species of birds. There were pigeons and pheasants and quail and snipe and plover and even turkeys. The country was incredibly rich in birds to eat. His mind grasped at the fact lusciously. And the revolver, which had seemed to him an entirely useless object, now became a magnificently important thing to possess.

It occurred to him then that it ought to be cleaned. Blore was wearing it and the webbing holster had slipped round to the middle of his back. Forrester leaned forward to take it out and in a second Blore sat bolt upright, violently startled, as if the revolver had really been fired.

'What the hell are you doing?' Blore said.

'Thought you were asleep,' Forrester said. 'Thought the revolver might need cleaning.'

'It's all right. No chance of it getting rusty in this climate.'

'It's damn funny how things do get rusty.'

'What would you want it for, anyway?'

'Thought we might shoot birds.'

'What birds?' Blore said.

'Well,' Forrester said, 'you know. Just when you haven't got your gun there goes a covey of pheasants.'

'Partridges. Covey of partridges.'

'This is Burma,' Forrester said. 'Not dear old England. They go in flocks here.'

'Yes: I see them.'

'Better let me carry it,' Forrester said. 'It'll be ready in case.'

'I can carry it,' Blore said, 'thank you.'

He struggled up, first on his knees and then on to his feet, and without another word began to walk on. From where he sat against the tree Carrington watched him go with a kind of sick astonishment. The boy had not spoken a word. And suddenly Forrester was troubled by the fact that he had not taken part in that curious and half-ironical discussion about the revolver. His face was very yellow. The gaiety that had turned aspirins into fried eggs had gone completely.

'Here.' He crawled over to where Carrington was propped against the tree. 'Here. What's up! Too many eggs for breakfast?'

'Oh! God!' the boy said. 'God.'

'What is it? What's up?'

The boy shook his head queerly. Running down from his lips a cold weak shudder took away a little more of the colour of his face, leaving it greyish-yellow, like wet stone.

'Oh, Christ!' the boy said. 'Jesus.'

He made a curious frantic grab at something in the air and Forrester caught his hands. They shocked him with their coldness. The young face seemed to age intensely for a moment and then stiffen, the eyes rolling back like the eyes of a doll, catching a flash of the awful glitter from the dust beyond the tree.

And in a second the idea of the boy dying suddenly there, without warning, after all the strenuous and cheerful gaiety, struck Forrester with bewildering terror. It lasted perhaps for about another three or four seconds. In that short interval the boy fainted right away and then came to himself with a terrific convulsion of pain and was suddenly sick. In his weakness the thin bright yellow sickness spewed down over his shirt and hung glutinous and raw on his lips until slowly Carrington came to life and spat it feebly away.

The sight of the living and spewing Carrington filled Forrester with more delight than anything the boy had said in his moments of wildest fun. He felt so unutterably glad of it that he forgot to shout to Blore and tell him to come back. He remained for a second longer on the edge of the ghastly and terrorizing moment of believing the boy was dead and then swayed forward, grasping and pressing the boy's head slowly down towards his legs, holding it down for almost a minute until he began to moan gently in answer.

It was only after he had laid Carrington on the sand and wiped his face and shirt dry and clean of sickness and given him half a cupful of water from the Thermos flask that he remembered Blore. He went out into the sun and began to call him. He could see that he was half-way between himself and the rock.

'Blore!' he shouted. 'Wait. Blore!'

For about twenty seconds Blore walked on without answering. Forrester called again and once more he had the irritating and antagonistic impression that Blore was going on alone.

And then to his relief Blore turned. He stood for a moment and then waved his hand. Forrester signalled with both hands, beckoning him, and after standing briefly there Blore began to come back.

In the few minutes of waiting for Blore he sat gently rubbing Carrington's hands. The boy lay with closed eyes. His legs, crudely bandaged with the towels, had an oddly clumsy and useless look. They seemed too large for the rest of the slight sick body, and the lids of the eyes were smoky-brown.

By the time Blore arrived, sweat pouring down from under his hat as if it were soaked with water, the chances of moving on seemed to Forrester very slim, and yet he was determined to make a great effort. The renewed antagonism of Blore and the sudden feeling that Carrington was really very ill made it seem more than ever necessary to go on, even if only a hundred yards at a time, before the real heat of the day began.

To his relief and surprise Blore was very cheerful. He did not seem to resent the necessity for coming back.

'I didn't want you to go on and then I couldn't lift him,' Forrester said.

'No,' Blore said. 'That was sensible. Is he fit to go?'

'Carrington,' Forrester said. The boy opened his eyes, grinning faintly. 'How's the old jockey?'

'My guts are boiling like hell. What happened?'

'Fainted.'

'Bloody silly.'

'How are you for going on?'

Carrington gave a flat sort of smile.

'Ready when you are.'

'It's getting a little warm out there,' Blore said. 'I'll lend him my hat.'

Forrester felt touched and endeared to Blore by that unprompted offer of the hat. They succeeded in getting Carrington back into a sitting position against the tree. Once again Forrester knelt between his legs and the boy grasped him about the neck and then slowly, Forrester staggering up off his knees and Blore bearing some of the weight behind, they lifted him up. The exertion had on Forrester the effect of being slogged on the head with a heavy sack. It sent him ponderously staggering about from side to side. He felt for a moment as if he must fall down. Then he made a great effort, biting his lips, and regained his balance and began to move on. Then he remembered that he had forgotten to put a pebble into his mouth and said to Blore:

'Get me a pebble to suck. A good round one. You'd better get one too. There's going to be no stopping this time.'

He looked at his watch and saw that it was nearly ten o'clock. Out on the shadeless enclosed river-bed the sun was touched already with the white glare of noon. Ahead of him the granitic dog-like rock scintillated darkly in the rising heat-haze, creating once more the illusion of being untouchably far away. He carried the boy without saying a word except a last warning to Blore to keep close to him and not go on; and was stimulated and surprised to hear him say, 'Of course. That stands to reason,' and then to see him take step beside him, slogging heavily forward on his dragging foot, so that for the first time they were walking together, in step, side by side.

Walking in the rising heat, his head down, the strain of Carrington's weight so dead that it sucked at the cords of his neck and pulled his lower lip open and down like the mouth of an idiot, he achieved a curious state of instinctive mobility. He began to walk half-consciously, sometimes with eyes closed. It did not matter very much now whether they were open or not. There was no path to wander from and whenever he did look up there lay before him, as far as he could see through the pearl-brown haze, the same devilishly glittering and simple arrangement of sand and rock and scrub, between two changeless borderlines of straw-white bamboo. All the languorous and tender colour of the tropical dawn had gone.

There persisted all through this state of dazed and terrible stupefaction the thought of birds. He began to be aware of a kind of hunger that was like the beginnings of lunacy. He walked as if light-headed. And with the thought of birds and the lunatic sensation of hunger there went the thought of Blore's revolver. It began to be a hunger in itself. It began to be a physical obsession that in some way had to be appeased, a hot and dazzling craziness that would not let him rest. It began to hold him as frantically clenched as the paralysis of blinding light striking up from the white sand. With the revolver he could, in the cool of the evening, if ever there was an evening after the blistering bitterness of the day, shoot birds; and with birds they could eat while they still had water. After the water had gone there could be no eating. Without water he knew that eating was death. He calculated the water would last rather less than three days. After that, thirst and sun would act very quickly.

Walking half-blindly, he was not aware of reaching the rock until Blore shouted. He looked up and saw then that they were close under it. And now it had something more than the shape of a shaggy dog. It was a spur marking a break in the low escarpment of the valley on the south side. Beyond it the valley opened out. It became a mile or more wide, flat and glassy, like a lake of white grey mud smoothed by monsoon water and glazed hard by sun. It stretched pitilessly into savage distances that were without tree or rock or scrub on the south side, the last fringe of bamboo thin and withered as a clump of torn reeds.

The light coming off this skimmed flatness had a white and

murderous brilliance. It came in long waves that attacked with painful pressure his naked and stupefied eyes followed by shorter waves of dark shadow, like swift black webs spun over the retina, so that for the moment before they passed he felt that he had gone blind.

Over on his left hand, on the north side, the fringe of bamboo, with a few shorter, thinner trees, still continued. He tried to stare away into the distance on that side in order to discover how far they went, but the glazed waves murdered his power of focus and in the nearer distance the bamboo seemed to diminish to the size of scattered match-sticks and the low grey trees were consumed like shadowy wreckage in the quivering haze.

Aware of the need for some sort of decision, he staggered to a standstill. They had the choice of lying under the rock through all the heat of the day, in passive madness, or of risking the chance of shade on the north side.

Before he could speak, Blore said:

'Better get on. Better get over that way.'

He waved his left hand and did not stop and Forrester knew suddenly that there was no need to answer.

As he caught up with Blore the sun began to have a brassy beating hammer-stroke. The sky had grown colourless under the heat. He walked again with eyes closed, partly in defence against the downward stream of sweat, partly against the long white waves of painful light that threw the repeated short web of blindness across his eyes. In terror he recalled what Harris had said of sun-stroke through the eyes. He recalled too what he had said in answer, but the terror had no persistence and stabbed only for a second like a white needle and then was gone. On his shoulder he could feel the boy's head lumped forward, the brim of the hat pressed on his own head, and he endured the weight of it because he was glad of the inch or two of shade.

A few moments later he staggered and began to be aware then of a new terror: the terror of falling down. Oppressed by it, knowing that if he fell now he would never get up, he gripped Carrington more tightly and forced himself to watch his feet. Taking rather shorter steps, he felt himself draw on a new reserve of strength. He seemed for a moment to probe deep down inside himself, scraping the bone of his endurance. And then as this strength came up his hunger also came up, in new hollow abortive waves, his brain ravaging madly once again like a little ugly animal fretting for food; and with the hunger came the idea of birds and with that the renewed idea of the revolver.

He did not know how long they walked like this. The glittering and vicious waves of light skimmed off the flat mud-bed with callous persistence. They had the regularity of a diabolically flashing pendulum. Sometimes he stared at his feet and did not look up for long intervals, and then only looked up in terror of falling down. But he could never wholly escape the attending pain of dazzle and the short relief of blindness that prepared him for new pain.

During all this time they did not speak to each other. It was only when he glanced up and saw thirty or forty yards ahead of him a tree half-twisted to earth by the force of flood-water, like an umbrella overturned by wind, that he heard Blore make any kind of sound. Even then it was not coherent. It was a kind of bubbling shout. And then he saw the shade of the tree. Only ten or twelve feet wide, it seemed on that vast expanse of glittering mud like an acre of darkness. He saw Blore, just ahead of him, fall flat on his face into it like a man flopping into a pool of water. And then he himself was there too, letting Carrington slide from his back and laying him down.

And with the weight of Carrington gone from his back he could not stand up. The terror he had successfully resisted out in the sunlight, the fantastic terror of falling down and never getting up again, became a reality. He fell flat on his face. And the feeling of being able to escape at last the vicious waves of alternating light was so great that he felt no pain as he struck the sand.

They lay there through the day on the small island of shade, lying mostly face downwards, on their stomachs, to ease the swelling of hunger. With Carrington this was very difficult and by noon he had begun to roll slightly from side to side, complaining terribly and for the first time of the pain of burns.

Getting up to give him water Forrester was appalled by the

situation of the Thermos flask. It had seemed to him in the early morning to be two-thirds full. Now as he poured water for the boy he saw how he had been deceived by the inner magnification of glass. What had seemed like two cups now became less than one. He poured this out and then poured half of it back into the flask, corking the flask down and wrapping it again in the towel. In the haversack the towel had dried to the unkindly roughness of a loofah husk.

He lifted up the boy and gave him water. The dryness of his lips had become very dark. They were pouched a little, with the beginning of swellings, and on the exposed edge they had something of the blackish unhealthy shade of meat turning bad.

'Lunch,' Forrester said. His mouth felt very brittle and the effort of forcing the single syllable seemed about to split it, and he saw on Carrington's mouth the same painful sort of effort to form a smile.

The boy drank slowly. Sweat had formed veins of greyish dust on his face as it poured from under the bush-hat. Forrester took the edge of the towel and wiped them away. In Carrington's eyes there lay a yellow glitter, curiously naked and stripped of all former buoyancy, that was like a weak reflection of the horrible and deadly glitter of the smooth-skinned dust across the valley.

All afternoon this light in Carrington's eyes troubled Forrester. He felt he saw in it the first glimpse of death. He saw that soon it would not be possible to carry the boy, who began towards the middle of the afternoon to stab weakly and desperately at the dust with his feet, as if trying to smash the tight constriction of pain. He gasped with small broken noises, trying to get his breath. Sometimes Forrester comforted him with a fresh sip of water and then by loosening the bandages about his legs and pouring a little of the antiseptic on them and tying them up again more loosely. Then he lay back on his stomach, pressing it in the dust, and tried to get back the breath he had lost in that small exertion. It came back to him always in horribly bitter waves. It drew in through his swollen mouth a new acidity of salt-sharp dust that burned into the cracks on the outer edges of his lips; and then the breath itself passed into his mouth like hot vapour, cruel as the breath of burning ashes, acrid and suffocating, so that in terror he had to turn over on his back and grope for breath that way, upward, to keep himself from choking.

All the time he fought for breath in the heat of mid-afternoon and thought of the diminishing and hazardous glitter in Carrington's eyes, Blore lay on his face, not moving or speaking. He had been too exhausted to unbuckle the webbing that held the revolver. Now it lay against the small of his back. And with his hand clutching at the dust above his head and the revolver uselessly buckled about his waist he had something of the attitude of a man instantaneously shot in battle. The identity of the rather pompous, meticulous, argumentative officer, the man who had not felt the early summer heat of the plain, had gone from him completely. He had become a dumb and anonymous figure of blind anguish. The heat seemed to have beaten out of him the last of the character that, in the night, had sent him on with violent independence down the wrong valley, alone.

And was it the wrong valley? Towards the end of that afternoon Forrester began to wonder. Through the daze of thirst aggravated by repetitions of his early obsession about birds and the revolver, there began to grow in him a savagely mutinous sort of doubt. Gradually it began to haunt him. And presently it began to be borne on him, through the last spiteful burnished glitter of the late afternoon, that soon, when the moon was up again, he ought to go back.

The shock of this thought made him sit weakly upright. The awful idea of slogging back, alone, to the point where he had found Blore under the ledge of rock seemed painfully preposterous. Under the net of shade the heat had bludgeoned him to jelly, as if there had been no shade at all. Until the heat died there could be no thought of walking. And yet he was haunted by the idea that something had gone wrong. The time-table by which they were so lightly to walk so many miles a day was now like a wickedly impossible dream. They would never keep it. It remained only to haunt him. Wretchedly he began to think that not only had everything gone wrong, but that he himself, obstinate and antagonistically opposing Blore, had been responsible.

He lay down again, turning his face from the sun that had now begun to whip in low, like a savage sword-cut, pressing back the shade. He was terribly thirsty and could not suck the pebble. There was no saliva on his tongue and his lips were heavy and parted like the lips of a frog, scorched and breathless and gasping for air in the sun.

He lay there for about an hour, tormented and haunted into a kind of light-headed stupor. Once he rolled over and crawled back to follow the receding edge of shade and then lay mindlessly flat on his face again. And in this state, tortured beyond coherence of thought, he drifted light-headedly into a dream-maze of vivid activity with the revolver. He was walking in the low forest scrub, looking for game. Bright scarlet and gold little jungle fowl, perky and proud and dainty as they fed among the dry low bamboo, danced elusively and without sound forty or fifty yards ahead of him. Although walking quite fast, he could never catch them. Presently they seemed to grow much larger. He saw the flash of trembling grey gills. He knew then that they were pheasants, and he held the revolver in his hands, ready to shoot when he came near. The metal of the handle was warm from the long fiendish afternoon and he could feel it perfectly. Then the pheasants rose in a little flock, diminishing prettily, becoming bright banana-green, a flock of small parrots, smooth and lively with small gill-arrows of sky-blue, disappearing like a quick cloud of emerald smoke into the leaves of a tree as dark and shining as the leaves of the margosa tree by Harris's dispensary in the village compound. Then suddenly there were no parrots. There was only the dark cool tree and himself sitting beneath it, waking out of that first tired doze to see the girl smiling down at his sleepy astonishment and Harris laughing fatly in the cane chair. There was only that first dream-surprise of seeing her from which he had never quite recovered: his first step towards a world of confidence and a desire to live.

A moment later he was within firing distance of the parrots and then suddenly something hit him in the back.

'Give it back to me! Give it back! Give it back!'

In the instant of being struck from behind and of hearing Blore's voice he realized two things. He knew that he really had the revolver; he knew that he was really walking through the broken scrub beyond the tree. He could not remember how the dream had so suddenly become a reality. He became supremely astonished to find Blore hitting him in the face. The blows were angry and weak and there was blood on one of Blore's hands, and the hand was like soft wet jelly on his face. Continually Blore was sobbing something about giving back the revolver. His mouth was dark and swollen and its monosyllabic agitated gabble gave it an awful fluttering open grin.

After the first moment of astonishment he tried to grasp Blore by the shoulders. He discovered that the older man had a kind of fatuous strength. He struck out with lolling fat hands. His face had an enraged and fanatical brightness about it, senselessly dark about the eyes and mouth, the skin yellow with sweat.

Forrester could not feel the blows that Blore swung out at him. There was only pain in trying to shout with his cracked mouth, out of which he made gabbling stupid sounds. He succeeded at last in getting Blore by the shoulders. At the same time Blore seized the revolver and after staggering weakly for a moment or two, locked together, the two of them fell down.

Because of his locked arms and because Forrester was behind him Blore fell heavily on his face, the weight of Forrester full on top of him. As he fell he let out a frantic scream of pain. It was like the gurgle scream of someone waking in a nightmare. It seemed to crush itself out as Blore buried his mouth in the dust.

He lay like that for some moments and Forrester had no strength to touch him. It was all he could do to roll away himself. And as he rolled away and lay on his back he felt the breath in his lungs trying to break out. It split through his ribs in great tortured upheaving gasps of pain. The sun came down through the flimsy web of grey shade and hit with the bitterest blinding whiteness at his naked and exhausted face, but he did not care. There was no way of moving. His breath would not come back. He was choking and there was nothing he could do. With terrible desperation he tried to turn over on his face, but the effort and his strength were not enough and he simply lay where he had fallen, letting the sun scorch him murderously, the air scalding as steam as he drew it down through his swollen mouth.

After some long interval he found himself on his knees. The colour sense had been killed in his eyes. There was only a vast expanse of dead whiteness about him and in front of him the black corpse-shape of Blore. The brutalized retinae had lost their power. He could not even accept now the little web of shadow that was spun at the end of the long, vicious waves of light.

Presently he had strength enough to see that Blore was alive. He crawled and bent over him. Then he discovered that he still had the revolver in his own hands. Some of his own life came back in a spark of anger as he dropped it, and then he spoke to Blore.

'Blore,' he said. 'Blore.'

The two words, dropped out of his mouth like words spoken by an idiot without the power of muscular coordination, were all he could gather strength to say. Blore did not answer except by trying vainly to focus his eyes. His fight for breath was dying out in a slow, long agony of upheaval. His tongue was stuck in his mouth and seemed as if it must choke him.

With a great effort Forrester raised him up. The movement startled Blore into fresh pain. The pain in turn seemed to split the stoppage in his throat. With a great retching gasp he sucked in breath. And after some minutes he could sit by himself upright. The hand he had cut in the crash was swollen and bright like a lump of decaying meat. Forrester saw him slowly raise the other hand and hold it to his chest, under his bush-shirt. It remained hidden there for about twenty seconds and then slowly Blore drew it out. It was covered with blood.

Forrester undid the shirt and saw how, in the fall, the broken rib had twisted itself, breaking the flesh. The bright blood on both of his hands seemed to fill Blore with terror. He stared at them and then up at Forrester with an expression of dark idiocy. He seemed to have lost hope. And all the time, as Forrester sat there, he had nothing to say.

Presently Forrester had strength enough to crawl back to Carrington. He was surprised to find that he had walked fifty or sixty yards away from him.

To his astonishment Carrington was cheerful and could talk. The struggle with Blore, the helplessness, the exhaustion and the fight for breath had played on him a ghastly trick of deception. He had been prepared for Carrington, like himself and Blore, to be half dead. He felt that all three of them had come very near the end. But now Carrington had the strength to smile and could frame a word or two of the old half-mocking banter. Lying in the shade of the tree he was incredibly and miraculously living.

'How's old horse?'

Forrester heard the words with startled affection. He wanted to jabber impossibly with relief. He made weak and abruptly grateful signs with his hands, trying to smile.

He crawled over to where the water-bottle lay with the haversack. The cork was very tight in the bottle and for some moments he was too weak to get it out. Then when he got it out he was too exhausted with exertion to take a drink. He sat once again helpless and gasping. His sweat streamed down over his hands, on to the bottle and even into the water.

At last he wetted his lips. He put back the cork and slung the water-bottle over his shoulder and began to crawl back to where Blore lay. From under the tree the boy called out, quite strongly, something that sounded incredibly like 'Hurray for the Burma Derby,' and Forrester felt an amazing desire to laugh at himself slowly crawling there on the hot dust, like a broken-down horse on its knees.

He had crawled like that, for about twenty yards, oddly encouraged by the last astonishing remark from Carrington under the tree, when he heard the revolver fire. He ducked his head instinctively down, as if Blore, impelled by a new and curious burst of antagonism, had really begun to shoot at him.

And then the shock of it made him stagger to his feet. He got up and with incredibly light strength began to run. It did not seem to require any kind of physical effort to run the other thirty or forty yards, between the light undergrowth of the scrub, to where Blore lay.

When he got there he discovered in himself a wonderful and terrible thing. His colour sense had come back. The sand was no longer dead white but gold with sun and in the distance, beyond the thin trees, there was the first tropical touch of evening purple, mounting to bronze, against the hills.

On the ground in front of him all the lower face of Blore was scarlet. He saw this ghastly thing as part of the bright dream of birds that had first brought him wandering out there with the revolver. He could not believe in the dead, self-shot Blore. And then the true ghastliness of it hit him with terrible revulsion. He saw the face of Blore moving, not dead but cruelly and fantastically still living, starkly conscious and aware of living and waiting for the death that was too slow to come.

After another second of watching him Forrester picked up the revolver from where it had fallen. And in that moment a curious thing happened. The colour sense was killed again in his eyes. Mercifully there was nothing to fire at except the black corpse-shape of Blore, without identity, in the white sand.

16

In the hard light of mid-afternoon Mr Prang was ferried over from the settlement to the other shore of the river, taking his bicycle with him. The tireless wailing song of the ferrymen as they padded up and down the flat ferry deck had no meaning for him and was only a means of impatience as he stood there in the heat, holding the bicycle and watching the boat-poles cleave against the snow-green currents that took the boat on a course of long angles down the dazzling stream.

He was impatient to see Mr Fresta: to whom the umbrella had been joyfully lent as an excuse for a second meeting. Mr Prang simmered with fervid admiration for the tall English pilot who was not too proud to kneel down before the children of the settlement and take their flowers. To Mr Prang he had appeared, kneeling there with Anna in the dusty compound, as a man of tenderest humility. Here, thought Prang, there were no white prejudices, no racial superiority, no British imperial humbug, but only humanity. Inspired by it, he had talked to the children that very afternoon of the flying man who had come from very far away and had honoured the little school by eating water-melon on its steps.

As the ferry came into the other shore Mr Prang lifted his bicycle carefully down on to the sand and wheeled it away ahead of the bullock teams waiting to disembark. Riding away along the river path, between the fawn-green fringe of bamboo, he did not miss the umbrella. It did not seem to him viciously hot. Certainly it was not as hot as Rangoon or as the days of the journey he had taken from Rangoon, cycling most of the way, three years before. A little wind from the river was already turning deliciously to and fro the papery fronds of bamboo and in an hour the lovely coolness of it would cover the plain.

In ten minutes he would be at the village; and there he would inquire from Anna and Miss McNab whether Fresta had the possibility to arrive. He had great hopes that Mr Fresta would already have had the possibility to arrive, or if he had not had the possibility that he had not already brought the umbrella. To get the umbrella back and not to see Mr Fresta would, he thought, be a terribly unfortunate thing.

Two hundred yards along the track the path went deep between the low forest of bamboo cane and suddenly as he cycled through it Mr Prang was sharply surprised by someone sitting beyond it, on the white strip of shore.

He got off his bicycle at once and leaned on it and called:

'Anna,' he said. 'Good afternoon.'

He spoke in English because he was very proud of the English he spoke and because he was prouder still, and very envious, of the English spoken by the girl.

'Anna!'

The girl did not answer and Mr Prang, leaning on his bicycle, waited. All his life he had felt a kind of academic affection for her. There were plenty of girls in Rangoon as lovely as she was in that pale aristocratic way, but he did not know one who spoke English so purely and so well. The English he spoke was the English of students and it was because he hoped to change that once and for all that he cherished the dream of going to London and working there; but the English of Anna was as English as the English of Mr Fresta, and he could think of no more exact or wonderful praise.

'Anna, I had somewhat of a spare hour and I was biking over,' he said.

He knew very well that that sentence was wrong, but it was the best he could do. Sometimes he found it hard to think in English. There were words, like somewhat and possibility, that haunted him, but three years under occupation, with no one daring to speak a word of English and no English to be taught in the little school, had cut short the refinement of study. When he got to England such words would have to go; he would have to be ruthless; it would all be different there.

The girl stood looking at the water, her face turned away. What he admired also about her was her grave poise and refinement; you did not get that in many girls. Her beauty was sometimes almost aloof, and then he felt, especially if at the same time she spoke English, a sense of grey and terrible inferiority that all of a sudden took away his power of words.

Suddenly he felt it now. Without warning it came like a grey web over his brain and made him mute. He could not call to her. He saw too that she had begun to walk away, still staring at the water, and as he watched her he was overcome by the depressive thought that she did not want to speak with a man who called himself a student of Far English. A fresh grey shiver of inferiority seemed to come over the glittering water and wrap about his mind.

'Anna,' he said again. 'Hullo there.'

He waited for another moment, but she did not turn and finally he got on his bicycle again and rode unhappily up the path, through the deep bamboos that had begun to sway at the tips with the wind of late afternoon. Abruptly he felt something about the day to be ill-omened; a terribly unfortunate thing. The springy confident joy of the journey to see Mr Fresta was punctured; the excuse of the umbrella seemed obvious and idiotic. All his buoyant ardour to conquer English died in him ashily and London seemed tragically unattainable and far away.

He resisted the idea of turning back and rode on far under the bamboos across the shadeless plain. The thought of cycling all the way to the town to see Mr Fresta lost all its charm in the hard white light of sun.

In the village he left his bicycle propped up against the gate of the compound and walked across the dust just as Miss McNab came out of the house. She had no hat on and the loose heavy mass of her dyed mahogany hair hung scraggily down, as if she had not brushed it all day. As he saw her Mr Prang's power of English came back. He said several good afternoons, and then:

'I had the possibility to spare some time and I came to exchange the umbrella lent to Mr Fresta.'

Miss McNab did not speak.

'Mr Fresta is not here?'

Once again she did not say anything and Mr Prang, looking

more closely at her, had suddenly the idea that she had been crying.

'The umbrella is here perhaps?' he said.

Miss McNab did not speak.

'Mr Fresta is a fine gentleman and it will be everlasting honour to have a second word with him.'

Miss McNab stared down at the dust. Mr Fresta? She stared in a dream until across at the fence some children rang the bell of Mr Prang's bicycle and the sound startled her into looking violently up.

'Mr Forrester has gone,' she said.

'To the town?' he said eagerly. 'Easy thing for me to bike there!'

Looking past him, she told him how it was.

'There has been an accident. Mr Forrester will not come back.'

He stood there mute again, petrified, his power of English gone. He was suddenly thinking hard. But curiously he was not thinking of Miss McNab or the things she had said or even of Mr Fresta, whom he admired so much and who would never come back. He was thinking of Anna, walking by the river, turned away from him, silent and never answering him as he called.

The reason for it all struck him with unpleasant violence. His open mouth began to work desperately up and down. The words of English he wanted to say so much could not release themselves from his idiotic muteness and it was not until the children rang the bell of his bicycle that he got the words out, stuttering and painful, in a cry.

'Anna is down by the river. She is walking there!'

Miss McNab looked very frightened.

'I called her a lot of times, but she did not answer.'

'Oh! God Almighty Father,' Miss McNab said. 'Almighty Father.'

She looked wildly and helplessly about the compound.

'I will bike!' Mr Prang shouted.

He rushed across the compound to the fence where he had left the bicycle. Beyond the fence the children who had been ringing the bell stood away like a bland half-circle of cream-brown moons.

Miss McNab, hair falling down, flung herself through the light bamboo-gate at the bicycle.

'For God's sake, I'm coming with you!'

By the gate the half-circle of moon-faces widened and then closed again, to stare with wonderful roundness at the sight of Mr Prang cycling wildly away under the trees, with Miss McNab, red hair falling fantastically down, clinging on behind.

17

Carrington confronted Forrester with an immediate question, 'Where's old Blore?' and repeated it several times as they lay there in the darkness after the sun had gone down. At first Forrester was shattered by exhaustion and recurrent and ghastly recollections of Blore and could not answer. Then with darkness and coolness he felt his strength come back. He invented, without thinking, the story that Blore had once more gone on alone. And it became, gradually, both for himself and Carrington, a true story. He began to think of Blore not as dead, destroyed by himself in a moment of crazy despair, but alone, walking ahead of them, independent as ever, seeking something by himself. It became the only story he could tell.

Somewhere between seven and eight o'clock he was rested and strong enough to get up. He had in his mind the idea to light a little fire. By the light of it he would be able to repack the haversack. He would get together the final necessary things: the water, the aspirins, the shaving cream, the antiseptic; and then discard the rest.

By doing these things, crawling about mostly on his hands and knees to find matches and then a pile of dry bamboo husks and at last lighting it and feeding it with bits of scrub and bamboo until the fire was a heap of white candescent flame, he felt his strength of mind come back. It emerged out of its heat craziness and became workable and sane. If he had had any sort of idea of not going on, even before the death of Blore, he could not remember it now. As he lighted the fire and sat watching it flame brilliantly up he remembered the fire he had lighted for Miss McNab in the compound. It brought back a swarm of memories. He remembered the skinless lump of flesh he had carried from some other compound under the palm trees, the lump that had been a child, living and laughing and falling trouserless from Harris's jeep in the dust, and it came back to him as a moment worse in fear and terror than any he was living now. He remembered too the light of the other fire. It had burned with amazing dry brightness. He remembered too how Miss McNab had scolded him, telling him a few home truths about himself. He remembered all she had said about the girl being afraid. It had made him feel very small. It had made him begin to look outside himself. And then he saw the face of the girl. He seemed to see it with almost unreal clearness, so much paler than the face of any English girl, the pink frangipani flower in her black hair, eyes calm and dark, deeply stoical. It had all the great Eastern fatalism in it, so attractive and hypnotically beautiful, and yet something else besides: a rare kind of wakefulness, as if that school in Rangoon had given her the start of a bright emancipation.

In the light of the fire, thinking of her, remembering how the frangipani flower had fallen from her hair and how it stood for immortality, he sorted out the things. He laid them by the haversack ready to pack. Then he took the aspirins, the water and the shaving cream over to the boy.

His lips were thick and swollen and he found it difficult to speak. He muttered a few words and then dipped his fingers in the shaving cream and began to rub it over his lips and face, and then gave the pot to Carrington. Slowly the boy rubbed his face with cream. For perhaps ten or fifteen minutes they looked at each other, half grinning, slowly rubbing their faces with cream that melted on the warm skin into a thin soothing grease that gradually brought back the life of lips and muscles. Once the boy dabbed a lump of cream absurdly on the end of his nose and then wrinkled his nose like a rabbit and Forrester, trying to laugh with his greasy cracked lips, was aware of a fierce kind of affection for the very livingness of the boy. It angered him impotently to think of it being uselessly destroyed there, dying with terrible painfulness under another day of sun. For it had become very obvious now that they had only one day more.

He got the boy with slow but almost savage determination to sit upright. The dark sky was wonderfully brilliant with stars. The flame of the bamboo fire burned straight upward in the windless silent tropical air, and the light of stars and fire was supremely comforting. The retinae of his eyes were normal again and all his terror of light had gone. He was very glad of the fire and was not even afraid of the heat of it as he sat there and held the boy by the shoulders and gave him all but the smallest drop of water remaining in the flask.

With the last drain in the cup he moistened his own mouth, feeling it touch his thick tongue with pain, and then spoke to Carrington.

'Got to go. Catch up with old Blore. Fit?'

'Ready when you are.'

He put some impossible brightness into his voice that heartened Forrester greatly.

'Got to stand up,' he said.

'Easy.'

'Got to get you against the tree first. Then stand. After that, hang on.'

'Fair enough.'

The fire was burning itself down to small yellow gems or flame. By the light of it Forrester got together the water-bottle and the haversack and slung them over his shoulders. Earlier in the evening he had taken off his shoes and socks and now his feet, rested in the cooling sand, were not tired. He remained for a few moments considering the revolver. It might conceivably have a use in firing signals, but the weight of the webbing belt was too much and he decided against it. Then at the last moment he changed his mind. He filled up the two chambers that had been spent and put the revolver in his trousers pocket. The boy said:

'Blore forgot the revolver.'

'Had it,' Forrester said. 'Won't need it now.'

'Heard him firing it,' the boy said.

'That was me. Shooting parrots.'

'Good show. When do we eat?'

'Tomorrow,' Forrester said. 'Eggs for breakfast in the morning.'

He could not go on talking and began to lift Carrington by the waist, pulling him so that only his heels touched the ground until at last he had him upright by the tree. For about a minute they both stood panting there and the boy, flat against the tree-trunk, fists clenched rigidly and body tautly pressed upright, grinning darkly with shining greasy face, looked strangely like someone crucified by the light of the fire.

And suddenly Forrester knew that he was fighting against pain. The grin in his face was no longer the grin of courageous foolery, but the grin of horror. It grieved him terribly to watch it. It seemed to smash his own suffering into something extraordinarily small and petty. All the bright and exhausting craziness of the afternoon, his thirst and the murder of his senses by the bludgeoning glitter of light and lastly the death of Blore became expunged from his consciousness by a frantic search for strength. He felt as if he were about to jump a chasm, and that the chasm was an inch wider than the normal limit of his power would take him, but that somehow, even if it meant tearing his heart out by the living roots, he had to reach the other side.

And as he lifted Carrington he felt he had done exactly that. His heart seemed to be torn upwards out of his chest. The naked core of himself, raw and deep, was wrenched out. He felt the last final cord of it pull like hot wire out of his guts and then all of it up through his chest and lungs, so that his heart was not there. He stood there with an inconceivably strange feeling of being disembowelled. He was about to fall forward, flat on his face. There was an awful, beatless emptiness in his chest. The little bamboo fire gave a sort of expanding dance of diabolical fern-like flame and went black before his eyes, the retina killed and unreceptive again so that the sky was starless beyond.

Then an amazing thing happened. Carrington, like a child playing on the back of its father, pulled his left ear. And instantly Forrester felt himself lunge forward, not of his own volition, but oddly and defeatedly impelled by the living playfulness of the thing. As he moved he had sense enough to take a look at the stars before he turned. He paused for a moment until he saw the Plough and the North Star on his left hand, and then, over the dark flat lake of sand he saw a star or two flashing green and rose, magnificently bright, above the black-purple mass of the farthest distances.

He knew then that his vision had come back again. And he went straight ahead.

The night seemed to have no distances and he did not know how far he travelled. To his surprise he found it easier to travel than to stand still. For a long time the sand was very flat where he walked and it stretched with the same monotony as far as he could see in the starlight across the valley. He moved forward by instinct, all the conscious guidance in himself expended. His instinct was not to become stationary for a single moment or to sit down. Behind the stupefied rhythm of his limbs there lay an unexpendable core of strength. He had blindly conceived that he was imperishable, that it was impossible to die.

After he had been walking for a long time he saw the shape of the horizon on his right hand, over to the south, thicken and grow darker. Soon it began to come nearer. Then by the refracted light of the moon that was not yet up he saw it take the shape of the valley-side. In about ten minutes it closed right in. And now something about the mass of rock and trees seemed altogether heavier and thicker than those of the valley that lay behind. He remembered dimly fighting with the idea of going back to the fork of the valley which Blore had explored the night before. In distress and exhaustion he had forgotten all about it. And now he was glad. It gave him fresh strength to feel that he had conquered the pitiless place that in the diabolical white heat of afternoon had almost killed him with its glare. The intolerable fierceness of it had to be beaten before the beginning of another day. Now he did not care so much. He could see that there would be thicker, deeper shade in the trees that, above the higher rock, were already with their branches beginning to blot out a few of the lower stars.

As he began to walk into the valley, dusty and crystalline and dry as ever, but now less than two hundred yards wide from one strip of trees to another, he saw the orange glow of moonlight begin to carve out the shapes of the farthest hills. Gold and dark, they lay far down the valley like sleeping tigers.

He watched them growing magnificently light for the next ten minutes or so, tiger-barred with orange where the rising light caught the tips of the lateral valleys. They seemed much nearer than he had ever seen them before. They were all tawny-purple below the orange burst of moon, which rose very rapidly, with overpowering tropical splendour that gradually turned the whole of the valley before him into a river-bed of yellow and rose.

And then, somewhere far behind him, distantly across the flat lake of sand, he heard a sound. It made him hesitate for a second. On his back he felt Carrington start uneasily. It was the sound of jackals: the sound that he could not bear in its crying piteous human wail. It brought back the times he had heard it across the plain from his tent under the pagoda and then from the village under the margosa tree. It made him think of Blore. Soon it was certain that Blore would be scavenged by either vultures or jackals, and of the two the jackals, working by night, seemed perhaps the more merciful thing.

The jackals seemed to be about five or six miles away to the south, and he began to be glad he had brought the revolver. And yet in a way he was also glad of the sound of them. They had a taste for civilization. They came down even to within the fringes of a great city like Calcutta and it was there he had first heard them, crying and wailing like women at the burning-ghats, with the bitter uncanny sound of mourning over the dead.

After a time their crying was silent. When they began again it was much farther away to the south. They seemed to be separated from him by a low ridge of hills. Once he stood still and listened hard and tried to calculate, from the stars and the sound of wailing voices, how far they were away, but the hills seemed to distort the sound. Then the weakness of his legs, inactive for a moment after the long mechanical slogging, became so stark that in another second his legs were not there. Underneath him was a horrifying pit of space and he was going to fall into it, face first, and never get up again.

Somehow the instinctive deathless slogging took him forward again. He watched the colours of the rising moon bleached out from orange and pink and rosy-purple to a deep yellow touched with green. It had the magnificence of a cold sun rising above the hills. And then the cool green-white monotony of the glare began. It flooded the valley with stark light. Once again he could see occasional rocks like stooping men, the grey thorn-icicled scrub, the bleached fringes of bamboo, not so stunted as the night before, and the flood-smoothed sand between the bars of muddy tea-brown shale. The valley began to fall, as on the previous night, a little more sharply, and once there was a place in the adjoining forest where a fire had swept down, skinning off from the escarpment all trees and bamboo and grass to a width of about half a mile. It was a fire of the dry season that had been arrested by the gap in the valley, so that now the height of the valley-side, burnt down to the naked rock, could be seen. It rose to about fifty or sixty feet and by the time he had staggered on to the end of the fire it had risen another ten or fifteen feet. The valley, narrowing in, seemed to be becoming a gorge between two precipitous slopes on which the bamboo had begun to grow to twice the height of a man. It became no longer a place of sand cut across by irregular bars of shale. In the white moonlight it looked more like the place of a great explosion. The flinty granite rock, breaking off like hard coal, glittered harshly as it began to cover the sand in long water-thrown ridges. Then soon there was no sand. The ridges of steely rock began to cut through the soles of his suède shoes and stab at his feet. He began to stagger wildly about with pain. Once he was slithering forward on his heels, the weight of Carrington pulling him back, the sound of his heels on the shale hard and metallically echoing down the gorge of rock like the echo of an exploding and receding wave on a shore. He saw before him a ledge of rock, dropping away six or seven feet below, and saw himself pitching over it, on his face, as Blore must have pitched over the night before. He experienced some of the terror Blore must have felt and understood his pain during the crack of a second before he dug his heels wildly down into the sand below the shale and brought himself to a standstill.

For a second he heard Carrington shouting and then he fell down. He fell sideways and as he fell he felt the boy wrench himself free, falling the other way. He had no strength to prevent the fall one way or the other. His body was stiff and unpliably weak from an awful tiredness and suddenly the very fall was a great relief. He wanted to lie on the earth, his face on the cool shade, the pain of his feet and shoulders gone,

Face sideways to the moonlight, he lay for a second or two defeated and did not care. All of his strength was smashed at last.

He seemed to go off into a sort of trance of stupefied weakness for about ten seconds before he came to himself and heard the shale still rolling down the slope. He knew in a ghastly way that Carrington was rolling down, helpless, over the edge. The terrible need for doing something to prevent this murdered what remained of his consciousness. He felt his mind go black. Then the moon glared into his face and by a curious trick of refraction he saw the boy actually rolling down.

He moved in a way that had no consciousness at all. He only knew that instantaneously he lay across Carrington's body, digging his heels against the edge of rock, and then a second later that he was not strong enough to hold the weight of both of them. They were going over and he could not prevent it. This was the end and there was nothing he could do. Incongruously for a moment he thought of Harris, then of Miss McNab and Burke, and then of the girl. Even the powerful evocation of her face, terribly and beautifully tender, was not strong enough now to keep away the moment of death. It seemed only to become part of the cool sweetness of relief after pain.

Slowly, after another second, they went over the edge of rock together. Even in that moment he covered the boy's face with his hands.

When he came to himself again the moon was full in his face. He lay under the rock, and the shelf was like a black ridge of steel shining six or seven feet above him. Something had knocked him out and the moon, blazing on his eyes with the same thundering beat as the sun, created for an awful moment the impression that it was day. The sickness in his mouth and stomach was exactly the sickness that came from lying in the sun.

He could think of nothing but Carrington and the water. He felt with one hand for the water-bottle and found it dry, the cork safely fixed on his chain.

The boy lay on his face. He lay in the attitude of a man about to fire a rifle down the valley: his head half-inclined on his

214

crooked arm, his legs stiffly outstretched. Something about this stiffly familiar attitude alarmed Forrester terrifically, and he sat up. He called Carrington's name with a mouth no longer capable of forming the syllables, passionately desiring the boy to be alive, and the result was a slobbing idiotic cry.

To his half-crazy relief the boy answered. He actually turned his face. It had a skull-like whiteness lying there against the blackish shale in the moon, but it seemed to Forrester a very wonderful thing. It evoked in him a frantic broken gaggle of words, asking mostly if the boy had been knocked out and was all right or in pain, and which he did not expect to be answered and which in fact was answered immediately. He saw the boy pointing down and across the valley to the far hills and the answer was a single word.

'Fire.'

He followed the direction of Carrington's arm. Across in the hill-forests he could see the smouldering crimson of fires immediately below the crests. They were very far away. Thirty or forty miles off, they were perhaps no more than forest fires started by the heat of sun, but they, too, seemed to Forrester a very wonderful thing. Like the crying of jackals they brought back into his pained consciousness the reality of the outside world.

The boy had a different idea about them.

'Been watching them,' he said. 'Could be bombing. Some chaps having a war.'

Forrester lay merely thinking of this. It worked down below his hammer dulled consciousness and revived him fully. He sat slowly up. The thought that the fires might be man-made coincided with his sight of the valley. Now under the clear moon he could see every rock and shadow of it. It looked more than ever like the precipitous place of an explosion. Deeper ledges of rock cut across it and were joined by evil reaches of glinting shale and everywhere now there was no sand. To walk down it would be something like walking down the debris of an avalanche.

The thought that he had come to the end of carrying Carrington filled him bitterly. He crawled to where the boy lay. Across the far valleys the fires in the high forests burned rosily, with sudden mysterious brighter glows of flame. It seemed to him a terrible thing that somewhere between themselves there might lie the line of war. The irony of not being able to reach it depressed him deeply. He felt very sick from the pain of the fall and there started up into his eyes every now and then a dull long thud of heavily-heated pain. As it receded it left him cold and quivering through the entire sweat-weak part of his naked body.

The boy spoke again, and Forrester grasped the fact that he had never been unconscious. Some of the old way of cheerfulness indomitably remained.

'Never get me down there,' he said.

'Bloody good try.'

'Talking cock.'

He found it difficult to frame his words, and something about the two words, incredibly comic, half made him want to laugh in answer. He let out a sort of blubber of protest instead.

'Only thing,' the boy said, 'you go down.'

'No.'

'Only thing.'

Forrester sat silent, partly from the pain of trying to frame his words, partly from a half-frightened notion that the boy was right. He wanted tremendously that they should remain together. For a long time he had seen death in separation. Sometimes as he walked with the boy on his shoulders he had had the odd impression that there crowded about him a persistent shell-like figure, keeping them company; it had an extraordinarily uncanny vigilance and was never tired. Now he felt that if he left the boy this figure would step in and take his place. It would take him finally away.

And he did not want that. He felt that Carrington had become irrevocably identified with the thought of living. He wanted the two never to separate. He was terribly haunted by the chill shell-like watchfulness of the figure that followed him and yet with equal terribleness he began to be convinced that the idea of going on alone was right.

He looked at his watch. It seemed very wonderful to think that it was still going. The time was about twenty minutes to eleven. Heavily and stupidly he sat looking at his watch and calculated the hours to daylight. If he got the boy into the shade of a rock or a tree and then rested a little he could count on five hours before the sun rose.

He considered this for some moments and then from far off, once again, he heard the crying of jackals. They were still five or six miles away, but the sound of them made him think once again of lighting a fire. It would be a comfort to Carrington and a guiding place.

He told the boy this. Carrington was watching the fires far across in the hill forests and said: 'There's a hell of a flare-up there sometimes. Wonder what?'

As Forrester climbed out of the shale bed into the low forest fringe and began to gather bamboo and broken branches he saw that the bamboo was thicker here. It would make pistol-shots as it burned. There was plenty of dead wood and among it were tough mountain acacia boughs covered with thorn. In places flood water had bared the whip-cord roots of over-hanging trees and had piled up beyond them shelves of silted sand. Here it would be possible for Carrington to lie, with the fire at his side. He built the fire on rock and when he lit it the flames again had that white candescent flare that made the moon-broken edge of forest a homely place.

It took him more than half an hour, crawling mostly on his hands and knees, to collect wood for the fire and light it. Once or twice he was overcome again by the peculiar light-headed exhaustion in which his brain was a little animal, peering out, fretful and ravenous, searching for food. In the middle of the night now the air was cool among the rocks and without his shirt he was not warm and was glad for a few moments of the heat of the fire.

He sat for a moment feeling the fire on his bare chest and then he crawled back to Carrington and collected the water bottle and the haversack he had left there. He calculated the water-bottle to be about half full. It was not much. He knew enough about the sun to know that a man without water could die in a day. It was remotely and painfully possible that Carrington could last two days. He did not know about himself. It was something that in his half-numbed state of consciousness he

217

was not quite capable of thinking about. He took the water-bottle and the haversack and laid them by the fire.

After that he went back for Carrington. The distance between the place where they had fallen and the place where he had made the fire was about fifteen yards. This time he picked Carrington up bodily, in his arms, and once again it was as if he had to jump a chasm too wide for the limit of his strength. He made a ferocious effort and staggered wildly forward, his mouth dragged down with a look of dry idiocy, his head banging with blows like the sickening thunder of sunstroke.

At last he succeeded in laying Carrington down. The boy had learned the trick now of not speaking whenever he was being carried, the trick of not making the slightest protest of pain, so that Forrester had no need to waste his strength in answering, and now for about three or four minutes they both lay by the fire, silent, while Forrester got back his breath.

It was the fire dying down that made him get up at last. The effort of getting to his knees drove the blood out of his head and for a moment he seemed to spin wildly, the fire dazzling him, so that he had difficulty in not falling down.

'Aspirin and some water before you go,' the boy said.

He shook his head.

'Orders.'

'Never take 'em,' he said. He grinned down with a hollow mouth of pain.

'Going to start now?' Carrington said.

He knew that it was useless to think of aspirins, and impossible to think of water. He could not swallow the dry powdery tablet now. But he fumbled in the haversack and struck the palm of his hand against his mouth and then tilted the water-bottle and put the metal cap of the cork against his lips, afterwards smacking the cork tight down with his hand.

'O.K. now,' he said and had the impression at the same time that the boy, staring carefully up at him in the light of the fire, was not deceived.

As he knelt down by the boy he knew that they had gone past deceiving each other. He unstrapped his watch, wound it a little more and strapped it on the boy's left wrist. The risk of separation had now to be calmly and simply faced.

'Listen,' he said. He spoke very slowly and it seemed to him that the boy's face had an immense loneliness as it lay there, staring and listening, very quiet, in the light of the fire.

'Keep the fire going.'

'Yes.'

'Make a signal at eight tomorrow morning. Fire a shot.'

'Yes.'

'Then another at twelve.'

'Yes.'

'Think that's all.'

'Good show,' the boy suddenly said. 'How's the old horse?'

'Bloody good. How's the jockey?'

'Up the Burma Derby.'

The boy gave a grin of wonderful and horrible cheerfulness. It turned his face into a twisted mask that Forrester could not bear to see. He got up and looked down the valley. All across it and across the great incrustation of hill forest farther away the moon had a chalky brightness. Suddenly he wanted to go. Then abruptly Carrington said:

'Funny we never caught old Blore.'

'Away in the old handicap,' Forrester said. 'Good start.'

'He shot himself with the revolver back there,' the boy said.

The words were calm and embittered and curiously brave and Forrester did not answer them. He saw on the boy's face in the firelight a look of imperishably bright affection. In a clear and unanguished way he understood what the revolver, lying there by the water, the haversack and the fire, now meant to him. It did not seem to Forrester that he was afraid. But suddenly he could not bear the thought of his lying there alone with nothing but a little fire and water for comfort under the stark moonlight; and then in the morning the sun and the revolver for the final moment; and later the vultures or the jackals to pick at the young decent face until it was clean blistered bone in the sun. It troubled him so terribly that without another word he lifted his hand in abrupt good-bye.

Carrington lifted his hand too. The watch on his wrist flashed in the light of the fire. At that moment a rod of bamboo in the fire gave off a crack like a pistol that against the enclosed rock of the valley echoed briefly round and round. Forrester's feet were noisy on the shale and Carrington whispered something that sounded incredibly like 'They're off' as he started down the valley.

18

Climbing down the long slopes of black shale in the moonlight
was easier than the long march with Carrington across flat sand,
and yet soon he was tired. He was oppressed by a new terror of
being alone. He turned several times and looked back. The
valley had become a long ravine, with something of the desolation of a shattered railway track, and on both sides the forest
was thicker and deeper, so that the moonlight made only fragmentary veins of light on the floor below the outer fringe of
short acacia trees. But the thing that kept his terror of loneliness
down to bearable limits was the small bright flame of fire back
among the rocks where he had left the boy. It burned there like
a reflection of the forest fires.

Each time he went on he felt the fire behind growing smaller
and farther away; and the hill fires, that had the look of something unreal and sacrificial with their sudden flares of light on
the half-dark hills, growing no nearer. After a time the comfort
they gave him turned to a feeling of isolation. For perhaps three
or four hundred yards he could hear the pistol-shots of burning bamboo very clear and crisp in the still tropical night air,
but soon he was too far away and then there came a time when
he turned round and the small stars of fire had become hidden
among the rocks and he knew he would see them no longer.

This feeling of isolation increased as he went on. The mind-
less and instinctive way of walking which had carried him
across the flat lake of sand was no use now. The sand had had
the effect of drugging him and he could not fall. Now the slopes
of shale, with deep cross-shelves of rock falling sharply away,
had to be consciously climbed. He could no longer stumble
forward in that drugged way. The physical effort, though it was
all downhill, began to make him terribly weary. He found it
hard to keep his swollen lips closed and as he took in his breath

it was as if he drew in long draughts of salt, sometimes icily sharp, sometimes scalding, as they hit the cracks of his mouth and his bloated tongue.

Every ten minutes or so he would lie down, pressing his stomach on the shale. His feet seemed to have swollen too. They pressed puffily against his shoes, so that they seemed too large for them, but he was too tired to take them off. He could only lie with his face on the cold broken rock, getting a tiny cool scrap of comfort from resting his lips there.

In one of those rests he went off into a stupor of exhaustion, a sort of moon-drugged daze, not really sleep, where he had dropped on the shale. He did not know how long it lasted. When he woke again he could hear the jackals still crying somewhere in the distance over the rocks. There was a flat cloud of mist, like bluish milky vapour, far down the valley, and the air was cold. Over the south-western slope of rock the moon had something of the glint of a tarnished spoon. It was growing daylight on the far hills.

The horror of missing the opportunity of travelling all night filled him with feeble rage. He got up and began to stagger down the valley. His eyes were still glutted with exhaustion and his jaws clamped together with the pain of thirst. He was filled with acid crying reproaches against himself for lying there and letting the night go past him. He could not see straight and wandered cruelly and blindly about for some minutes before he fell down.

The fall seemed to wake him. It expunged the stuffy sleep-blindness from his eyes. With it went most of the bitterness of the reproaches and he began to feel very wakeful and clear and strong with the prospect of fresh horror: the light of day. Thirst had been his chief reason for travelling in the night. Now he had to travel by day.

He got up and stood where he was and listened. The jackals had ceased crying with the rising daylight. All down the valley and through the low forest there was no sound. He was caught up once again by a solitude that frightened him. He thought once again of birds and remembered, for some curious reason, the crying of the Sergeant's monkey in one of the tents near his own. The recollection of these sounds aggravated everything:

the silence, the solitude and the absence of life, but most of all his fear of the sun. In an hour it would begin to blast him. The intolerable glare of whiteness would begin to shatter his senses. And suddenly he felt that he could not bear it and began to stumble down the valley with long ghoulish steps, his swollen mouth open and dark as if he were going to spew.

After about twenty minutes of this he stopped again. Daylight was coming with a horribly beautiful net-cloud of rose and orange over the purple hills. The fires on the forest slopes could no longer be seen. In front of him the valley seemed to go on and on and he was sick with the feeling that he would never conquer it. The sun was coming up to blister the blood out of him for the last time. Already the shale, dark and cool all night, had on it the rose-orange glitter of first light that would become, in an hour or so, the killing glitter of sun that would murder him by afternoon.

Hysteria beat him for a moment and he thought of going back to Carrington. The evil of going on alone seemed suddenly more terrible even than the prospect of slogging back up the valley. There, at least, he could die with the boy.

For a few seconds he ached for the companionship of death. Then he noticed ahead of him, thirty or forty yards away, a break in forest on his right hand. A landslip, brought about perhaps by the torrential force of the last monsoon, had broken down through the tree-belt. The trees, through the long dry season, had not grown up again. Bare steps of rock went up the valleyside for fifty or sixty feet, and came out in a sort of scrubless plateau between the highest trees.

He went slowly on and began to climb. He did not remember consciously making any decision to climb; he did not consider what he would see when he reached the top of the gap. He climbed very slowly. Acacia boughs sharp with thorn had fallen everywhere and under long bitter heat had dried like a rusty tangle of barbed-wire among the rocks. Stamping against them, he once again fell down. In his weakness he put his hands forward to save himself and fell flat against crowded thorns that drove into his naked chest and hands. The scratches of his chest and hands began to bleed and he could not drag himself up again between the fissures of rock without feeling as if the flesh

223

of his palms was being combed with broken glass. Then as he dragged himself up, his body riddled with the new pain of thorns, he began to be troubled by an hallucination. The shell-like figure had come back. But now the figure of queer persistent vigilance was not quite the same. It was simply a face now. Then after it had persisted in front of him for some time he knew that it was really two faces. He knew that the face of his young wife, cruelly blown into utter darkness by the bomb, and the face of the young girl, waking him softly to a new thought of living in the shade of the margosa-tree, had come together. They were very beautiful and now they were also an indissoluble part of himself, so that he was afraid and alone no longer.

As he pulled himself finally over the top of the ledge of rock above the valley something hit him in the face. It was the sun. And for several moments it fantastically blinded him with the power of its level glare.

He lay flat on his face and shut his eyes. He could feel again the bitter pain of his bleeding chest and hands and the still more bitter pain of his gasping mouth. The two faces that had come together and had kept vigilantly with him as he climbed had gone. He did not want to open his eyes again. All he wanted now was to lie in darkness. He wanted passionately to wait for the faces that he loved to come back and help him defeat the power of the sun. In some way the fusion of the faces was the coming of death.

He lay for a little while longer, waiting for death to come. There was no sound at all in the deathly tropical air except the faint noise of a stone or two falling away where he had climbed the slope below.

It was a small sound and every few seconds it came again. Then he realized, very dimly through his darkening consciousness, that it was not the sound of a falling stone. It was a nearer, quieter, more living sound. It had something of the lightness of a falling leaf.

For the first time since reaching the ledge he opened his eyes. He saw before him an astonishing thing. A small yellow-green lizard was running among the dry acacia twigs and out on to the flat rock a few yards in front of him. It was like the lizard the child had killed by the pagoda. As he opened his eyes it died protectively, eyes wonderfully bright and tiny hands out-stretched on the flat face of the rock. And then, like the lizard the child had tormented, it came to life again in the sun.

He began to cry very weakly as he saw the lizard. As he went on crying his eyes were watered into crazy mistiness by acid and difficult tears. And then when he could see clearly again the lizard, frightened by the small noises of his mouth, had gone. But down in the valley below him he could see something that even beside the wonder of the bright living lizard was like a miracle.

Down below him a white egret was walking daintily among the tall grass of the jungle. The thought of seeing a bird was so crazily wonderful that he staggered up on his feet. And the egret, as if disturbed by the sound he made, seemed suddenly to fly.

And then he saw that it was not an egret. He saw that it was a small column of smoke. He saw it rising pearl-grey as the feath-ers of an egret from the dry ring of grass. Beyond the fire was a narrow dust-white road and between the road and the little fire he suddenly saw the movement of men. They were small brown men and incredibly one of them carried a rifle in his hands.

He knew then that they were Naga bearers and he began to run down the slope towards them, waving his arms with feeble jubilation and senselessly crying with new tears and no longer caring about the sun.

19

Three days later they flew him out from the forward field hospital in an ambulance L5 that itself had something of the lightness of an egret flying over the dark ranges of hills. That afternoon he said good-bye to Carrington in a long cane hospital basha where nurses walked coolly between shaded beds, by which stood tables of bamboo, bright with pots of marigold and rose and flowers of the near jungle, scarlet and yellow-green, whose names he did not know. He had signalled dutifully to Aldridge, and had sent another to Harris which said, among other things, 'Put in an Allelujah and a spasm or two for me in the bass notes.' It had gone off on Easter Sunday.

Today was Tuesday. A young nurse of more human and feminine temperament than Burke hung about Carrington's bed and with tender attention arranged the marigolds in the barred shade. But whether the attention was for Carrington or himself or the flowers he never knew. She had incredibly sweet blue eyes and living yellow hair and been magnificently lenient and kind.

Her name was Mavis and for some reason or other it had become impressed on her that he and Carrington had known each other for years. It had begun in fact to seem like that to Forrester. The distrust, the antagonism and the ghastly irritations of a week ago seemed very far away. The boy lay with his legs in a kind of low tent and was very cheerful and very tired. In two days they would fly him back to Calcutta.

They had shaken hands twice and now, as on the ridge up the valley where the Naga search party had finally found Carrington shooting at flocks of imaginary parakeets, Forrester did not want to leave the boy.

'You ought not to talk any longer, Mr Forrester,' the sister said.

'Mavis,' the boy mocked from the bed, 'or may I call you blackbird?'

'You may call me blackbird.' She creased the sheets closer about his neck. 'And you may say good-bye.'

'Not fair,' he said. 'Mr Forrester and I have a lot to talk about.'

'Say it in Rangoon.'

'I don't want to go to Rangoon. The L5 can take two cases. Why can't I go with Forrester?'

'Mr Forrester's going to Rangoon,' she said, 'aren't you, Mr Forrester? Sooner or later we're all going to Rangoon.'

'Mr Forrester's hell!' the boy said. 'He's streaking off to Cal. There's a girl named Anna there.'

Forrester stared at the boy grinning up, thin and imperishable, from the bed, and could not believe what he heard.

'How do you know about Anna?' he said.

'Please,' the sister said. 'Don't let's start that.'

'Always talking about her. That's how,' the boy said. 'What is she? Brunette or blonde?'

The young nurse grew very severe. She found it hard to grow very severe because of the indomitable blue sweetness of her eyes, but she said, quite harshly:

'Now please, that's enough.'

'Mavis,' the boy mocked for the last time. 'Blackbird.'

'This is where you go, Mr Forrester,' she said.

She pushed Forrester away from the bed, and in going he raised his hand.

'See you in Rangoon.'

'Good-bye,' the boy said. He suddenly seemed resigned and very tired. 'Thanks for the ride.'

'Thank the jockey.'

'Out!' the girl said, and he raised his hand for the last time.

In half an hour the light ambulance plane was flying him back. His eyes were still tender and cautious; they could not accept the distances in the white noon haze. He was alone in the plane and after looking down once or twice at the dark encrustations of jungle between the thin white waterless valleys he lay down and shut his eyes. Incredulously he remembered what

227

the boy had said: 'Always talking about her.' The unreality of the days in which he had struggled somewhere through the valleys below began to stand more and more apart from him, unrelated. He began not to be able to believe in what he had endured of the glitter, the harshness and the horror of sun.

When at last he felt the plane begin to lose height and he sat upright and saw below the familiar foreshortened tents lying like brown seashells among the palms that grew everywhere like tiny feather dusters, the white glitter of pagodas, the glassy squares of water-holes, the pencil scar of oil-dark road running out across the plain, he felt some of the sick excitement of a man coming home. He watched as if he had never seen them before the corrugations of wheel-marks criss-crossing like ancient trackways the yellow dust about the airstrip, the aircraft dispersed about it like dust-thick moths, and the brown-blue muscles of the river beyond. All of it had a cool toy-bright detachment that did not oppress him now.

And then suddenly the small plane was down, almost vertical in descent, the palms and the tents and the dust were all rushing up to meet him, and he became aware of the great heat of the afternoon. Blinding white as the dust, it beat up with a moment or two of revived horror that clashed on the retina of his eyes and left them dead.

For a moment the cross of the ambulance standing on the edge of the runway changed from crimson to black. Then flared white and then in the blazing glare of haze vanished altogether. As he stepped down from the plane he felt the dust rock sideways under his feet. He stood poised against the hot air like a drunken man. He had not realized how weak he was and as if to demonstrate the stupidity of it he waved his arm savagely at two Indian boys running enthusiastically at him with a stretcher.

The light of sun beat him about the face, making him stagger; and then he heard the voice of Burke, thin and sharp as vinegar as it lashed the Indians. 'Ah! for God's sake, you clots, for God's sake!' And then Harris caught his arm.

'H'ven't we met?'

'Seems to be something familiar about the face,' he said. He seized with dry joy the sweaty hands of the chubby doctor.

'Into that ambulance,' Harris said.

'Not on your life.'

'You're a sick man,' Harris said. 'You need rest.'

'For God's sake,' Burke said. 'Don't let's have any fooling.'

'No,' he said, 'for God's sake.'

'As stubborn as a damn camel still,' she said. 'With the hump, too!'

He grinned again and felt the power of his eyes come back. He saw Burke and Harris regarding him with dry professional concern. Harris, quiet now and watchful and a little troubled, was wearing a large bush hat that reminded him curiously of Blore, and behind him the two Indian boys stood panting with the stretcher. Something about the idea of being borne away on a stretcher after all that had happened to him seemed very funny and he began to laugh, but to his surprise Harris did not laugh in answer and he was puzzled. He did not know that to Harris his face, dazzled by the glare of sun, had something of the hollow dark-mouthed stare of a face gouged out of a yellow turnip.

'Better get into the ambulance,' Harris said.

'Take the other arm, sir,' Burke said. She was professionally holding his left arm. 'What in the name o' God d'ye suppose we're here for?'

'I wouldn't be knowin',' he said. 'Just the welcome committee.'

'Back that ambulance down!' she shouted.

As the ambulance reversed slowly down to him Forrester waited. Harris's jeep stood just beyond the plane.

'Easy,' Harris said. 'Come on now.'

'What the hell!' he said. 'You know where I'm going.'

'You're going in the ambulance, that's where!' Burke said.

'Go home and have tea with Johnson,' he said.

'Johnson is in Comilla! Come on now.'

'You can get there for tea in the mail,' he said. 'Harris knows where I'm going and I'm going now.'

'Sir,' she said to Harris, 'do you stand for this?'

'He does and he likes it.'

'I don't like it,' Harris said.

'I should say not for God's sake!' Burke said.

'All right, sister,' Harris said. 'Let him come with me.'

Savagely Burke let go his arm and slowly Harris walked over to the jeep with him. The hood of the jeep was raised and Forrester pulled himself up by the supports of it and sat down inside. Without a word Harris walked round and got into the driver's seat on the other side. In the moment before he started the engine Forrester heard from the direction of the ambulance the voice of Burke drilling the bearers as if she were an enraged firing squad.

'Get the bloody thing out of the way, you dead beats! You clots, get the damn thing away!'

He heard her and grinned. She looked very offended and angry and yet lonely as she stood shouting between the ambulance and the little plane.

Harris drove the jeep slowly away across the strip. The haze of dust was glaring gold above the purple distances and, as always, the only thing that moved in the scorched barrenness beyond the shaded road were a few white egrets daintily feeding on the yellow rice fields. The afternoon had all the staggering unreal brightness of the day when Harris had first driven him out there, but now Harris did not talk and did not drive madly in and out of the bullock-tracks and the sun bouncing off the dark road and the little railway track and the hard crystalline dust did not trouble his eyes. The light seemed almost kind after the light he had known and it did not seem that that first journey was only a week away.

It was past five o'clock when they drove in under the shade of the tamarinds and palms at the village edge. Across the river the sun was going down with smoky copper fire and the leaves of the bananas were a strange tender green in the fiery light and already the shade was dark and cool on the track between the palm-frond fences below. He caught the acrid smell of village fires. He saw a few villagers in purple waist-cloths squatting about them in the dusty compounds, then suddenly from out behind the fences of bamboo came the small brown boys, flat-faced and laughing shrilly, running to ride with Harris along the dusty track.

As Harris stopped the jeep all the boys clambered about it like cream-yellow laughing monkeys.

230

'Tired?' he said. 'Eyes ache at all?' He looked at Forrester closely.

'No.'

'Let's look at your tongue.'

Forrester put out his tongue and wagged it comically up and down so that all the boys on the back seat of the jeep screamed with laughter.

'Can't keep a good man down,' Harris said.

'Was I always good?'

'No,' Harris said, 'you were bad.'

'Very bad?'

'You were bloody awful. You were lucky nobody hit you. I could have hit you myself,' he said.

'Thanks,' Forrester said.

Harris smiled, decently, and without a word. Slowly he let in the clutch and drove along the track of shade. About fifty yards from the house he stopped the jeep, not violently, so that the boys fell off, but quietly, parking it under a tree. The boys seemed very disappointed at not being thrown off the jeep and they remained on it like puzzled monkeys waiting to be fed.

'We'll walk the rest,' Harris said. He waved his hand to the puzzled almond faces.

They did not speak as they walked together to the house. In a few moments he was under the deep-scented shade of the margosa tree, the fragrance of it overpowering and painfully sweet as he smelled it for the first time. Miss McNab was coming across the compound from the house. The mother came out of the house too and stood on the steps of the veranda like a dark cream idol and the elder sister came slowly after her, but he did not see the girl.

Miss McNab came running forward and began to cry. Holding his hands she could not speak and she did not look like the excited dominant Miss McNab he had known.

From the veranda the mother and sister came to speak to him. 'I will make some tea,' the sister said. They too shook hands.

'Where's Anna?' he said.

Miss McNab suddenly calmed herself and began to smile and

in irritation at herself brushed back the thick mop of her dyed mahogany hair.

'I'll take you in,' she said. 'Crying like a loony now, if you ever heard such a thing. Tears in my eyes and I can't see.'

She savagely tried to brush the tears from her face and succeeded only in wiping the wetness of them across the blue-pink powder in a smear.

He followed her across the compound and into the house. In the room where he had sung 'Allelujahs' with her and had seen the floor strewn with the wounded and the dead she turned to him and spoke in a whisper.

'She's in here,' she said. 'Asleep, I think. She hasn't slept much until today.'

He stood waiting. The pinkish tear-wet powder on her face was touching in its ugliness.

'You can go in,' she said.

She spoke very simply, in a whisper, pointing to the curtain of dark purple cloth that separated the room from another.

'I ought not to wake her,' he said.

'No need to wake her,' she said. 'You look as if you haven't slept much yourself.'

'No. No sleep,' he said.

'Go in and lie down and sleep with her,' she said. 'Nothing will be said in this house about that sort of sleep together.'

She smiled very softly again with the most tearful powdery ugliness and then suddenly went out of the room and left him there. He stood for a moment listening. There was no sound in the heat of the afternoon. He waited for another moment and then pulled back the curtain and went into the room beyond.

Anna was lying asleep, fully dressed, on the wide low bed of bamboo. He stood for a moment looking down at her face. It was exhausted and quiet and dead with sleep and the rosy crimson frangipani flower had fallen on to the bed from her black hair.

He took off his shoes, the same dusty suède shoes that had taken him down the valley with Blore and Carrington, and stood looking down at her face. He looked at her for a few moments longer with tenderness and then lay down beside her on the bed. He was very quiet and she did not stir. He lay there for some moments without moving, listening to the great silence of the burning plain outside, the burning, savage, glittering plain he had so much hated, slowly breathing in the deep scent that had begun to fall from the margosa tree and overpower the hot smell of dust and mingle with the scent of the fallen frangipani flower in the heat of the late afternoon. From all across the hot distances of the plain there was no breath of sound. In the small bare room with its bamboo-shaded windows there was no glitter of sun. He picked up the stem of the frangipani flower and held it in his hands. The flowers were still blooming, as the girl had said they would be, with rosy half-opened buds of blossom, and he remembered now that they stood for immortality.

Breathing in the scent of them in a great gasp that was like an agony of relief and pleasure, he lay with his body against her and shut his eyes. Her body felt young and trembling with the breath of sleep and now there was nothing more he asked for but to lie beside it and sleep too.

Outside, the plain was purple in the falling dusk, and the long day was over.

The Scarlet Sword

H. E. Bates

Kashmir, 1947. Partition has provoked political crisis and the fierce Pathans and Afridi of northern India come sweeping down from the hills to take part in the riot and massacre.

A small Catholic mission is in their path, and for ten days its inhabitants suffer the nightmare of murderous attack and occupation.

Without melodrama H. E. Bates shows how heroism can be simply the preservation of human reason and emotion amidst the surrealism of violence and tragedy.

'An inspiring study of fear and heroism' – *Daily Telegraph*